Tales from
HIGH
HALLACK

the collected short stories of
ANDRE NORTON

Volume: 2

OPEN ROAD
INTEGRATED MEDIA
NEW YORK

978-1-4976-6101-1

This edition published in 2014 by Open Road Integrated Media, Inc.
345 Hudson Street
New York, NY 10014
www.openroadmedia.com

FOR JODY LYNN NYE

CONTENTS

INTRODUCTION

A good short story is a work of literary art, and Andre Norton was a master of the form. Science fiction, fantasy, contemporary, historical . . . no matter the genre she could weave a solid, complete tale in a minimal amount of space.

And often she would sprinkle in cats.

I became friends with Andre because of a short story.

I edited Historical Hauntings, a DAW anthology, and Andre had a wonderful story in it. I needed to include little biographies about each author in the book, and I hadn't yet collected one from her. The packager told me not to worry; that they had a "stock bio" on hand and that it would suffice. But to me, a stock bio wouldn't be good enough. This was my first anthology for DAW, and I wanted it as close to perfect as I could manage.

So I found Andre's phone number, and I called her. I expected to get a secretary or somesuch, but she picked up the phone. Her voice was thin and musical, like wind chimes. I told her I'd like a little biography to run with her story, and she said: "Bless you."

Andre said no one had asked her for a new "about the author" paragraph in quite some time. She wrote one up, e-mailed it to me, then called to make certain is was satisfactory. We shared pleasantries, Andre talking about her cats, me talking about my dogs, and we promised to stay in touch.

For many years we exchanged letters once or twice a month, random phone calls, and always cards for special occasions. She would send me hand-written lists of books she recommended that I read, and copies of magazine articles focused on archaeology (a shared interest). I would send her SF or fantasy books I'd read and thought she would enjoy, and sometimes I sprinkled in cat toys. Later, when she closed her High Hallack Library, she gave me a fine chunk of her medieval history books, and they are properly displayed on the shelves in my office—and are often and lovingly referenced.

Andre edited a DAW anthology with me, Renaissance Faire, teaching me more than a little bit about the art of the short story. Later, I had the honor of collaborating with her on three novels. We were plotting a fourth when she became ill. She was a joy to work with—an amazing writer, but an even better friend.

Enjoy these tales. They're worth reading more than once.

Jean Rabe

FREEDOM
Cleveland Press, September 1943

This is Freedom—
America bought it—for a price—
From scalping knives and red war hatchets
In ragged clearings about burned cabins
This is Freedom—
America bought it—for a price—
With long rifle and starvation
At Brandywine and Saratoga,
Valley Forge and Yorktown
This is Freedom—
America bought it—for a price—
With frigates' broadsides
To proclaim seas free to all nations
This is Freedom—
America bought it—for a price—
With bayonets at Chateau Thierry and Belleau Wood
And in the shattered forests of the Argonne
This is Freedom—
America buys it—at a price—
In the air and distant seas
And on the beaches of ravaged lands,
With our hands and bodies and those minds
Trained to act and work
That this Freedom shall not perish from this earth.

OMNIUMGATHUM POEMS
Cats

Cats curl upon my bed,
Hieroglyphics yet unread.
Those who worship moon-eyed bast,
Sleep the future, dream the past.
Satin fur, sineuwy limbs,
Jeweled eyes, never dim.
Wisdom unknown to my kind,
Alien thoughts, alien mind.
Yet we are linked, will to will,

Uneasy bonds time can not still.

SONG OF THE
BARBARIAN SWORDSMAN

What grins at me from the cherry tree?
Bone, unfleshed and hanging free.
What towers high in the market place?
A pile of skulls I must face.
Who rides with fire and sword?
Soldiers bought by Death's Dark Lord.

THE LAST COHORT

Mithra, God of the Morning,
Thy trumpet arouses the wall!
Mithra, Lord of the Dawning,
Who hath given rule over all.
With my sword and my shield before me,
And the spears of my men at my back,
Mithra, Lord of the Dawn Light,
March we now to attack.
For the legions have gone from Britain
And the Wall is broken stone.
Mithra, God of Soldiers,
Must we fight on alone?
The ravens scream above us,
Our square is breaking now!
Mithra, God of the Dawn Light,
Remember thou our vow.
For we are the last to hail thee,
In thy shrines to bow the knee.
Mithra, Our Lord of Sunlight,
How came this thing to be?
Do gods die with men who call them?
Lie they also among our dead?
Mithra, the Soldiers' Sheild Man,
We do not believe you fled.

SWAMP DWELLER
Magic in Ithkar (1985) TOR

I am Quintka blood, no matter my mother. Shame-shorn of skull, snow-pale of skin, her body crisscrossed by lash scarring, her leg torn by hound's teeth, lying in a ditch, she bore me, to hide me in leaves before death came. The Calling was mine from the first breath I drew, as it is with all the Kin. And Lari, free ranging that day, heard, pawing me free, giving me the breast with her own current nurseling, before loping back to Garner himself to show her new cubling.

Quintka I plainly was by my wide yellow eyes and silver hair. Though my mother was of no race known to Garner, and he was a far-traveled man.

The Kin paid her full death honors, for it was plain she had fought for my life. Children are esteemed among the Kin, who breed thinly, for all our toughness of body and quickness of mind, gifts from Anthea, All Mother.

Thus did I foster with Kin and Second-Kin, close to Ort, Lari's cubling, though he was quicker to find his feet and forge for himself. However, I mind-spoke all the beast ones, and tongue-spoke the Kin; thus all accepted me fully.

Before I passed my sixth winter, I had my own team of trained ones, Ort as my seconding. I was able to meet the high demands of Garner, for he accepted only the best performers.

Because I was able so young, the clan prospered. Those not of the blood seemed bemused that beasts such as orzens and fal, and quare, clever after their own fashion, head-topping me by bulk of bodies, would obey me. Many a lord paid good silver to have us entertain.

Nor had we any fears while traveling, such as troubled merchant caravans that must hire bravos to their protection. For all men knew that the beasts who shared our covered wagons, or tramped the roads beside us were, in themselves, more formidable weapons than any men could hope to forge.

Once a year we came to Ithkar Fair—knowing that we would leave with well-filled pouches. For Garner's shows were in high demand. Lords, even the high ones of the temple, competed in hiring us.

However, it was not alone for that profit we came. There were dealers who brought rare and sometimes unknown beasts—strange and fearsome, or beautiful and appealing—from the steppes of the far north or by ships plying strange seas. These we sought, adding to our clan so.

Some we could not touch with the Calling, for they had been so mishandled in their capture or transport as to retreat far behind fear and hate, where the silent speech could not reach. Those were a sorrow and despair to us all. Though we oft times bought them out of pity, we could not make them friends and comrades. Rather did we carry them away from all that meant hurt and horror and sung them into peace and rest forever. This also being one of the duties Anthea, All Mother, required of us.

I was in my seventeenth year, perhaps too young and yet too aware of my own powers, when we came that memorable time to Ithkar. There was no mandate laid upon me to mate—even though the Kin was needful of new blood—but there were two who watched me.

Feeta's son by Garner—Wowern. Also there was Sim, who could bend any horse to his will, and whose riding was a marvel, as if youth and mount were of one flesh. Only to me my team was still the closer bond, and I felt no need to have it otherwise.

The fair-wards at the entrance hailed us as they might some lord, though we scattered no gold. From his high seat the wizard-of-the-gate, ready to make certain no dark magic entered, broke his grave mask with a smile and waved to Feeta, who also makes magic, but of a healing kind. Our weapons were few and Garner had them already sheathed and bundled, as well as the purse for our fee ready, so there was no waiting at the barrier.

We would pay a courtesy visit to the temple later, but, since we were not merchants dealing in goods, we made only a silver offering. Now we pushed on into that section where there were beasts and hides, and all that had to do with living things. Our yearly place was ready for us—a fair-ward waiting, having kept that free for our coming. Him we knew, too, being Edgar, a man devoted to Feeta, who had cured his hound two seasons back. He tossed his staff in the air to pay us homage and called eager questions.

We all had our assigned tasks, so we moved with the speed of long practice, setting up the large tent for the showing, settling in our Second-Kin. They accepted that here they must keep to cages and picket lines, even though this was, in a manner, an insult to them. But they understood that outside the Kin they were not as clan brothers and sisters, but sometimes feared. I know that some, such as Ily, the mountain cat, and Somsa, the horned small dragon, were amused to play dangerous—giving shudders to those who came to view them.

I had finished my part of the communal tasks when Ort padded to me, squatting back on his powerful hindquarters, his taloned forepaws lightly clasped across his lighter belly fur. His domed head, with its upstanding crest of stiff, dark blue fur, was higher than mine when he reared thus.

"Sister-Kin . . ."—the thoughts of beasts do not form words, but in the mind one easily translates—"there is wrong here. . . ."

I looked up quickly. His broad nostrils expanded, as if drawing in a scent that irked him. Our senses are less in many ways than those of the Second-Kin, and we learn early to depend upon what they can read by nose, eye, or ear.

"What wrong, Brother-Kin?"

Ort could not shrug as might one of my own species, but the impression of such a gesture reached me. There was as yet only simple uneasiness in his mind; he could not pin it to any source. Still I was alerted, knowing that if Ort had made such a judgment, others would also be searching. Their reports would come to those among the Kin with whom they felt the deepest bond.

The Calling we did not use except among ourselves and the Second-Kin—and that I dared not attempt now. But as I dressed for fairing, I tried to open myself to any fleeting impression. A vigorous combing fluffed out hair usually banded down, and I placed on midforehead the blue gem I had bought at this same fair last year, which adhered to one's flesh, giving forth a subtle perfume.

Ort still companied me. Mai, Erlia, and Nadi, the other girls, were in and out of our side tent. But there was no light chatter among us. The tree cat, that rode as often as was possible on Nadi's shoulder, switched its ringed tail back and forth, a sure sign of uneasiness. And Mai looked distracted, as if she were listening to something afar. She was like Sim with horses, though also she had two Fos deer from the mountain valleys in her team.

It was Eriia who turned from the mirror to face the rest of us squarely.

"There is . . . " She hesitated for a moment with her head suddenly to one side, almost as if she had been hailed. Still facing so, she added, "There is darkness here—something new."

"A distress Calling?" suggested Mai, her face shadowed by concern. She faced that portion of the fairgrounds where dealers in beasts had their stands and where we had found those in pain and terror before. Erlia shook her head.

"No Calling—this rather would hide itself—" She brushed her hand across her face as if pushing aside an unseen curtain that she might sense the better.

She was right. Now it reached me. There are evil odors to sicken one, and evil thoughts like dirty fingers to claw into the mind. This was neither, yet it was there, a whiff of filth, an insidious threat—something I had never met before. Nor had these, my kinswomen, for they all faced outward with a look of questing.

We pushed into the open, uneasy, needing some council from any who might know more. Ort snarled. The red glare of awakening anger came into his large-pupiled eyes, while the tree cat gave a yowl and flattened its ears.

Wowern, his trail clothing also changed, stood there, his hand resting on the head of his favorite companion, the vasa hound that he had bought at this same fair last year—then a slavering, fighting-mad thing who had needed long and patient handling to become as it now was. That, too, was head up, sniffing, as Wowern frowned, his hand seeking the short knife that was all fair custom allowed him as a weapon. As we joined him he glanced around.

"There is danger." The vasa lifted lip in such a snarl as I had not seen since Wowern had won its trust at long last.

"Where and what?" I asked. For I could not center fully on that tinge of evil. Sorcery? But such was forbidden, and there was every guard against it. Not only was there a witch or wizard by every gate to test against the import of such, but those priests who patrolled with the fair-wards of frequent intervals had their own ways of snifling out dire trouble.

Wowern shook his head. "Only . . . it is here." He made answer, then added sharply, "Let us keep together. The Second-Kin"—once more his hand caressed the hound's head—"must remain here. Garner has already ordered it so, for Feeta urges caution. We may go to the dealers, but take all heed in our going."

I was not so pleased. All of us usually spread out and explored the fair on our own. Within the breast pocket of my overtunic I had my purse, and I had thoughts on what I wanted to see. Though first, of course, we would visit the dealers in beasts.

Heeding orders, we moved off as a group, Sim joining us. Nadi set the tree cat in its own cage, and Ort returned reluctantly to the tents. I felt the growth of uneasiness in him, his rising protest that I go without him.

There were other beast shows along the lane where our own camp had been set up. One was manned by the people from the steppes who specialize in the training of their small horses. Then there was a show of bright-winged birds, taught to sing in harmony, and at the far end, the place of Trasfor's clan—no bloodkin to us, yet of our own race. There we were hailed by one hurrying into our path.

Color glowed on Erlia's cheeks when he held out hands in a kinsman's welcome.

"Thasus!" she gave him greeting. I believed that this was something she wished and was sure would happen. By the light in his golden eyes, she was right.

"All is well?" He broke the gaze between the two of them, speaking to all of us as if we had parted only yesterday. "The All Mother has spread her cloak above you?"

Wowern laughed, giving Erlia a tiny push toward Thasus. "Over this one at least. You need have no fear for her, brother."

Erlia did not respond to his gentle attempt at teasing. Her head turned away and on her face lay again a shadow of distress. I had caught it, also, stronger, more determined—that echo of darkness and all evil.

This time it was as if I had actually picked up a foul scent—the kind that clung to swamps, places of death and decay ruled by tainted water. Then it was gone, and I wondered if I had only made a guess without foundation. There are those who sell reptiles and crawling things, yes. But they are set apart from our beasts and have their own corner. One which I, for one, did not spend time in exploring. Yet I was sure this was no stench of animal or of any living thing—

It was gone as quickly as it had come, leaving only that ever-present uneasiness. Still, I dropped a little behind and tried in a very cautious way to pin upon that hint of evil.

"What is with you, Kara?" Wowern matched his stride to mine.

"I do not know." That was true, yet deep within me something stirred. I was certain that never before had this unknown touched me. Still. . .

Once again I caught that rank stench. It was stronger, so that I wavered—and, without being aware of what I did, steadied myself by a touch on

Wowern's arm. He, in turn, started as might a horse suddenly reined in.

"What—" he began again as I swung halfway about to face an opening between two smaller stalls.

"This way!" As certain as if a Calling drew me, I pushed into that narrow opening, heedless whether the rest of the Kin followed.

Ahead was a second line of booths fronting another lane. From these came the chatter of smaller animals, squawks and screams of birds. This was the beginning of the area where merchants and not showmen ruled. Yet it was toward none of these that that trace of need—for need did lie beneath the overlayer of evil—drew me.

I entered the section I had always hitherto shunned—that portion of the mart where dealers in reptiles and scaled life gathered. Dragons I knew, yes, but they are warm-blooded in spite of the scaled bodies and in their way sometimes far more intelligent than my own species. But the crawlers, the fang-jawed, armor-plated creatures, were to me wholly alien.

"What—" Again Wowern broke my preoccupation. I threw out a hand, demanding silence.

The afternoon was nearly spent. Flares outside booths and stalls blazed up—adding their acrid odor—not enough to cover the ill smells of the wares. A deep, coughing bellow drowned out whatever protest my companion might have uttered. Whether the others of our company still followed I did not know nor care.

I stood before a tent perhaps a third the size of ours. But where the leather and stiff woven walls we favored were brilliantly colored, gay to the eye, these walls were uniformly a sickly gray, overcast with a yellow that made me think of decay and pustulant nastiness.

Over the tent-flap the light of a torch brought to life a device such as might be the mark of a noble house. However, even when one stared directly at this (it was as dull as tarnished and unkempt metal) it was difficult for the eye to follow its convolutions. This might be a secret seal only a mage could interpret.

Shivering, I looked away. There was an impression of dark shadow angling forth, as might the tentacle of an obscene creature questing for prey. Still, I must pass under, for what I sought lay within.

No merchant stood to solicit buyers. Nor was there any glow of lamp. What did issue as I walked slowly, more than half against my will, toward that dark opening was the effulgence of a swampland wherein lay evil and death.

There was light after all—a greenish gleam flaring as 1 passed the flap.

I could see, fronting me, a short table of the folding sort, some lumpish stools, like frozen clots of mud. Around the walls of the tent were cages, and from them came a stealthy, restless rustling. Those within were alert . . . and dangerous.

I had no desire to walk along those cages, peer at their occupants. I had no wish to be here at all. Still, my body—or an inner part of me—would not allow me back into the open air. Out of the gloom, which pooled oddly in corners as if made up of tangible hangings, emerged a figure so muffled by a thickly folded robe, so encowled about the head, that I could not have said whether I fronted man or woman.

The green glow that filled the tent, except in those shadowed corners, appeared to draw in about the newcomer, forming an outline, yet not illuminating to any great extent. There was an answering glow of dullish light from the breast of the robe. A pendant rested there—gold, I thought, but dull. I could make out (as if it were purposefully expanding and drawing color just to catch my eyes) the shape of a head—beautiful but still evil. The eyes were half covered with heavy lids, only I had the fancy that beneath was true sight, so I was being regarded by something reaching through the metal—regarded and measured.

"Lady." The voice from beneath the hood, shaped by lips I still could not see, was clear. "You would buy." It was not a true question, rather a statement, as if any bargain we might make was already concluded.

Buy? What? I wanted nothing from any of those cages whose contents I still could not see. Buy?

My gaze was pulled—away from the robe-hidden seller—until I looked over his or her left shoulder. There was one cage apart from the rest, a large one. And within it—

As one walks in one of those troubled dreams wherein one is compelled to a task one dreads, I moved forward. I still had enough control over my shivering body to make a wide circle, not approaching either that table or the one who stood by it.

The cage was before me, and here the shadows were thick curtains—the light did not reach. Nor could I discern any movement. Yet there was life there—that I knew.

I heard a sound from the merchant, out of my sight unless I turned my head. Did he speak or call? Certainly what he uttered was in no tongue I knew.

In the air above the cage appeared a ball of sickly yellow which cast light—no flame of any honest torch.

A creature crouched low upon the floor of the cage, so bent in upon itself that at first it was difficult to see any exact shape. Its skin was a dirty gray, like the tent walls, not scaled, but warty and wrinkled, hanging in folds. There were four limbs—for now it uncoiled to rise. When it reached its full height, it stood erect on hind limbs, its feet webbed and flat. It was taller than I, matching Wowern's inches.

There was a thick growth of ugly yellow wattles about the throat and a ragged comb-crest of the same upon its rounded head. The forelimbs reached forward as massively clawed digits closed about the bars of the cage, scratching along the metal. There was no chin, rather a wide mouth like that of a frog, above that a single slit, which must serve it as a nostril. Only—the eyes . . .

In that hideous nightmare of a face they were so startling that they brought a gasp from me, for they were a clear green—like wondrous gems in an ugly and degrading setting. Nor were the pupils slitted as one would expect in a reptile or amphibian—but round, somehow as human as my own. Also . . . in them lay intelligence—intelligence, and such pain as was a knife thrust into me when our gaze locked.

What the creature was I could not tell. Certainly I had never seen its like before. A flutter of movement to my left, and the robed merchant moved closer. From one of those long sleeves issued a hand as pale as that of any fine lady, very slender and long of finger. This waved in a surprisingly graceful gesture toward the still silent captive.

"A rare bargain, lady. You shall not see the like of this perhaps again in your lifetime."

"What is it—and from where?" Wowern's voice was loud and harsh. He moved in upon my right and I could sense his growing uneasiness, his desire that we both be away from this hidden-faced one and his or her strange wares.

"What is it?" the other repeated. "Ah. It is so rare we have not yet put name to it. From where? The east."

Then I felt cold. All who roved knew what lay to the cast—that swampland so accursed that no one ventures into it—about which all kinds of evil legends and tales have been told for generations.

"A bargain," the merchant repeated when neither of us made comment. "All know of the Quintka—that you delight in your trained beasts—that you seek ever new ones to add to your company. Here is one which will bring many flocking to see it. It is not stupid. I think you can train it well."

Those green eyes—how they demanded that I look upon them! That feeling of pain, of sorrow so deep that there were no words to express it—flowed from them to me.

"It is a monster!" Wowern caught my arm in a grip so tight that his nails near scored my flesh. I could sense fear rising in him—not for himself but for me. He strove to pull me back a step or two, meaning, I understood, to take me out of this place.

"Five silver bits, lady."

The caged creature made no sound; I felt rather than saw its compelling gaze shift a fraction. It looked now to the robed one, and within those green eyes was a flare of deep and abiding hatred. Within me arose an answer.

Those eyes, did they trouble me with some fleeting memory? How could they? This was an unknown monster. Yet at that moment this feeling of emotion was as much a true Calling as if mind-words passed. Our meeting was meant to be.

I brought out my purse. Wowern's hold on me tightened. He protested fiercely but I did not listen. Rather I jerked free, and, without the usual bargaining, I counted forth those bits. Not into that long-fingered graceful hand; rather, I turned and tossed them on the tabletop. I wanted no close contact with the merchant. Nor did I want to linger here, for it seemed those heavy shadows reached farther and farther, drawing out of the tainted air any hint of freshness, leaving me breathless,

"Loose—" I got out that part order, past a thickening of my throat, not sure that even a Quintka could control such a creature. Still, when I met again those eyes so wrongly set in that hideous face, I was not afraid.

The robed one uttered a queer sound, almost as if he or she had choked down jeering laughter. There was no move to draw any bolt or bar locking that cage. Instead, the slender hand went to the pendant lying heavy on the robe, fingers closed tightly about that, hiding the beautiful, vile face from view.

There sped a puff of darkness from that hand—thrusting outward to the bars of the cage. The creature had retreated, standing with shoulders a little hunched. I smelled a sickly sweetness which made my head swim—though I stood well away from that black tongue.

It wreathed about the bars and they were gone. For a long moment the creature remained where it was. From all the other cages about uprose not only a frenzied rustling, as if the other captives aroused to demand their own freedom, but also gutteral grunts and croakings, hissings—

That thing I had so madly purchased shambled forward. I was aware, without turning my head, that the robed one moved even more quickly, retreating into a deeper core of shadow. That retreat pleased me, made me less aware of my own recklessness. Did this merchant fear the late captive? If so, no such fear was mine. For the first time I spoke to the monster, using the same firm tone I would with any new addition to my team. "Come!"

Come it did—treading deliberately on hind legs as if that came naturally, its taloned paw-hands swinging at its sides. I turned, sure within myself that where I went it would follow.

However, once outside that tent I paused, for whatever compulsion had gripped me faded. Also, I realized that I could not return to our own place openly. Even though the twilight gathered in, this creature padding at my heels as if he were a well-trained tree cat, was far too obvious and startling. Though it was often the custom for one of the Quintka to parade a member of his or her personal team through the fair lanes as an inducement for a show, none of us had ever so displayed a creature like unto this.

Wowern wore his trainer's cloak hooked at the throat, thrown back over his shoulders. I had not brought mine. The feeling that we must attract as little attention as possible made me turn to him. There was no mistaking the frown on his face, the stubborn set of his chin.

"Wowern . . ." It irritated me to ask any favor, still, I was pressured into an appeal. "Your cloak?"

His scowl was black, his hand at the buckle of that garment, as if to defend himself against my snatching it from him. Behind him the monster stood quietly, his eyes no longer on me, for his bewattled head was raised as he stared at the device above the tent-flap door.

At that moment I swayed. What reached me was akin to a sharp blow in the face, a blast of raw hatred so deep—so intense—as to be as sharp as a danger Calling! Wowern must also have been struck by it. Hand to knife hilt, slightly crouching, he swung half-about ready to defend himself. Only there was no attack, just the creature, its arms still dangling loosely at its sides, staring upward.

His eyes narrowed, his scowl fading into something else, an intentness of feature as if he strained to listen, Wowern surveyed that other. Then, with his left hand, for he still kept grip upon the knife, he snapped open cloak buckle and swiftly spun the folds of cloth about the creature in such a skillful fashion that its head was covered as well as its body to the thick and warty-skinned thighs.

"Come!" He gave the order now. Again he seized upon my arm with a grasp I could not withstand, propelling me forward to the opening of the same narrow side lane that had brought us here, taking no note of the muffled creature, as if he were entirely certain it would follow. Thus we came back to the place of the Kin, Wowera choosing our path, which lay amid such pockets of shadow as he could find. I allowed him this leadership, for I was in a turmoil within myself.

I realized that we two had been alone. The others of our company must have gone on when I had been seized by the need to hunt out the dismal, shadowed tent. Which was good—for the moment, I could have made no real explanation of why I had done what I did.

Ort met me at the edge of our stand, his head forward, voicing that anxious, half-growling sound he always used when I left him. Sighting what accompanied us, he snarled, lifting lip to show gleaming teeth, his claws well extended as he brought up both paws in the familiar stance of challenge. Before I could send a mind-message, his growl, which had risen to a battle cry, was cut off short. I saw his nostrils expand, though since we had left that foul tent I had not been aware of any odor from the creature.

Now Ort fell back, not as one afraid, rather as one puzzled, confronted by a mystery. I picked up the bewilderment which dampened his anger, confused him to a point I had never witnessed before.

"Brother-Kin," I mind-reached him. Though the muffled monster betrayed no sign of anger, I wanted no trouble. Ort had never been jealous of any of my team. He knew well that he was my seconding, that between the two of us there was a close bond which no other could hope to break. "Brother-Kin, this is one who . . . " I hesitated and then plunged on, because I was as sure as if it had been told jne that I spoke the truth. "Has been ill-used—"

Ort shuffled his huge hind paws; his eyes were still on the creature as now Wowera caught his cloak by the edge and whipped it away from that ugly body, plainly revealed in the torchlight.

The monster made no sound, but its bright eyes were fast on Ort. I saw my Brother-Kin blink.

"Sister . . ." There was an oddness in Ort's sending. "This one—" His thought closed down so that I caught nothing more for a long moment. Then he came into my mind more clearly. "This one is welcome."

The stranger might be welcome to Ort, but with Garner and the rest of the clan it was a different matter. I was told that I had far overstepped the bonds of permissiveness, taking upon myself rights none had dared before. I think that Garner would have speedily dispatched my monster to his former master and cage, save that Feeta, who had been silently staring at my purchase, broke into his tirade. The rest of the clan had also been facing me accusingly, as if, for the first time in my life, they judged me no Kin at all.

"Look to Ort," Feeta's voice arose, "to Ily, Somsa—" She pointed to each of the Second-Kin as she spoke.

We stood in that lesser tent where our smaller teammates were caged, or leashed, according to fair custom. She made us aware of the silence of all those four-footed ones, the fact that they regarded the newcomer round-eyed—and that they had broken mind-link with us.

Garner paused in mid-word, to stare from one to another of those seconding our teams. I felt his thought, striving to establish linkage. The flush of anger faded from his face. In its place came a shadow of concern, which deepened as he beat against stubbornly held barriers.

Feeta took a short pace forward, raising her right hand so that her forefinger touched the forehead of the monster at a point between its brilliant eyes. Then she spoke to me alone, as if there were only the three of us—healer, monster, and I.

"Kara . . . "

I knew what she summoned me to do. In spite of the deep respect and obedience she could always claim from me, I wanted to refuse. Such a choice was denied me. Was it the power of those green eyes that drew me, or the weight of Feeta's will down-beating mine? I could not have said as I went to her, taking her place as she moved aside. My hand came up that my finger, in turn, filled the place where hers had touched.

There was a sick whirling, almost as if the world about me was rent by forces beyond my reckoning. Also, I sensed once more that overshadow of faint memory out of nowhere. This was like being caught in a vast, sticky web—utterly foul, utterly evil, threatening every clean and decent thought and impulse. Entrapped I was, and there could be no loosing of that bond. No! There was also resistance, near beaten under, still not destroyed.

The net was not mine. That much I learned in a breath or two of time. Just as that stubborn, near despairing resistance was not born from any strength within me!

Danger—a murky vision of thick darkness, within which crawled unseen perils all so obscenely alien to my kind as to make the very imagining of them fearsome. Danger—a tool, a weapon launched, set to strike—but a tool that could turn in the user's hand, a weapon whose edge might well cut the wielder.

"What threatens us?" I demanded aloud, even as I also hurled that thoughtwise, threading it into that wattled head through my touch.

I felt Feeta catch my free hand, hold it in a tight grip between both of hers. From the creature came a pulsating flow—sometimes sharp and clear, sometimes fading, as if the one who sent it must fight for every fraction of warning.

Evil, dark, strong, rising like a wave—

There lurked within that darkness the beautiful face of the pendant. It leered, slavered, anticipated—was arrogantly sure of victory. I heard a gasp from Feeta—a single word of recognition.

"Thotharn!"

Her naming made my vision steady, become clearer. Names are potent things, and to call them aloud, our wise people tell us, can act as a focus point for power.

Thotharn I might not know, though of him I had heard, uneasy whispering for the most part, passed from one traveler to another as veiled warnings. There were the Three Lordly Ones upon whose threshold Ithkar stood, there were other presences within our world which my kind recognized and paid homage to—did not we look to the All Mother? But Thotharn was the dark, all that man feared the most, shifting westward from swamplands into which no man, save he be outlawed and damned, dared stray.

It is an old, old land—the swamp country. We who tread the roads collect tales upon tales. It is said there was once a mighty nation in the east—greater than any existing today, when small lordlings hold their own patches of land jealously and fight short, bitter wars over the ownership of a field or some inflated pride. The north was ravaged when I was a small child, by the rise of a conqueror who sought to bring diverse holdings under one rule. But he was slain, and his patchwork of a kingdom died with him, by blood and iron.

Only in the east was no tale of a lordling with ambition. No—there was far more, a rulership that impressed itself on all the land and under which men lived in a measure of peace, no lord daring then to raise sword against his neighbor. There came an end, and tradition said this end was born of evil, nourished in evil, dying evilly, even before the Three Lordly Ones came to us. With the breaking of this power the land fell into the depths of night for a space. All manner of foulness raved and ravaged unchecked. Was Thotharn a part of that? Who knows now?

But in these past few years rumor spread again—first in whispers, and then openly.

Thotharn's priests walked our roads. They did not preach aloud, as did the friars or the wise ones who serve All Mother, striving thus to better the lives of listeners. Nor did they shut themselves into a single temple pile and impress their weight of service demands as did those who outwardly acclaim the Three Lordly Ones. They simply walked, while from them spread an unease and then a drawing—

From the creature I touched flared red rage, strong enough to burn my mind. Thotharn—yes! That name awakened this emotion. But it was against the dread lord of shadows that that blaze was aroused. Whatever this creature might be, he was no hand of the east.

No hand. It caught at my turn of thought, seized upon it, hurled it back to me, changed after a fashion. Obey the will of Thotharn—no, not that, ever! When I acknowledged that fraction of half appeal, that need to make clear what lay inside the other's brain and heart, there was a swell of triumph through the sending—a quick flare like a shout of "Yes, yes!"

I spoke aloud again. Perhaps some part of me wanted to do so, that I make very sure of what I learned.

"They believe you serve them?"

Again a burst of agreement. There is this about mind-send: a man may cloak his values and his desires when he uses words, but there can be no hiding of the truth while sending. Any barrier becomes in itself a warning and injects suspicion. That this hideous thing out of the swampland could hide from me in thought was not to be believed. But, knowing this, why then would any follower of Thotharn—such as the robed merchant must surely be—thrust upon a Quintka possessing sending powers a creature so easily read?

That thought, also, was picked up. The churning within the other became chaotic in eagerness to answer.

Thoughts were so intermingled, came so swiftly, that I could not sort one from the other. I heard far off, as if she were now removed from me, though still our hands were locked, a gasped moan from Feeta. I guessed that it was only our linkage, her power and mine together, that made this exchange possible at all.

There were scraps of information—that the robed one of Thotharn knew of the Quintka, had marked them because of their far traveling. They were readily welcome in lords' keeps, even the temples—that the people who gathered for our showings were many in all parts of the land. Where a wandering priest or priestess of suspect learning could not freely go, one linked with us might penetrate. However, the swamplanders did not truly know the Quintka. They accepted us as trainers of beasts, not realizing that, to us in our own circles, there was no Kin and beast—two things forever separated—rather there was Kin and Second-Kin linked by bonds they did not dream existed.

This one had been prepared (the plan had been a long time in the making—and it was their first such) to be sent out as a link between their great ones, who did not leave the swamp, and the world they coveted so strongly. The first—there would be others. The robed one I had dealt with—I learned in that half-broken communication with my purchase—had believed I was under the influence of Thotharn's subtle scents and pressures when I bought it.

"Why do you betray so easily your masters?" I strove to find some flaw in this flood of explanation. "You were made for what you do, yet now you freely tell us that you are a thing designed to be all treachery and betrayal—"

"Made!" Again a flare of intense anger—so painfully projected into my mind that I flinched and near dropped my finger contact. "Made!"

In that bitter repetition I understood. This thing, in spite of all its grotesque ugliness, was near mad from the usage it had received. It had lain under Thotharn's yoke without hope—now it took the first opportunity to strike back, even though any blow it might deliver could not be a direct one. Perhaps it also had not realized the Quintka had their own defenses.

It was even as I caught this that there dropped a sudden curtain of silence. But not before, it seemed to me, a whiff of foul air blew between me and this purchase of mine. The green eyes half closed, then opened fully. In them I read appeal—an agony of appeal.

Feeta loosed her grip, caught at my wrist, jerking me back from that touch which had brought us such knowledge.

"What is it?" I rounded upon her.

"They are questing—they might learn," she half spat at me. Never had I seen her so aroused. "Is that not so? Blink your eyes if I speak the truth!" She spoke directly to the creature.

Lids fell over those green eyes, rested so for a breath as if to make very sure that we would understand, then arose again.

I heard a swift, deep-drawn breath from Garner where he stood, feet a little apart, as one about to face an enemy charge. Feeta spoke without turning her eyes from the swamp thing.

"You mind-heard?"

Garner bared his teeth as Ort might do. "I heard. So these crawlers in the muck would think to so use us!"

"To plan is not to do." I did not know from whence those words came to me but I spoke them, before I addressed the swamp dweller.

"These you serve, do they have a way of setting a watch upon you? Blink in answer!" Again, deliberately those eyes closed and reopened.

"Do they know of our linkage? Blink twice if this is not so." I waited, cold gathering within me, fearing one answer, but hoping for another. That came— two measured blinks.

"So . . ." Garner expelled breath in a mighty puff. He dropped a hand on Feeta's shoulder and drew her to him. The tie between them was so old and deep that I did not wonder he had been able to link with her during that exchange. "Now what do we do?"

I had one answer, though whether he would accept it I could not tell. "To return this would arouse their suspicions, lead them to other plans."

He snorted. "Think you that I do not understand that?" He regarded the creature measuringly. Then he made his decision.

"This one is yours, Kara. Upon you rests the burden."

Which, of course, was only fair. Garner and the others left me with the self-confessed spy of evil. Only Second-Kin—Ort, the rest of the beasts— remained. They continued to watch the stranger with unrelenting stares.

We had no cage large enough to accommodate the being, and somehow it did not seem fitting to set a rope loop about its neck, tether it with the four-footed ones. Where was I to keep it? Soon would come time for the night shows, and it should be under cover before our patrons came to look at the animals as was the regular custom.

Ort answered the problem with action that surprised me greatly. He padded to the baskets of trappings set along one side of the tent, came back to me, a wadding of cloth in his forepaws. I shook out a cape with a hood, old and worn, which had been used to top and protect the stored "costumes" our teams wore. It was a human garment and the folds appeared adequate to cover the creature.

Wowern had already taken back his cloak; now I flung this musty-smelling length about the thing's shoulders, fastened the rusty throat buckle. To my astonishment the creature, as if it were indeed a man and not grotesque beast, used its forepaws to pull the hood up over its misshapen head, well forward so that its ugliness was completely hidden. I could almost believe that I fronted a man—not a monster.

Ort chirped, one of those sounds my human throat could not equal. Our disguised one swung about, stumping after my seconding, out of the tent and into the shadows beyond. With an exclamation I hurried after.

Ort apparently had no such thing as escape in mind, nor did the other, who was certainly powerful enough to leave if it wished, deviate from the path shown it. Rather, it squatted down at the end of the row where our mounts were tied, concealed behind the bales of hay now stacked as a back wall. In those shadows the dull gray of the cloak was hidden, one would not have known that anything sheltered there.

The horses and ponies had stirred uneasily at first, but Ort paced down their line, giving voice to that soothing throat hum which he had used many times over to reassure nervous beasts. They accepted this newcomer because of his championship.

I hurried to change clothing, catching up some cold food to eat between the doffing of one robe, the donning of another, the fastening of buckles, the setting of sham jewels about my throat, wrists, and in hair strings. Nadi and Erlia were already prepared and on their way to lead forth their teams, but Mai stood before our mirror applying a thicker red to her lips.

"What do you plan to do?" she asked bluntly. "To carry with us a spy— even though it seems to have no liking for its true master—that is to endanger all of us. Why do you bring this upon us, Kara?" There was no softness in her voice, rather hostility in the eyes that met mine within the mirror.

"I—I had no choice." To me that was truth. I had clearly been drawn to the merchant's booth; once there I had been enspelled . . . . Enspelled? I shivered, the cold was well within me now and I could not rid myself of it.

"No choice?" She was both scornful and angry. "This is foolishness. Would you say you are englamored by this bestial ugliness out of the dark? Ha, Kara, you cannot expect the rest of us to risk its presence."

She swept away and I knew that she gave a truthful warning. Those of the clan would not long accept—even at Garner's and Feeta's bidding, if I could depend upon that—this addition to our party. I did not want it, either. I—

Yet I had paid that silver without a question. Unless . . . . Again I shivered and stood very still, my hands clasped tightly on the handle of my team leader's wand. Unless there was something in me which that robed one had been able to touch, to tame to his or her will, even as I lead my team! If that were so, then what flaw lay inside me that evil could reach out so easily and twist to its own usage? At that moment I knew fear so sharp it made me waver where I stood, throw out a hand to the edge of the mirror table and hold fast, for it seemed that the very earth moved under my feet.

I heard the thump of drums in the show tent. Habit set me into motion without thought. Nadi was dancing with her long-legged birds now—next I must be ready with my marchers. I staggered a little, still under the touch of that fear. Ort awaited me, his hand drum slung about his thick neck. Behind him, in an ordered row, were Oger, Ossan, Obo, Orn—just as they had been for months and years. Tall all of them, their talons displayed in order to astound the audiences, their bush combs aloft, and their long necks twining back and forth to the beat of the drums.

Nadi's music faded. She would be issuing from the other side of our stage. I breathed deeply twice, steadying my nerves—putting out of my mind with determination all except that which was immediately before me—the need to give my part of the show.

We had finished the first appearance of the evening and Garner was talking to several who wore the shoulder ribbons and house marks of lords, making arrangements for private performances. Those would be steady for us all during the two ten-days we were in Ithkar. However, another stood in the lesser light just at the edge of the torch beams as if waiting his or her turn at bargaining. Enveloped in a cloak, it might well be a woman—and of that I was sure when a hand bearing a ring-bracelet came out of hiding to draw closer the cloak. She made no effort to push forward until Garner had finished and the others were gone. I saw her speak and Garner raise his head, stare across the crowded yard between our tents where fairgoers came to see closer our teammates. He looked at me, nodded, and I could not escape that silent order.

So I went to join him and the other. Her gem-backed hand touched her hood, pushing it back a little. I saw a face, deeper brown in color—some southern-born lady, I thought. Her features were thin and sharp, with an impatient line between her straight brows. No beauty—but one who was obeyed when it pleased her to give orders.

"Speak with this one." Garner was also impatient. "What we know is her doing." He left abruptly. The lady regarded me as 1 would a beast unknown—curious, perhaps. However, there was a sting in that survey. I lifted my chin and eyed her as boldly back.

"You made a purchase." She spoke abruptly. There was a slurring in her speech new to me. "It was one not meant for you."

"I was asked a price and I paid. The merchant seemed satisfied," I returned. This might be the answer to our problem. If she wanted the swamp dweller, then let her have him. But I would not strike any bargain until I knew more. At this moment it seemed to me that I saw between the two of us those wide green eyes.

"Paugh!" Her lips moved then as if she would spit, as might any common fair drab, highborn though she seemed. "That merchant exceeded his instructions. I have come"—a second hand appeared from beneath her robe, in it a purse weighing heavy by the look—"to buy what is rightfully mine. Where is he?"

"Safe enough." I made no move to take that purse. The hand holding it had come fully under the light and on the forefinger I saw the ring—the same smiling face of the merchant's pendant formed its bezel.

"Summon him." She moved a little, almost as if she wanted to be well away from us. "Summon him at once!"

Had they then learned, these followers of Thotharn, that the swamp creature had betrayed their purpose, and so were eager to reclaim him? What would be his fate at their hands? I knew that Garner would report to the temple all we had learned. These could reclaim the creature, slay it, and deny all. What proof would we have then that they had tried to move so against the peace of Ithkar?

"I—" Fear I had known, even disgust, when I had made that purchase; still, I would betray no living thing. For the Quintka might not deny refuge to the Second-Kin. Second-Kin—a swamp creature out of the dark land? Yet Ort and the others had made it welcome after their own fashion, and their instincts I trusted.

"Summon him!" Her order was sharp; she waved the bag back and forth so it gave out a clink of metal. It must be well filled with coin. "I give you four—five times what you paid. He is mine—bring him hither!"

I heard the guttural throat sound from Ort and looked over my shoulder. My Brother-Kin led a cloaked shape into the open, the swamp creature. Still, Ort lifted his lips a little, showing fangs, and I knew that what he did was not in obedience to such as she who stood with me, nor even to me. He moved for himself—and perhaps another.

Those who had come to see the animals had passed along—I heard the boom of a gong signaling the second part of our performance and the thud of hooves as the horses moved out into the circular space beyond. We were alone now—the four of us.

"Ran . . . " Her voice was far different from that with which she had addressed me. "Ran, I came as I had promised—freedom!" She swung up the purse to give forth again that clinking.

I saw a warty paw in the open, tugging at the hood so it fell free upon his broad shoulders. His nightmare face was clear. She bit her lip and could not suppress the shadow of distaste, near of loathing. She is not, the thought flashed into my head, as good an actress as she believes.

"Take it!" Again she shoved the bag in my direction.

I put my hands behind my back as the green eyes turned toward me. I could not pick up any clear mind-speech, and I dared not touch him to establish linkage. But somehow I felt again that blaze of red rage—not for me, but for this woman.

"I will not," I said firmly. Though I could not find any true reason why— except those eyes.

"You shall!" She thrust her head forward and her hood fell away, her eyes bored into me. Then I saw her gaze change a fraction; she caught her breath. "No. . ." Her voice was a half whisper. "Not that—the blood—"

I am no voice of the All Mother, I wear no robe of the Three Lordly Ones—I am no shaman of any tribe. Still, there awoke in me then something that I had sensed twice before this day—an ancient knowledge. Nor was that of the Quintka. Partly of their blood I might be—yet who knew what other strain my dead mother had granted me?

What I did came in that moment as natural as breathing—I brought forth both hands as I took two quick steps toward my monster. He pawed at the buckle of his cloak and that fell away from him, leaving his nightmare body bare. My hands fell to his shoulders, the roughness of his skin was harsh under mine. He had to bend a little from his height. All that filled the world now were his green eyes—and in them was a flashing light of eagerness, of hope reborn, of pain now fading—

"By the thorn and by the tree,
By the moon and by the sea,
By the truth and by the right,
By the touch and by the sight,
Let that which is twisted,
Straightened be.
That the imprisoned go free!"

I pressed my lips to the slimy cold of his toad mouth. Fighting revulsion— pushing it utterly from me.

When I drew back I cried aloud—words that had no meaning, yet were of power—and I felt that power fill me until I could hold no more. My fingers crooked, bit into his odious flesh. I tore with my nails—the skin parted, as might rotted cloth. As cloak so old that nothing was left but tatters, that skin gave to my frantic hands, rent, and fell away.

No monster, but a man—a true man—as I shredded from him that foul overcovering. I heard a shriek behind me—a keening that arose and arose. Then the man I had freed flung out one arm, to set me behind him, confronting the woman. She had her beringed hand up, held close to her lips, ugly and open, as she mouthed words across the surface of that head-set ring. Frantically she spilled forth spells. His hand shot out, caught hers. He twisted her finger, pulled free the ring, and flung it to the ground.

There was a barking cry from Ort. One of his ponderous hind feet swept between the two at ground level, stamped that circlet into the beaten earth.

The woman wailed then spat before she fled. Where the ring had been pounded there was a small thread of smoke. Ort leaned forward and spat in turn, full upon the thread, setting it into nothingness.

"So be it!" A deep voice.

A well-muscled arm swooped, fingers caught up the cloak, once more twisting it about a bare body, but this time a human body. "So be it."

"You are a man—" The power that had filled me vanished as quickly as it had come. I was left with only amazement and a need to understand.

He nodded. Gone from him was all but the eyes—those were rightly his, marking him even through the foulness of the spell. "I am Ran Den Fur—a fool who went where no man ventured, and by my folly I learned. Now . . ." He gazed about him. I saw the cloak move as he drew a deep breath, as if inhaling new life to rid him of the old. "I shall live again—and perhaps I have put folly behind me."

He looked at me with the same intentness as when he had tned to link earlier.

"I have much to thank you for, lady. We shall have time—now—even in the shadow of Thotharn, we still have time."

GET OUT OF MY DREAM!
Perilous Dreams (1976) DAW

Every world had its own rites, laws, and customs. Itlothis Sb Nath considered herself, in position of a Per-Search agent, well adjusted to such barriers and delays in carrying out her assignments. But inwardly she admitted that she had never faced just this problem before.

Though she was not seated in an easyrest, which would automatically afford her slim body maximum comfort, she hoped the woman facing her got the impression she was entirely relaxed and certain of herself during their interview. That this . . . this Foostmam was stubborn was nothing new. Itlothis had been trained to handle both human and pseudohuman antagonism. But the situation itself baffled her and must not be allowed to continue so.

She continued to smile as she stated her case slowly and clearly for perhaps the twentieth time in two days. Patience was one of the best virtues for an agent, providing both armor and weapon.

"Gentle Fem, you have seen my orders. You will admit those are imperative. You say that Oslan Sb Atto is one of your present clients. My instructions contain authority to speak with him. This is a matter of time, he must be alerted to the situation at his home estate. That is of utmost future importance, not only to him, but to others. We do not interfere on another world unless the Over-Council approves."

There was no change in the other's expression. By the Twenty Hairs of Ing! Itlothis might as well be addressing a recorder, or even the time-eroded wall behind the Foostmam.

"This one you seek," the woman's voice was monotonous, as if she were entranced, but her eyes were alert, alive, cunningly intelligent, "lies in the dream rooms. I have told you the truth, Gentle Fem. One does not disturb a dreamer. It would be dangerous for both your planetman and the dreamer herself. He contracted for a week's dreaming, provided his own recorded background tapes for the instruction of the dreamer. Today is only the second day . . ."

Itlothis curbed a strong desire to pound the table between them, snarl with irritation. She had heard the same words, or those enough like them to seem the same, for six times now. Even two more days' delay and she could not answer for success in her mission. Oslan Sb Atto *had* to be awakened, told of the situation on Benold, then shipped out on the first available starship.

"Surely he has to wake to eat," she said.

"The dreamer and her client are nourished intravenously in such cases," the Foostmam replied. Itlothis did not know whether she detected a note of triumph in that or not. However, she was not prepared to so easily accept defeat.

Now she leaned forward to touch fingertip to the green disk among those she had spread out on the table. Her polished nail clicked on that ultimate in credentials which any agent could ever hope to carry. Even if that disk had been produced off world by an agency not native to this planet, an agency which held to the pretense of never interfering in local rule, yet the sight of it should open every door in this city of Ty-Kry.

"Gentle Fem, be sure I would not ask you to undertake any act which would endanger your dreamer or her client. But I understand there is a way which such dreaming *can* be interrupted . . . if another enters the dream knowingly to deliver a message of importance to the client."

For the first time a shade of expression flitted across the gaunt face of this hard-featured woman, who might well have played model for some of the archaic statues Itlothis had noted at this older end of the city where the sky towers of the newer growth did not sprout.

"Who? . . ." she began and then folded her lips tightly together.

Within Itlothis felt a spark of excitement. She had found the key!

"Who told me that?" she finished the other's half-uttered question smoothly. "Does it matter? It is often necessary for me to learn such things. But this can be done, can it not?'

Very reluctantly the other gave the smallest nod.

"Of course," Itlothis continued, "I have made a report to the Council representative of what I wish to do. He will send the chief medico on his staff, that we may so fulfill regulations with a trained observer."

The Foostmam was again impassive. If she accepted that hint as a threat or a warning, she gave no sign that Itlothis's implied mistrust caused her any dismay.

"This method is not always successful," was her only comment. "Annota is our best dreamer. I cannot now match her skill. There are unemployed only . . ." She must have touched some signal for there flashed on the wall to her right a brilliant panel bearing symbols unreadable to the off-world agent. For a long moment the Foostmam studied those. "You can have Eleudd. She is young but shows promise, and once before she was used as an invasion dreamer."

"Good enough." Itlothis arose. "I shall summon the medico and we will have this dream invasion. Your cooperation is appreciated, Foostmam." But not, she added silently, your delay in according it.

She was so well pleased at gaining her point that it was not until the medico arrived, and they entered the dream chamber, did Itlothis realize that she was facing a weirder adventure than she had in any previous assignment. It was one thing to trace a quarry through more than one world across the inhabited galaxy, as she had done for a number of planet years. But to seek one in a dream was something new. She did not think she quite liked the idea, but to fail now was unthinkable.

The dreamers of Ty-Kry were very well known. Operating out of the very ancient hive presided over by the Foostmam, they could create imaginary worlds, adventures, which they were able to share with anyone able to pay their high fees. Some of the dreamers were permanently leased out to a household of the multi-credit class inhabiting the upper reaches of the sky towers, where their services were for the amusement of a single individual or house-clan. Others remained at the Hive, their clients coming to them.

While entwined mentally with a dreamer, that client entered a world seeming utterly real. And an action dreamer of A rating was now fashionably expensive. Itlothis surveyed the room in which her quarry now lay lost in his dream.

There were two couches (the Foostmam was overseeing the preparation of two more which would crowd the room to capacity). On one lay a girl, thin, pallid of skin, half her head hidden in a helmet of metal which was connected by wires to another such covering Oslan's head where he rested on the adjoining couch. There was also an apparatus standing between their resting places hung with bottles feeding liquid into the veins of their arms.

Itlothis could see little of Oslan's face, for the helmet covered it to nose level. But she identified him. This was the man she had hunted. And she longed to put an end to her frustration at once by jerking off that dream cap, bringing him back. Only the certain knowledge that such an action was highly dangerous made her control her fingers.

The Foostmam's attendants had set up one couch beside the dreamer and a tech made careful linkages of wires between that of the cap now worn by the girl, and the one waiting to be donned. While a second couch was placed beyond Oslan's, another cap adjusted to match his.

That uneasiness was growing in Itlothis, akin now to fear. She hated beyond all else to be under another's will in this fashion. On the other hand, the need for bringing Oslan back was imperative. And she had the medico to play guard.

Though she showed no outward reluctance as she followed the orders of the Foostmam, settled herself on the waiting divan and allowed the helmet to be fitted on, yet Itlothis had a last few moments of panic when she wanted to throw off that headgear, light and comfortably padded within that it was, to run from this room . . . .

They had no way of telling into what kind of an adventure Oslan had been introduced. No two dreams were ever alike, and the dreamer herself did not often foresee what pattern her creations would follow once she began the weaving of her fantasies. Also the Foostmam had been careful to point out that Oslan had supplied the research tapes and not relied on those from the Hive collection. Thus Itlothis could not know what kind of a world she might now face.

She could never afterward be sure how one *did* enter the dream world. Was there a moment of complete unconsciousness akin to normal sleep before one opened one's eyes upon . . . this?

Itlothis only knew that she was suddenly standing on the rough top of a cliff where rocks were wind-worn into strange shapes among which a flow of air whistled in queer and mournful moaning. There was another sound also, the drum of what she recognized as surf, from below.

But, she *knew* this place! She was at Yulgreave, on her own home world! She need only turn away from the sea's face to see the ancient, very ancient ruins of Yul in all their haunted somberness. Her mind was giddy. She had been prepared for some strange, weird dream world, then she had been abruptly returned to the planet of her own birth! Why . . . how . . .

Itlothis looked for Yul, to make sure of her situation.

But . . .

No ruins!

Instead heavy and massive towers arose unbroken, as if they had grown out of the cliff's own substance, as a tree grows from the earth, not as if they had been laid stone upon stone by man or manlike creatures. The ancient fortress in all its strength was far more imposing in every way than the ruins she knew . . . larger, extending farther than the remaining evidences of her own age suggested.

And, remembering what her own time deemed Yul to be, Itlothis shrank back until her shoulders scraped against one of the cliff pinnacles. She did not want to see Yul whole, yet she found she could not turn away her eyes, the dark rise of tower and wall drew her.

Yul had been in ruins when the first of her own species had come to Benold's world a thousand planet years ago. There were other scattered traces of some very ancient civilization to be seen. But the least destroyed was Yul. Yet, eager as her own kind had always been to explore the mysteries of those who had preceded them in rulership of any colonized world, the settlers on Benold did not willingly seek out Yul. There was that about the crumbling walls which made them uneasy, weighed so upon the spirit of any intruder that sooner or later he withdrew in haste.

So, though it was viewed from a distance, as Itlothis viewed it now, and tri-dees of it were common, those were all taken from without. Why had Oslan wanted to see Yul as it might once have been?

The puzzle of that overrode much of her initial aversion. That this dream had a real purpose she guessed. It was not merely a form of pleasant escape. The girl moved away from the crag against which she had sheltered and began to reconsider her mission.

Oslan Sb Atto, he was heir to the vast Atto holdings, after the custom of Benold. Thus when Atto Sb Naton had died six planet months ago it had been very necessary that his heir take up Clan-Chief duties as soon as possible. His brother, Lars Sb Atto, had hired Itlothis's agency to bring back with the utmost dispatch the heir who had cruised off world. Later, when the continued absence of the Atto heir had taken on political ramifications, the search became a Council matter.

But why had Oslan come to the dreamer's planet, sought out the Hive, and entered a dream set on his own home world in the far past? It was as if he, in turn, might be searching something for importance. Itlothis thought this the truth.

What *did* he so hunt?

Well, the sooner she discovered that, the sooner they would both be freed to return to the right Benold and Oslan's duties there. Though Itlothis hated the very thought of what must follow, she began to walk toward Yul, certain, as if Oslan himself had told her, that there lay the core of this tangle.

At least the visible forms of life familiar in her own time had not altered. Overhead swooped the seapars, their crooning cries carrying above the boom of surf, their brilliant orange, blue, and green plumage bright even on this day when the sun was cloud-veiled. Among the rocks grew small plants, almost as gray-brown as the stones about them, putting out ambitious runners toward the next cupful of soil caught between the crags.

Itlothis kept a wary watch on Yul. Though its walls were now entire, its towers reaching high, unbroken, she could detect no sign that it was any more inhabited than in her own time. No banners were set on those towers, nothing showed in the windows, which were like lidless eyes staring both seaward and toward the rise of sharp hills to the west.

Yul lay on the edge of the Atto holdings. Itlothis had seen it last when going to confer with Lars Sb Atto before leaving Benold. They had flown hither from Killamarsh, crossing the mass of ruins to reach that inner valley beyond the hills.

In fact, the House of Atto could claim this cliff and the ruins had they so wished. But the ill repute of Yul had made it no man's territory.

Determinedly Itlothis scrambled over the rough way, listening to the cries of the seapars, studying the grim pile of Yul. She had thought that plunged into Oslan's dream, she would meet him immediately. But apparently that did not follow. Very well, she must hunt him down.

As she approached the now unbreached outer wall, the huge blocks of its making added to her uneasiness. There was a gate in that wall, she knew. Oddly enough it did not face the interior of the land, but the sea. And, if she were to reach that, she must follow a perilous route along the verge of the cliff.

There was no road, nor even path. That there had been none such had always baffled the experts among her own people. Why had the only gate not fronted on some road impressive enough to match the walls? Also there was no trace of harbor below, no sign this had ever been part of a port.

Itlothis hesitated, surveying the way before her with a doubt which began to shake her self-confidence. She had initiated this quest believing that all her experience and training prepared her for any action. After all, she was a top agent, one with an unbroken number of successfully concluded cases behind her. But then always she had been operating in a normal world . . . normal as to reality. Here she felt more and more cast adrift, all those familiar skills and safeguards challenged.

In any *real* world . . . she drew a deep breath. She must make herself accept for the present that this was a real world. If she could not regain her confidence she might be totally lost. After all many of the planets on which she had operated with high efficiency had been weird and strange. Thus, she must not think of this as being a fantasy Benold, but rather one of those strange worlds. If she could hold to that, she must regain command of the situation.

The way ahead was very rough, and she did not know whether the strip was under observation from Yul. She kept glancing up at the windows, to see nothing. Yet she could not escape the feeling she was being watched.

Setting her chin firmly, Itlothis crept forward. The space between the edge of the cliff and the wall seemed very narrow, and the thunder of the surf was loud. She set her back to the wall, slipping along sidewise, for she had the feeling she might tumble and fall out and down.

There were many upward jutting rocks and by each she paused. Then she crouched into hiding, her heart beating wildly, her breath shallow. For more than seapars now soared over the waves!

Whatever the thing was, a flying craft perhaps, it came at such speed as to make her wonder. And it was homing on that sea gate toward which she crept. Like an arrow shot from some huge primitive bow it sped into that opening with the same unslacking speed.

Craft . . . or some living monster? Itlothis could not be sure which. She had a confused impression of wings, the body between them shining with metallic brilliance. Man-made . . . or living?

She was startled by a flicker of movement overhead and glanced up. There, well above her, she was certain that someone, or something, had moved into a window opening.

Itlothis leaned far back against the rock which sheltered her. Yes, head and shoulders were framed in the window opening. And, by comparison of size, either the stranger she sighted or the window itself was far out of proportion, for the body was dwarfed by the frame about it.

He was climbing out on the sill!

The girl gasped. Was he going to jump? Why?

No, he was moving cautiously, hunkering down to swing over. Now he appeared to find some support for his feet. But how did he *dare?* He was pressed tightly to the wall, inching down, with hands and feet feeling along the stone for grips.

Itlothis was tense with empathy for the strain of that descent. That he was able to find a way seemed to her a miracle. But he moved surely, if slowly, seemingly certain he could find the holds he sought.

The sight drew Itlothis from her shallow hiding place to the foot of the wall immediately below where he hung so perilously. She lifted her own hands to skim that surface, unable by eye to distinguish any break in it. Then her fingers dropped into a kind of niche cut so cleverly that it must have been fashioned for no other purpose than to so afford an invisible ladder for a climber.

She stepped back a little the better to watch the man descending the wall. There was a familiar look about his head, the set of his shoulders. Her eyes trained to value such points identified him.

Oslan!

With a sigh of relief Itlothis waited. Now she need only make contact, explain the need to break his dream. Then they could return to the world of reality. For the Foostmam had admitted that Oslan's desire held the dreamer's efforts in balance, that, whenever he wished, he could awake.

Perhaps he had already completed whatever purpose had brought him to this ancient Yul. But at any rate Itlothis's message was important enough to keep him from lingering any longer.

Having made sure of his identity, she noted he was wearing clothing alien to any she had seen. The covering clung tightly to his body but was elastic, as if fashioned from small scales, one fitted to slightly overlap the next. Only his hands and his feet were bare. The exposed skin was brown enough to match the stone down which he crawled.

His hair made a smooth cap, dark enough to show better. Itlothis knew, though she had not yet seen his face, that he had the well-cut features of his clan; he could be counted handsome if in the tri-dees she had seen there had been any expression to lighten a dull, set countenance.

Still a way above cliff level, he loosed his hold, ending his descent with a leap. He breathed heavily as he landed. Itlothis could guess the cost in effort of that long trip down the wall.

For a moment he remained where he was, gasping, his hands and feet both resting on the ground, his head hanging as he drew air into laboring lungs.

"Clan Head Oslan," Itlothis spoke with official formality.

He flung up his head with a jerk, as if he had been so hailed by some monster out of the sea below. His gaze centered on her as he scrambled to his feet, planting his back against the wall. His hands balled into fists, prepared to front some attack.

She saw his brilliant green eyes narrow. There was certainly no lack of expression in his face now! No, what she faced was raging anger. Then his eyes half closed, his fists fell to his sides, as if he saw in her not the danger he had expected.

"Who are you?" His question came in almost the same monotone as the Foostmam used, his voice might be willed not to display any revealing emotion.

"Per-search Agent Itlothis Sb Nath," she replied briskly, "Clan Chief Oslan, you are needed."

"Clan Chief?" he interrupted her. "Then Naton has died?"

"In Ice Month Two, Clan Chief. You are badly needed on Benold." Itlothis was suddenly struck by the oddity of their present position. They *were* on Benold. A pity the dream world was not the real one. It would save so much valuable time.

"You have not only clan affairs to settle," she continued, "but there is a need for a new treaty over the output of the mines, a Council affair much pressed by time."

Oslan shook his head. Once more a look of mingled alarm and anger crossed his face.

"No way, no way, agent, do you get me back yet!" He moved closer.

In spite of herself, Itlothis, to her annoyance, retreated a step or two.

"Now," he said with a whip-crack note in his voice, "get out of my dream!" It was as with each word he aimed a stun bolt at her.

However, his open opposition brought a quick reaction. Itlothis no longer retreated, standing firm to meet his advance. This was not the first time she had faced an unwilling quarry. And his negative attitude steadied her.

"This is a Council affair," she replied briskly. "If you do not . . ."

He was laughing! His head was flung back, his fists resting on his hips, he laughed, though his amusement was plainly fired with anger.

"The Council and you, Per-search Agent, what do you propose to do? Can you now summon an armsman to back you—*here?*"

Itlothis had a momentary vision of yet another couch, another dreamer, if any such could be crowded into the Hive chamber, an armsman ready to be transported. That was utterly impossible. On this case she did, indeed, have only herself.

"You see," he took another step closer, "what good is any Council authority here? The Council itself lies uncounted years in the future."

"You refuse to understand," Itlothis retained her outward calm. "This is of the utmost importance to you, also. Your brother Lars, the Council, must have your presence on Benold by High Sun Day. I have the necessary authority to get you on the nearest hyper ship . . . "

"You have nothing at all!" Oslan interrupted her for the second time. "This is my dream and only I can break it. Did they tell you that?"

"Yes."

"Well, then you know. And you are my captive here, for all your powers and authorities, unless you willingly agree now to let me send you back."

"Not without you!" Even as she retorted, Itlothis wondered if she were making some fatal choice. However, she had no intention of giving up as easily as he seemed to think her willing to do.

"Do you wish to be cited as relinquishing your clanship?" she added quickly. "In this matter the Council has extraordinary powers and . . . "

"Be quiet!" His head turned slightly toward the walls of Yul. So apparent was his listening that she did also.

Was that deep humming note really a sound, or a vibration carried to them through the rock on which they stood? She could not be sure.

"Back!" Oslan flung out his arm and caught at her, to drag her to him until they both stood pressed to the wall. He was still listening, his face grim, his head at an angle, as he stared up at the outer defenses of Yul.

"What is it?" Itlothis asked in a whisper as the moments lengthened and he did not change position.

"The swarm. Be quiet!"

Highly uninformative, but his tension had communicated to her the necessity for following his order. This was Oslan's dream and he had come out of Yul, therefore he plainly had knowledge she lacked.

There came a burst of light, like that of an alarm flash, aimed at the air over the sea. Another and another, issuing from the cliff-facing gate and shooting over the waves so rapidly Itlothis could not see more than what seemed balls of fierce radiance. Then these were gone, quickly lost far out over the water.

As he stood body against body with her, Itlothis felt the tension ebb from Oslan. He drew a deep breath.

"They are gone! There will be a safe period now."

"Safe for what?"

Oslan looked straight into her eyes. Itlothis did not quite like that searching stare, it was as if he wished to read her thoughts. Though she wanted to break free, she could not. And her failure brought resentment. She did not wait for him to answer her question but repeated her own message as bluntly as she could.

"If you do not break the dream, now, you will lose Atto. The Council will confirm Lars as Chief in order not to waste time."

His smile was tinged with anger as his laughter had been.

"Lars as Chief? Perhaps . . . if there is an Atto left for him to rule over."

"What do you mean?"

"Why do you think I am here? Why do you think I crossed half the star lanes to find a dreamer to put me in Yul's past?"

His stare still held her. Now his hands fell on her shoulders and he shook her, as if that gesture would emphasize his words.

"You think Yul is a ruin, a masterless place in our own world. Men have repeated that since the first of our kind explored Benold. But Yul is not just tumbled walls and a feeling of awe. No, it is the encasement for something very old . . . and dangerous."

He believed this; she read the truth in his voice. But what? Itlothis did not get a chance to ask her questions, words poured out of him now in a torrent of speech.

"I have been in this Yul. I have seen . . . " he closed his eyes as if to shut out some sight. "Our Yul above ground may be three-quarters erased by time. Only that which is the heart of Yul is not dead. It lies sleeping, and it begins to stir. I tell you I have speculated on this for some years, searched out all accounts. A year ago I dared take a scanner within for a reading. I sent the data to the central computer. Do you want to know the verdict?" He shook her again. "Well, it was that the new mine tunnels spreading east had alerted, awakened something. That thing is ready to *hatch* . . . ."

Itlothis realized that he believed so fervently in what had brought him here that she could raise no argument he would listen to, the fantasy possessed him.

"To hatch," she repeated. "Then what is *it?*"

"That which once filled Yul with life. You have just seen its swarm take flight. Well, that is only a thousandth part of what Yul can produce. Those flying things are energy, and they feed on energy. If one came near you, your body would crisp into ash. There are other parts to it, also." She again felt him tense. "That which lies in Yul can appear in many forms, all utterly alien and dangerous to us.

"Men, or beings not unlike men, reared Yul, made those other cities we can trace on our Benold. Then . . . *that* came. Whether it sprouted from some experiment which went wrong, or broke through from another dimension, another world . . . there is no record.

"Only those who found it made it a god, fed it with life energy until it was greater, the absolute lord of the planet. Then it blasted away the men it no longer needed, or thought it no longer needed.

"But when there was no more life energy, it began to fail. Instead of spanning the planet, it was forced back to this continent, then into Yul alone. It knew fear then and prepared a nest. There it went into hibernation . . . to sleep away the years."

"But the mine-search rays awoke it. Those fed it new energy. It grows again. Benold has new food for it. And . . . "

"You must warn the Council! Wake us."

He shook his head. "You do not understand. This monster may not be destroyed in our time. It can feed upon the minds of those who face it, empty their bodies of lifeforce. There is no shield. Only in the past can it be defeated. If its nest is sealed against it, then it will starve and die. Benold will be free."

Itlothis was shaken. Oslan must be mad! Surely he knew this was a dream! What could they accomplish in a dream? Perhaps if she humored him a little . . . .

"I gathered all the reports," he continued. "I brought those to this dreamer. They can use such research to back a dream. Clients are often interested in the past. I had her concentrate on my readings."

"But this is a dream!" Itlothis protested. "We are not really on Benold in the far past! You cannot do what . . . "

This time the shake he gave her was savage. "Can I not? Watch and see! There are dimensions upon dimensions, worlds upon worlds. Belief can add to their reality. *I* say that this is the Benold which foreshadows the Benold that is now." Oslan swung away from her to face the wall. "It has sent out its feeders, it will be concentrating only on them. This is my time!"

He reached above for a hold, began to climb.

Itlothis moved too late to prevent him. She could not leave this madman here. If she went with him, agreed outwardly that what he said was true, might she lead him to break the dream? Ever since she had entered this fantasy she had felt at a disadvantage, shaken out of her calm competence. She now could only cling to the hope that she could influence Oslan in the future if she kept with him.

She sat on the rock, pulled off her boots. With her fingers and toes free, she searched for the wall hollows, started up the wall of Yul.

Luckily she possessed a head for heights. Even so she knew better than to look down. And she feared and hated what she was doing. But, determinedly, she drew herself up. Oslan was already at the window. Now he reached over to aid her. And they pushed from the wide sill down into a shadow-cornered room.

"Best you did come," Oslan remarked. "Otherwise *that* might sense your presence. You must be quiet for you cannot begin to imagine what your folly in entering my dream might cost you."

Itlothis choked down her anger. This was a madman. He could not yet be influenced by any argument, no matter how subtle. So she offered no protest, but crept after him along the wall, for he shunned the center portion of the chamber.

The stone walled, ceilinged, floored room was bare. What light came issued from the window behind them. Oslan did not head to the door Itlothis could sight on the other side. Instead, he halted halfway down the wall, and felt above him at the full stretch of his arms, as if seeking another place to climb.

However, he did not swing up as she half expected him to do, to no purpose, since the ceiling, though well above their heads, appeared entirely solid. There sounded a grating noise. Three massive blocks before which he stood thudded back, to display a very dark opening.

How had Oslan known that to be here? Of course, in a dream, an imagined wall passage was entirely possible. Only the seeming reality of this shadowed room continued to war with logic. How *could* a dream appear so real?

"In!" he whispered. When she did not move at once he jerked her into the hidden way. She tried to break free as the blocks moved to seal them in a dark which was more horrible because now she was conscious of an intangible sense of wrongness, that which dwelt in the Yul she knew.

"Here is a stair," his grip on her wrist was mercilessly tight. "I will go first, keep hand on the wall beside you."

Now he loosed her. Itlothis heard only the muted sounds of his moving. There was no way back, she had to follow orders. Setting her teeth, more afraid than she had ever been in life, Itlothis cautiously slid one foot forward, feeling for the drop at the end of the first step.

Their descent was a nightmare which left her weak of body, drenched with sweat. That there was any air to fill their lungs was a minor marvel. Still always the stair continued.

Oslan had not spoken since they left the room above. Itlothis dared not break silence. For about her was the feeling that they now moved, in a caution born of intense fear, past some great danger which must not be alerted to their presence within its reach.

A hand on her arm brought a little cry from her.

"Quiet!"

His grasp drew her beside him. There her bare feet sank into a soft cushion, as if centuries of dust carpeted this hidden way. Once more Oslan was on the move, towing her with him. In the utter darkness she was content to cling to him as she dared not think or face what might happen if she were to lose contact.

Finally, he dropped his hold and whispered again: "Let me go, I must open a door here."

Trembling, Itlothis obeyed. An oblong of grayish light appeared ahead. After the complete dark of their journey this was bright. Across it moved a dark bulk of what must be Oslan. She hurried to follow. They stood in what was nearly twin to the room far above, save that its ceiling was much lower and one full wall to the left was missing. Thus, they could look out into a much larger space. That was not empty. What light there was, and Itlothis could not locate the source of that wan glow, made clear a massive park of wheeled vehicles jammed closely together.

Oslan paused, his head turned a little to the right as if he listened. Then he beckoned to her, already on his way toward the outer area.

There was only a narrow space left open around the wall through which they could move. Oslan hurried at the best pace he could keep in such cramped quarters. Now and then he paused to inspect one of the strange machines. Each time, seemingly unsatisfied, he pushed on again.

At last they reached another open wall, and there he halted abruptly, his nostrils expanding as if he caught a warning scent. She had seen a vast hound do so on settling to hunt.

Here was another of the strange vehicles directly before them and Oslan made for its control cabin. When Itlothis would have gone after him he waved her back. A little mutinous, she watched him climb into the driver's seat, study a control board.

The rigid line of his shoulders eased. He nodded as if in answer to his own thoughts, then beckoned again. Itlothis wriggled through to join him.

The seat on which she crawled was padded, but both short and narrow, so his body pressed tight to hers. Oslan hardly waited for her to settle before he brought the palm of his hand down on a control button.

There was an answering vibration, a purr, as the vehicle came to life, moved forward, down the open way it faced. Itlothis waited no longer for an explanation.

"What are you going to do?"

"Seal the nest place."

"Can you?"

"I will not know until I try. But there is no other way."

There was no use in trying to get any sense out of him while he was so sunk in his obsession. She must let him follow his fantasy to the end. Then, perhaps, he would break the dream.

"How do you know how to run this?" she asked.

"This is my second such visit to Yul. I came at an earlier time in the first part of my dream, while there were still men serving *Its* needs."

He had been two days deep in the dream when she had located him and she supposed a dream fantasy could leap years if necessary. That did have some logic of its own.

The vehicle trundled forward. Now the passage began to branch, but Oslan paid no attention to the side ways, keeping straight ahead. Until a rock wall blocked them. At that barrier he turned into the passage at the left.

This new way was much narrower. Itlothis began to wonder if sooner or later they might not find themselves securely caught between the walls. From time to time Oslan did stop briefly. When he did so he stood upon the seat, reaching his hands over his head to run fingertips along the ceiling.

The third time he did this he gave a soft exclamation. When he sat down he did not start the vehicle again. Instead he crouched closer over the control panel, peering at the buttons there.

"Get out!" he ordered without looking up. "Go back, run!"

Such was the force of that command she obeyed without question. Only she noticed, as she jumped to the floor, his hands were flying over the buttons in a complicated pattern.

Itlothis ran back along the corridor. Behind her she heard the vehicle grinding on. As she turned, pausing, she saw Oslan was speeding toward her, the machine moving away on its own. Satisfied he had not deserted her she began to run again.

He caught up, grasped her arm, urging her to greater efforts. The sound of the vehicle receded. They gained the mouth of the main tunnel. Oslan pulled her into that, not lessening his furious pace as he pounded back the way they had come. The fear which boiled in him, though she did not know its source, fed into her, making her struggle ahead as if death strode in their wake.

They had reached the cavern holding the machines when the floor, the walls, shook. There came a roar of sound to deafen her. After that, darkness . . . .

Something hunting through the dark . . . a rage which was like a blow. Itlothis hid from that rage, from the questing of the giant anger. Shaking from fear of that seeking, she opened her eyes. Inches away from her face was another's which she could see only dimly in this light. She wet her lips. When she spoke her voice sounded very thin and far away:

"Clan Chief Oslan . . . "

She had come here hunting him. Now someone, some *thing*, was hunting her!

His eyelids flickered, opened. He stared at her, his face wearing the same shadow of fear as possessed her. She saw his lips move, his answer was a thread of sound.

"*It* knows! *It* seeks!"

His mad obession. But perhaps she could use that to save them. She caught his head between her hands, forcing him to continue to look at her. Pray All Power he still had a spark of sanity to respond. Slowly, with pauses between words, summoning all her will, she gave the order:

"Break the dream!"

Did any consciousness show in his eyes, or had that same irrational and horrible fear which beset her now driven him into the far depths of his fantasy where she could not reach? Again Itlothis repeated those words with all the calm command she could summon.

"Break the dream!"

The fear racked her. That which searched was coming nearer. To lapse herself into madness, the horror was worse than any pain. He must! He . . .

There was . . .

Itlothis blinked.

Light, much more light than had been in that cavern below Yul. She stared up at a gray ceiling. Here was no scent of dust, nor of ages.

She was back!

Hands had drawn away the dream helmet. She sat up, still hardly believing that she, they, had won. She turned quickly to that other divan. The attendants had removed his helmet, his hands arose unsteadily to his head, but his eyes were open.

Now he saw her. His gaze widened. "Then you *were* real!"

"Yes." Had he really imagined that she was only a part of his dream? Itlothis was oddly discomfited by that thought. She had taken all those risks in his service and he thought she had only been part of his fantasy.

Oslan sat up, looked about as if he could not quite believe he had returned. Then he laughed, not angrily as he had in Yul, but in triumph.

"We did it!" He slammed his fist down on the couch. "The nest *was* walled off, that was what made *it* so wild. Yul is dead!"

He had carried the fantasy back with him, the obsession still possessed him. Itlothis felt a little sick. But Oslan Sb Atto was still her client. She could not, dared not, identify with him. She had performed her mission successfully; his family must deal with him now.

Itlothis turned to the medico. "The Clan Chief is confused."

"I am anything but confused!" Oslan's voice rang out behind her. "Wait and see, Gentle Fem, just wait and see!"

Though she was apprehensive during the hyper jump back to Benold, Oslan did not mention his dream again. Nor did he attempt to be much in her company, keeping mostly in his cabin. However, when they reached the spaceport on their home planet, he took command with an authority which overrode hers.

Before she could report formally, he swept her aboard a private flyer bearing the Atto insignia. His action made her more uneasy than angry. She had dared to hope as time passed that he had thrown off the effect of the dream. Now she could see he was still possessed by it even though this was not the Benold the dreamer had envisioned.

As he turned the flyer north he shot a glance at her.

"You believe me ready for reprogramming, do you not, Itlothis?"

She refused to answer. They would be followed. She had managed to send off a signal before they rose from the port.

"You want proof I am sane? Very well, I shall give you that!"

He pushed the flyer to top speed. Atto lay ahead, but also Yul! What was he going to do?

In less than an hour planet time, Itlothis had her answer. The small craft dipped over the ruins. Only this was not the same Yul she had seen on her first flight to Atto. Here only a portion of the outer walls still stood. Inside those was a vast hollow in which lay only a few shattered blocks.

Oslan cut power, landed the craft in the very center of the hollow. He was quickly free of the cabin, then reached in to urge her out with him. Nor did he loose his hold on her as he asked:

"See?"

The one word echoed back hollowly from the still standing outer walls.

"What . . . " Itlothis must admit that this was a new Yul. But to believe that action taken in a dream on a planet light years away could cause such destruction . . . .

"The charge reached the nest!" he said excitedly. "I set the energy on the crawler to excess. When the power touched the danger mark it blew. Then there was no safe place left for *It* to sleep in, only this!"

She had, Itlothis supposed, to accept the evidence of her eyes. But what she saw went against all reason as she knew it. Yet whatever blast had occurred here had not been only weeks ago, the signs of the catastrophe were ages old! *Had* they been sent eons back in time? Itlothis began to feel that *this* was a dream, some nightmare hallucination.

But Oslan was continuing:

"Feel it? *That* has gone. There is no other life here now!"

She stood within his hold. Once in her childhood, when she was first being trained for the service, she had been brought to Yul. Then only just within the outer wall, beyond which few could go, and none dared stay long. She remembered that venture vividly. Oslan was right! Here was no longer that brooding menace. Just the cry of seabirds, the distant beat of waves. Yul was dead, long ago deserted by life.

"But it was a *dream!*" she protested dazedly. "Just a dream!"

Oslan slowly shook his head. "It was real. Now Yul is free. We are here to prove that. I told you once, 'Get out of my dream.' I was wrong; it was meant to be your dream also. Now this is our reality . . . an empty Yul, a free world. And, in time, perhaps something else."

His arms about her tightened. Not in anger or fear. Itlothis, meeting that brilliant green stare holding hers, knew that dreams, some dreams, never quite released their dreamers.

OF THE SHAPING OF ULM'S HEIR
Tales of the Witch World (1987) TOR

When my Lord Ulric put aside his wife, the Lady Elva, because within two years she had borne naught but dead babes and those far ahead of the time of normal birthing, there was much whispering in the Dale—both of keep folk and of those who dwelt on the land. Yet the majority of those who spoke behind one hand and kept an eye out for any talebearers were inclined to agree with their lord's action. Ulmsdale must have an heir, all knew that. For a Dale where there was no one of the right blood to sit on the High Seat of the hall had wretched times of quarrels, and sometimes its folk were forced to live under a strange banner of some invading lord. Evil and danger one knew was better than what might lie ahead.

Not that Ulric was either an evil or a danger to his own people. He was a man soured by what he considered a major misfortune and which others muttered was the curse of his house. That, since the days of his father Ulm, and that one's impetuous despoiling of a treasure house in the waste, there had been born no living children to the blood of his line—Lord Ulric himself being fathered before that venture. One did not steal from the Old Ones, even though they be gone, without some harsh payment in return.

My lord's first wife had died in childbed—though that was not too uncommon a thing. However, even then the whispers began, for no follower of Gunnora tended her, and all knew that when things go amiss in the ways of womankind the Lady of Fruitfulness can well move to set them aright.

My lord did not even wait the full year of mourning before he was a-wooing again and this time his selection was my dear lady. It was my pride that her choice of first chamberwoman fell upon me, who am also accursed in my own small way, and live in the keep only by sufferance. For my father was marshal on that fateful trip into the Waste under Lord Ulm, and, in his sin and folly, also wrought ill for his blood. For I was born with a beast one's face—my upper lip split like that of the free running hare. So that people ever turned from me in disgust, from the time I was able to understand my deformity.

Only the Lady Elva never showed such aversion to me. Instead spoke me fair and praised my skill with my needle and my soft touch when putting to order her long hair. Long and beautiful was that hair—lighter than any I have ever seen—closer to the sheen of gold—waving of itself when it was loosed from the formal loops of a matron's styling. Hidden now beneath a dark veil yet she is content to have it so.

For after my lord, speaking in a strange high voice unlike himself and looking everywhere but at her whom he addressed, had said the words of dismissal, she made no plaint but withdrew to the Abbey at Norsdale and there took the secondary vows of one who comes from the world, having been a wife. Though before her all such were widows ready to find a safe refuge from the world.

I begged her to let me go with her, and that was when I first learned that, though she was of pure Dale's blood, she had the Seeing, or some portion of such power. For, even as Lord Urlic's eyes had turned from her as he had ordered her forth from his household, so now did she look beyond my shoulder as if she saw no wall of stone but that which was alive.

"Ylas, there is that ahead which will concern you, and more than you. Here you must abide until that hour when what you shall do will be greater than you know and will change much for others." Then she took from around her neck the chain which held an ancient carving which she had worn ever under her robe so that none save me had ever marked it. Worn by years and handling it was, still there was no mistaking its shape—for it was an amulet of the Great Lady Gunnora who smiles on womankind. And this the Lady Elva put around my own neck and then laid her hand upon it, pressing it against me so that I felt its weight even through robe and under smock, and she said, "This will be shield to you, dear heart, when the time is here. Think often upon her whose sign this is and when the evil creeps upon this place call to her."

Thus she went from us, to be swallowed by the abbey walls and no more have any touch with our world. Sore was that parting for me, very sore— once more I was the outcast one. But I think that my lord might have had second thoughts concerning his act—though the need for an heir ruled him so straightly—for he gave me freely the foretower top chamber and said that I was no longer to be the butt of other's foul humors and laughter. Clever with my needle I remained, and thus I felt that I earned my bread, for I made clothing and worked upon hangings for the walls.

My lord did not remain long without a lady. Save this time he needs must go far afield, since the whispers had run beyond the valley walls, and he was looked upon by the neighbors as a cursed man. His new wedding brought us the Lady Tephana out of the north.

She had no right to stand against any curse, for men said—or their wives whispered—that she, too, was from an uncanny House. Her kin had had dealings with some of the remaining Old Ones of the Waste so that strange blood flowed even within her own body.

As my own dear lady had been fair, so this one was dark with a pale skin which seemed more of the moon's giving than any healthy sun-touched flesh. She was small, and quick but graceful in her movements, and she laughed much, though it seemed to me that good humor never touched her dark gray eyes.

Though I was no longer chamberwoman she sought me out and gave into my hands various lengths of fine stuff which my lord had gifted her for her bridal, showing me with well-drawn pictures what she wanted made for her adorning. Though she would have her own maid do the measurements, as if she would not have upon her my touch. I did not care, for it seemed to me that there was that about her which was like a thin grayish mist. And always, I noted from the first, when she was nearby, the amulet my dear lady had given me seemed to chill, as if in some queer warning.

Her own chamberwoman she had brought with her from the North. She was a dour, sour-faced creature, much older than her mistress. They said that she had been the lady's nurse and that the lady had grown up always with her tending.

Her name was Maug and she made no friends in the keep, though she had presence even as if she were of the high blood, for people moved quickly to do her bidding. She need only to look sharply at any of the folk and straightway they were eager to do as she wished to get rid of her.

But to me she did not use whatever small power she brought to bear upon the others. Though I was aware that she watched me whenever I was in her lady's presence, almost as if I were some bold raider and she was a loyal guard.

The Lady Tephana was not a bride more than a month before she went forth from Ulmsdale saying that she would consult with a wise woman who had settled near Gunnora's hill shrine that she might do her duty according to my lord's great desires.

She had already borne one child, yet he was not with her but dwelt in her people's keep for a while. So it would seem that the lady had already favored her, and my lord had done well for himself in finding a fruitful lady. Still, when she rode forth with Maug and two of the guards, I noted from my tower window that she did not make the turn to the path which led to Gunnora's shrine but passed that by. Then curiosity moved in me and I changed house robe for a shorter tunic and put stout climbing boots on. Taking a shoulder bag with food for a double day's journey, I slipped out of the keep at twilight and made my own way over the women's road.

Why I thought thus to spy upon my new mistress I could not even understand myself, save that the need for my going gnawed in me like a hunger and would not be appeased.

It was close to midsummer and the moon was new, thus I felt that I had naught to fear for myself. Still I took with me a stout staff of ash over which I had rubbed my amulet along with the crushed leaves of illbane. Although I knew no spells, I called with my heart and mind upon the favor of Gunnora, trusting that one so much the greater would know that I meant no harm but that there was that which I must know.

The track was a winding one, for it had never been laid or cut by men but patterned so by the feet of women who sought the care and favor of The Lady. I had taken it many times before, since I had sworn service to the Lady Elva seeking with my own petitions to bring her the wish of her heart. Thus, even in the half dark, I trusted to my feet, which seemed of themselves to know each dip and straightway.

None in Ulm had a part in the building of the shrine toward which I traveled. Like much within the Dales THOSE WHO HAD BEEN BEFORE had laid the stone of its walls and planted about its doorway the sweet-smelling herbs which carried in their scent something which would lighten even the most dour heart for a space. But at the coming of our people to this land women were drawn to the place, and, within a generation of our people's lives, the power which dwelt here was recognized.

I came out upon the hillside at the top of which stood the place I sought. But there were no horses in pickets, no sign of the two guards, and I needed not even that to tell me that the Lady Tephana had not come this way.

Yet I went to the door and set my hand upon a place where the ancient wood was rubbed smooth and bare by the countless fingers which had touched there before me. There was the clear sound of a chime and the door opened, though none stood within. However, there was light, soft and golden as always, and into my face puffed the air which was deep scented with all the odors of the harvest time.

I came into the first room, laying my staff and my pouch of food upon the floor. Then, daring as I did only in time wherein my heart was sore, I brought forth the amulet and held it out so that which waited could know me for a daughter come for council. I went on into the inner shrine where shafts of light stood as towers on either side of a block of golden stone. In the center of that was a hollow which perhaps would hold as much liquid as I could scoop up in my two hands. By that hollow was a pitcher wrought of gold and bearing Gunnora's pattern of harvest sheath bound with a cording of vine, the fruit ripe upon it—all winking in the light with the glory of gems.

Going to that table I twice advanced my hand to that pitcher, twice withdrew it, as the force of what I would do brought with it fear. Yet I could not now turn aside. Thus on the third try I picked up that flagon and dribbled from it a clear bluish liquid which gathered into the pool. Just to the brim and no more was I careful to pour. Then I took from off my neck the chain of my amulet and that I laid by the pool. To me came words not of my choosing but as if something had stirred within me and spoke now through my lips.

"Lady—this one asks with all humbleness—to know—"

There was a swirl across the water which came of itself and not from any troubling of my doing. It grew dark—dark as a shadow of the midnight. Something moved through that darkness and then it cleared because a smoking torch shown within.

There were two cloaked and hooded figures, very small as if I gazed at them from a far distance. One raised herself even as I watched and laid her body upon a stone. That stone had to it a reddish look almost as if it had once been dipped in blood.

The other one therein the pool stepped forward and pulled at the first's cloak. I saw the Lady Tephana, and I did not doubt that that other was Maug. From beneath her cloak Maug brought forth a short rod or wand, and holding this above her lady she drew it back and forth in patterns. Also I was sure that

I saw come out of the dark where that torch did not light, faces and forms which appeared and disappeared so quickly I could not be sure of them. Yet I knew that they were wholly evil, so much so that I quaked with the dread of what I watched.

Then the torch was gone, the water in the pool no longer murky, and somehow the bridle on my tongue was loosened once more and I cried aloud to the lights, the stone, the very walls: "What would you have me do, Great One? What evil is being wrought this night and where?"

"When the moment comes you shall know—" Did that answer come out of the air itself, or was it in my head, a thought from another? I did not know, but I was also aware that there would be no other answer.

That the Lady Tephana dealt with evil was plain. That I was to have a hand in some great matter, that was also clear to me. As I took up my amulet and put it about my throat once again it seemed to me that the ancient bit of carving had grown heavier and that I was ever aware of a kind of warmth which comes before a full fury of flame.

I rested that night in the outer room of the shrine and I dreamed, that I knew. But on my waking I could not remember the stuff of my dream save there had been some great peril and there was a need to prevent some act— and that prevention was mine.

I left upon the table in the outer room my offering: a ribbon of fine weaving ornamented with the best my needle. And with the sun's rising I went from that shrine bearing not the comfort I had hoped but rather a sense of purpose I did not yet understand.

The lady was already returned when I came back to the keep. And I heard that she had indeed visited the shrine and prayed the night through that she might give her new lord the gift he wished—a son of his body.

Yet what shrine—not Gunnora's. Though the two guards swore that they had stood their watch apart from that—no man going within that gate. Whoever she had sought it had not been The Lady, and had she set dreams upon the guards to hide that?

I had chance to meet Maug that eve as I sought my own tower room, and it seemed to me that she hesitated as if she wished to speak with me and then thought the better of it. But I did not like the look which she gave me—as if she knew well that I had spied and how I had done so.

Again I dreamed, and this time I remembered after I awoke, the moonlight still shone full upon my bed. I had been somewhere else. And the feeling of that carried so fully with me that for more than a quick breath or two I looked about my tower room expecting fully to see that other place—a long hall with tall pillars and in the distance a white light—a moon silver one toward which I was drawn. There at the heart of that lay what I sought, a chest of crystal in which lay—

But the light burst forth as I tried to see who or what was within. Yet I knew that it was needful that I should do this.

I put forth my hand into the blazing light. It did not sear my skin as I thought it might. Rather my flesh prickled and I felt that into it entered some power which it was needful that I retain—even though I was no wise woman nor one of the Old Ones.

Now as my dream released me, I looked down at my hand and it appeared even in the full of the moonlight to have a broad band like unto a burnished ring encircling each of my fingers. Even as I watched in wonder, those faded from sight, but not from touch. I felt a constraint and weight on each as I moved them, curled and uncurled bone and flesh.

As I lay back again upon my narrow bed, I rested that hand on my breast when it chanced to cup to my body the amulet of The Lady. And that warmed from the power, sending through me now a strength such as I had never before known. My mind shaped words and spun them into phrases, though they were strange to me and it was as if I were repeating a ritual which I did not understand but which had been so drilled into my memory.

Nor did I sleep the rest of the night, though I lay quietly, wrapped rather in the warmth of what was now within me. And I strove to remember each small portion of the dream while I wondered at what had lain within the crystal chest and why some Great One made use of such a one as I.

It was a strange day which followed. I was uneasy and could not sit still at my stitchery for long at a time, but paced now and then my chamber. When I went down into the kitchen I heard the snickering of the maids and saw them watching from the corners of their eyes now and then a tall figure tending a brew pot on the hearth.

Maug, who seldom left her mistress's chamber was there, and to that which bubbled before her she added now and then a pinch of this, a dried leaf of that. While the scent of it was rich but sickly, liken to the smell of meat which is near spoiled and yet covered with spices to hide its nastiness. While she measured and tended so she was humming—not any tune such as might be sung as one went about one's work, but rather a mumble of sound which seemed to pierce into one's head and yet carry no meaning. And I saw that those gathered there made a wide circle about her, even the cook, all powerful here, keeping a good distance.

But not such a distance as I myself chose. For upon seeing her back I thrust under the edge of my upper jerkin my strangely weighted hand and ate bread and cheese awkwardly with my left. For that feeling of cold evil gathered about me and dulled all the pleasure one could take in this homey place.

I hurried away from the kitchen as soon as I had choked down a few mouthfuls and came again into my chamber. For now there settled upon me a feverish need to be about a certain piece of work over which I had dawdled earlier. This was a scarf of that same brave color sun's setting left upon the sky. This was to be patterned with birds the like of which I had never seen. However, Maug had brought to me two days earlier a picture of such, lined out on a thick shaving of wood. They shone bravely in shades of red, but where one might have set gold to give them majesty, the pattern had black lines, providing them with feet, bills and crests of that murky hue. Nor did I like to work upon them, for I had a queer feeling now and then that when I finished a crested head it would turn a fraction and the eye I had set therein fastened upon me.

I had never had such fancies before and I pushed these sternly out of mind. It also seemed, now that my hand was weighted by those rings I could not see, that the stitches I was setting precisely came very slowly into line. Yet also there was driving me this need to be done with the thing and have it off and away, back to she who would wear it. So doggedly did I labor that the sun was still above the hill crest when I set the last stitch, shaking out the folds to inspect them carefully, making sure that I had not skimped the pattern in any place. Then I folded it over my arm and took up also the pattern chip from which I had worked and went forth to deliver my handiwork.

Lady Tephana had been given the west tower for her own biding place, and I hurried along the outer defense wall rather than take the longer way of descent to the courtyard and up again. There were no sentries about since Ulmsdale, to our knowledge, had no enemies to try our strength. I saw a wink of light from a window ahead where that portion of the keep was in the beginning of twilight.

I raised a hand to knock, but instantly, as if she had foreseen my coming, Maug opened the door and beckoned me within. So I entered the scented warmth of the inner chamber where the lord's new lady sat before a mirror gazing steadily into it, not seeming in pleasure at her own features, but as if she saw there something of vast importance. Such strange fancies did fill my mind that day.

"Ylas." She said my name without turning. "Lay it about me—carefully now!" Her voice was sharp as if the placing of the scarf were some weighty matter which occupied all her thought for the moment.

I had expected Maug to take the wispy stuff from me, but now I obediently laid the picture from which I had worked down on a table nearby and shook out the scarf, letting it fall gently even as she said, about her shoulders. There was a movement to one side and I caught a glimpse of Maug taking up the wooden plaque I had put down and tossing it into a brazier.

But what was much more important to me was that as soon as I arranged the scarf to the Lady Tephana's liking those weights on my fingers vanished, and it was only when I backed away a step or so that the sensation returned again.

The lady gathered up the scarf, wrapping it tighter about her with small quick tugs which again made those ill-omened birds seem to move. But the color became her darkness very well and she appeared in that moment more beautiful than I had ever thought. Now she smiled into the mirror and laughed.

"You have done well, Ylas. My lord will be pleased. We shall deal together again, you and I."

That sounded with too much emphasis, as if it was more than work with the needle she had in mind. However, I somehow found the words to say that I was glad to have pleased her. She dismissed me with a wave of her hand, and Maug moved in with a comb to deal with her long locks which were as black as the bills and legs of those uncanny birds.

So it was that they were both occupied as I turned to go. Only my eyes lit upon what sat on the edge of the table—a small tray of copper well burnished bearing a goblet of gold. And from that stemmed cup, which was fancifully wrought with strange faces of beasts such as no man has seen, there came a whiff of the scent given off by the mixture Maug had been a-brewing earlier that day.

My hand jerked out as if fingers had closed about my wrist to twist it so that my fingers fluttered over the brim. And—I was aware of that as much as if I had seen it happen—from those fingers had slid those rings of power. There was a moment's troubling of the substance in the cup.

Then I knew fear such as I had never felt before in my life, maimed and kinless though I was. And I sped from that chamber out into the rising night wind on the wall, to hasten back into my own small room.

What sorcery had made me a part of it, I could not know. But that I had been used for another's purpose as one might use a goose wing to sweep an ashy hearthstone, that was a truth I did not deny. Thus I ran then until I was within my own room, the door closed tight behind me, both of my hands to my mouth where my breath came fast. My heart pounded and I gasped, at last sinking upon my bed, rubbing that ringless hand with my other one, for it seemed that with the going of those invisible rings my flesh was icy cold and must be brought back to warmth again.

I did not dream that night, nor the next, though I dreaded what sleep might bring me. Nor were there any more strange happenings to make me wish I had some safe person in whom I might confide. However, as the days passed dully one upon another I did not forget, and often, when I was sewing, I would stop and look upon my hand, spreading wide fingers, striving to understand what had happened to me on that one day.

It was not long until we heard that our lord's hopes had again risen—that the Lady Tephana was quick with child. As a favor to her he had brought her son Hylmer to the Keep and made much of him. He was a child in which there was little to admire or please, being large for his age and swift to tattle or hinder one. But in my own place I saw little of him, and I heard that my lord took pleasure in noting his sturdy health, foreseeing that as a promise for his own coming heir.

He also urged upon the Lady Tephana the calling of one of the wise women from a neighboring Dale, one who was reputed to be a Handmaid to Gunnora. However, his lady refused, saying that Maug had been at her own birthing and knew more than any strange woman, no matter how high the art she claimed. Had she not successfully seen Tephana through the first birth of her son and as all living might now see—was he not a sturdy manchild?

It was in the eighth month after the lady had given her joyful news that once more I dreamed. Again I was in that hall where lay the chest of clouded light. I stood by it and, at an order I did not hear nor fully comprehend, I stretched both hands into its gleam.

This time I brought back no rings from that meeting. Rather did I have always with me the sensation that over each finger, across each palm, was drawn taut the thinnest and finest of gauzy cloth. At first I hesitated to take up my needle again lest in some manner that coating I bore would be loosened upon the cloth to betray me to those to whom I was naught but a maimed one dwelling apart. But when I tried, that did not happen, and it was the very day I discovered that with growing confidence that Maug summoned me to the Lady Tephana.

She was lying back upon cushions, her swollen belly now giving her no ease. But by her was a pile of cloth—pieces of two colors—one shining white which was usual for the receiving cloth which was any babe's first garment in the world, and the other of a filmy red.

"Ylas, once more the best of your needle skill is needed," she told me, stroking with both her hands the burden beneath her flesh. "Make a birthing cloth which will be the finest ever seen in this or any other Dale. And with this," she put forward one hand to touch the red length, "you shall skillfully line with certain patterns Maug shall give you. For it is the custom of my House to so ask the protection of High Powers, that the sons we bear shall be straight and strong of body and fair of countenance."

Nor could I say no for in me arose that compulsion which had moved me before. I accepted the cloth and the piece of painted parchment which Maug had ready. Thus burdened, I returned to my chamber. I say burdened, for that I was. The parchment which I had not yet unfolded to look upon I could not carry easily. Light and thin it seemed, still it weighed as if it were a block of sword steel.

I threw it on the table in my chamber with the feeling that I had handled filth. Even yet I did not open it, but rather sat for a space nursing one hand within the other, feeling still upon the both of them that coating as if I went gloved. At length I brought out my threads and the packet which held my needles. And I laid the cloth out, finding it twice as long as was the custom, guessing then that it was to be folded about the red stuff so that would pass unseen.

It was when I at last made myself unfold the parchment that the full blow of unknown power struck at me. That feeling of handling filth was strong. It seemed to me that I breathed in rank odor as I leaned closer, holding a lamp to see. For though it was day without, here the shadows crept from the corners and there was a murk like drifting smoke to hide those lines of red and direst black.

That this was a thing of the Dark I now had no doubt, and I wondered that they had so revealed their purposes even to me who had no place among the Keep folk. It was as if they thought of me as someone beneath their need to consider.

But that I would stitch such with any needle unto a birthing cloth! What did they think of me—or (and cold spread through me) did they also have a plan in which I would be silenced once my work was done?

I have since many times thought that I was controlled by one greater than myself, and that Maug or perhaps even the Lady Tephana had taken care to bespell me into this labor and were not aware that I had not fallen helpless into their trap.

Now I pushed the parchment back into its folds and sat on my stool considering for a long moment what I would do. That I must stitch the red cloth between the layers of white was plain, for when I experimented, putting one over the other, there was a rosy sheen to the upper layer. But that I would use the symbols of the dark—NO!

Then I marked out for myself with a charred end of ash (which in itself was a powerful talisman against all evil) two other patterns. There was that borne by the amulet of Gunnora and the other—why, the gryphon which was my lord's own sign and under the banner of which we lived.

Looking upon these I set about with my stitchery and my needle flew with such speed and ease that it might have wrought of itself without my urging. The length had room only for four symbols, the two repeated, but they grew out of my best work and I wrought them in silver thread—moonglow such as is blessed by The Lady in her own shrine. Then quickly I laid the cloth within the other and sealed the sides with stitches so small that my eyes should have ached when I made them—yet I suffered neither that nor any fatigue as I worked, upheld by an inner strength which was new to me.

When I was done I folded it with care, making sure that the rose shine was visible, but I wondered if those symbols I had not used might have been visible too. That was a risk I must take.

I had worked the night through, still my head was clear, I had no aching of back, no redness and pain of eye. Not yet would I return it, I thought, let them think that the task was such a labor that I was kept to my needle for hours yet.

Opening my casement to the brightness of the morning I drew a deep breath of the freshness of the air before I turned again to where my work lay and performed one last task—that of passing above the folded cloth the amulet I wore. In my hand as I did so there was a pleasant warmth. Then all at once all the weariness I had earned came upon me and I stumbled to my bed, not taking off my jerkin or skirt, and fell upon it, sleep already sealing my eyes.

It was late afternoon that I awoke to another's shaking and saw above me Maug's lean, ill visage and smelled that sourish, bitter odor which she carried always with her.

"Fool—where is the work!" She raised her hand as if to slap me and then dropped it as one who would bide her time a little to deliver punishment.

"There—" I said, and pointed to the table.

She turned swiftly and snatched up first the parchment, tucking it into some pocket hidden within her fusty robe. Then her grayish-skinned fingers came to the folds of cloth. But she did not quite touch it. Instead she now shook forth another fold of material and gestured for me to place my handiwork upon that and cover it well.

With this she left me, but at the door she turned her head a little and I saw on her face a smile which was more the grimace of one steeped in malice. Again I suspicioned that those two meant me no good. Yet that suspicion did not really trouble me. It was as if I were sure that I wore armor against the worst they could attempt, and I gave thanks to Gunnora. For I truly believed that it was her amulet which had so hearted me. That and what still clung gloved tightly to my hands and which tingled a little now.

It was three days later that the news spread through the Keep that the Lady Tephana, wishing to make sure that her lord not be disappointed again, would go for the birthing to the very shrine of Gunnora where she could be sure that The Lady's favor would be hers. My lord was quick to give in to this plea of hers. But it was unexpected that she also asked for me to accompany them, her plea being that I was a devout follower of The Lady and was known to have her favor.

Thus, though there were clouds hanging over the crown of the not too distant hills we set out. The Lady Tephana was in a horse litter, the mares it was slung between being hand-led by my lord's men, Maug striding on foot by her side, while I rode behind with two of the castle maids who were experienced somewhat in the mysteries of birthing.

We went at a slow pace in spite of the gathering of storm warnings, and I was not surprised that we did not turn aside at the hillside path leading to the shrine, for no horses, even the most, surefooted, could make that climb. Instead we were to go around, to approach from the other side taking the slight risk of traveling on one of the Old One's roads which for the most part the Dalesmen avoided.

Our snail's pace brought us but barely on that road when the threatening storm broke and Lady Tephana cried out that she could not travel through its fury. The only shelter nearby was one of those half ruins which the Old Ones had erected at places along their roads. Into this we reluctantly crowded.

Luckily there were two half chambers left, and, having loosened the litter, the men bore Lady Tephana into the inner one whereupon we who had been chosen to serve her crowded.

It was then that she began to writhe on her resting place and cried out that the babe was coming too soon and in an evil place and she misdoubted that anything would be well. Maug held her hands and spoke to her softly but still she uttered cries, and it was plain that her time was indeed upon her.

Thus we made ready to do what we might for the babe, and I prayed to Gunnora that it would come alive and well. For—though I believed its mother to be tainted by some shadow I could not understand—the small new one would come sinless into the world.

Come it did, and it was a son, squalling lustily. It was I who received him upon the birthing cloth while Maug tended her mistress. And when I looked down at what I held, I near dropped the child. For the well-formed small legs ended not in feet but in hooves such as one sees upon a kid, and the eyes which opened wide when I rolled the cloth about him were as gold as the glint of that metal in the sun!

Maug swung about as I uttered a cry of my own and reached for the babe. Only at that moment there was a sound which rose above the fury of the storm and the faint moans of the lady. It was like the passage of wings through the air, and so did I indeed see what seemed to be a great wing, larger than anything living could weld, and this swept down between Maug and me. At the same time there was a voice—though whether it spoke aloud or in my head I could never afterward decide.

"Son sealed to me!" There was triumph in it and I saw Maug cower backward with both hands over her eyes and I heard a sharp cry of fear from the lady. But to me came peace, and I knew that this was well and good and what I held was no demon's brat but only one marked by nature with a brand even as the one I wore. And there was in me a vast pity as I cuddled him tight against a breast which would never know the weight of a child of my own.

The wing was gone and I heard sounds from the two maids who were crowded back against the wall shaking, their eyes squeezed shut as if they had been near struck blind. As I turned to give the child unto his mother as custom demanded that I should so that she could have the naming of him, Maug threw herself between us.

"Demon's get!" she mouthed and would perhaps have struck the babe out of my hold, and the Lady Tephana screamed full voice and thrust also outward, warning me off.

That was the way of it. They brought us back to Ulmsdale, but the lady would not look upon the child. Those who had been with us were quick to blame it on both the curse of the house and the fact that he had been birthed in a place of the Old Ones.

Since she would not feed it or even look upon him, the babe was mine for a measure of days and I was forced to allow him to suck warm milk from my finger. Yet he throve, and despite his eyes and those hooves he was a child good to look upon, and I came to cherish him.

But the Lord Ulric was determined that, having gotten his heir, he was fane to raise him. So he called in a forester with whom he had himself been fostered for a space when he was a child—the two of them being as brothers. To him the babe Kerovan was given and thus disappeared into the far reaches of the Dale. It was quickly made known by the will of my lord that no one was to speak of his son's deformity. The maids who had been present at the birthing were sent with him. As for me, I asked for speech with Lord Ulric and spoke of what had long been close to my heart, that I go unto Norseby and be with my lady there. He made me swear upon the mighty amulet which guarded the keep that I would not speak concerning Kerovan, and this I agreed to very willingly.

There was only a small glimmering thereafter of all which had been my lot. For the tingling invisible gloves were gone from me when I gave the babe to his foster mother. I could not forget, but neither could I speak. And, when I reached Norseby, I had much else to occupy my mind, for I found my lady ill of a deep cough and saw well that death was not far away. Out of their kindness they allowed me to nurse her. And there was one summer night when the moon was full that she spoke to me alone, for the Lady Sister who helped her with potions had gone to get more of a cordial which stifled the cough.

"Ylas—"

I had to bend very close to hear her faintest of whispers. "The foreseeing— you have done what the Powers would have of you. He—he—" she sucked in air as if she could not get enough to hold her with us—"he who—was—so— born—has his heritage. No demon as those two tried—no demon—" and so saying she crumpled back a little into the pillows about her and I knew that she had gone.

For me thereafter there was no more ensorcelment. I was given charge of the linens and the robes. Only in my dreams did I seek other places— which were always just a little beyond my reach. Yet never did I forget that great voice which greeted Kerovan at his birthing and thereafter my own dear lady's words concerning his destiny.

RIDER ON A MOUNTAIN
Friends of the Horseclans (1987) Signet

Nancee pushed back under a screen of drooping willow branches. The wad of wet clothing she had snatched from the stream launched a runnel of water between her small breasts. Her skin was roughened by more than just gully breeze as she quivered and shook from raw bursts of fear and pain in her head. This was not hearing—though she was also dimly aware of shouts and cries from the camp over the hill behind—this was rather a feeling which racked her slim, near-childish frame.

There was pain and death, and also a wild excitement and need to cause both pain and death—running with it a cold calculation which was like a stab between her narrow shoulders, a greed which fed upon attack, the lust for death. She crouched, as frozen as a rabbit cornered by a tree cat, the sandy gravel of the river's edge grating against her legs and buttocks.

That mind thread of pain arose to torment—then snapped as might a cord pulled too tightly. She smothered an answering cry with her hand, her teeth scraping her knuckles. Someone had died—someone close to her. Now the triumphant greed wreathed about like the smoke of a wild fire. If she stayed here—

She had learned well wariness and resolution during the past half year. Now she burrowed yet farther into the thickness of the willows until she had her back to the trunk of the largest, the rough bark grinding into her shoulders.

Would the raiders come questing along the stream? Did they realize that one of their prey was missing? She began to pull on the limp dampness of her clothing. How soon?

Would they come pounding over the hill where the river made a turn, or would they ride upstream in the stream bed itself?—the water ran shallow enough. She chewed on her lower lip.

Loincloth, then divided shirt weighted with water, but still smelling of horse and her own sweat, the shirt which her fingers fumbled so that she could hardly fit lashing cords to hole.

She squeezed the water out of her hair and knotted back the lank strands with a greasy thong, trying the while to stifle her hard breathing as she forced herself to accept the worst which must have happened—inwardly marveling that she had this small fragment of time still unhunted. She must prepare—

For Dik Romlee. Her lips stretched in a mirthless line.

Nancee studied the ground around her. Weapons? She remembered the Horseclans woman with whom she had shared a fresh roasted rabbit only two days ago. Then she and her uncle had still been part of the caravan, before Dik showed his hand. That prairie rover had had weapons in plenty, a knife hilt showing an inch or two above boottop, another at her belt, a sword of deadly promise, a bow—

The girl wiped her sweating hands on the skirt. She had nothing but those hands and her teeth. And she might well consider herself already captive. Except she was a Lowree of the House of Bradd.

Her head jerked as she raised her pointed chin. A Lowree was not truly mastered except by death. If she could not defend herself she could use those same teeth to open her own veins. Did not the Song of the House of Bradd tell of just such a deed when Mairee of the Sun Hair was taken by the Lord of Kain? Little good *he* got from that!

Firmly she closed her mind to that other's cold triumph, which beat at her as if a fist thudded into her face. She tried to pick up any call, the slightest hint of message from Uncle Roth, from Hari or Mik. There was only blankness to answer. So she was truly alone—

But she was startled out of that grim thought for a moment by a high squealing sound, a battle cry of another kind. Boldhoof—they had the greatest treasure left to Bradd's line, the giant Northhorse. She could use—

Only she could not. The Horseclan guards could bespeak their mounts at will. With the Northhorse Nancee had no such a bond. Her mindspeak was limited more to a sensing of emotion—the identification of those who had been long known to her. She could not now stir Boldhoof into any rebellion which would count. Rather did she already feel the reassurance which was flooding the camp. That mind which had betrayed itself with greed and cruelty was now striving to bring the huge horse into obedience. And Dik would certainly win. She had seen him with animals before. It was the one part of his character she could not understand, for it was not part of the evil which walked two-legged under his name.

He would not be satisfied with the loot he had taken, the deaths which already answered the steel of his followers. Her body would not lie there, and he would come seeking—

Nancee dropped to her belly, her head raised only inches from the gravelly soil, as she began to wriggle from the temporary shelter she had found farther along under the screen of the willows. This was another hunt in which she was the quarry, only this time there were none of those who had been with her before.

Back in the east where Bradd's Hold had once stood tall and defiant against the sky there had been swords in a plenty. Until that black-mouthed traitor Dik Romlee had caught them from their blind side—where they had had no watchful eyes, since no man expected treason from an oathed kinsman.

Uncle Roth, his right arm useless from the witch curse Dik must have laid upon him, had gotten the two of them out and away. She might not be as dear to him as a daughter in truth, but it was from her body—Nancee levered herself up a fraction on one elbow and listened with ear and mind. Yes, only she could birth an heir the kin would accept. And Dik was sure to lay within her his treacherous seed should he take her. Her outstretched fingers dug painfully into the gravel and she pulled determinedly ahead.

Still there gnawed upon her that belief that they would come a-hunting. What chance had she against the foul pack of them? Already they had accomplished half their plan. Dik had maneuvered the Traders' trail chief into leaving them behind, spreading his tale of their being outlawed in the west on Uncle Roth's first trip hither—that the Horseclans would not treat with any from a train giving them shelter. It was Dik's word against her uncle's. And Dik's hand deep in a money purse as he said it all. Gold pieces were few on the frontier—those looted from Roth's own strongbox had sentenced him to death in the end.

She turned her head to the river, of which she sighted only a little between the well-leaved branches. There was an inner core there with a current, but she could not swim. With a piece of the dried storm wrack which was between the rocks farther on could she hold herself afloat? Yet she would be in the open, easy for them to take.

Tentatively she tried a mindsend toward the hidden camp. And snapped it free and away as she breathed fast and shallowly. No one there except those who followed Dik. But not even Dik now—which meant—

She could look ahead to that pile of drift which had drawn her this far. No spear, no bow, no keen-bladed knife. What she might have—

Her hand loosed its tight grip upon the gravel and she made a quick grab with hooked fingers which closed iron-tight on a length of sun-and-wind-dried sapling.

What Nancee jerked into her willow screen was bone-yellowed wood ending in a mass of snapped and broken roots. She broke off several of those and hefted her find. A club of sorts—at least the best weapon she was to find except for some water-smooth stone. But a sorry and useless thing with which to meet a well-armed raider.

Yet they were not going to take her until—

She started, one hand dropping back to the ground to steady herself, her eyes wide in her sun-browned face. What—

"Where are the wagons, two-legs? This one is sore-pawed—also hungry—"

No foggy beam of hate or fear or calculating menace—this was as clear in her head as if she heard it by ear instead of by mind!

"Two-legs—"

Again that imperative and irritated call. She hunched over the crude club, her hands rubbing along its length. Then there came a quiver of leaves ahead, a swinging of branches, and a fur-covered head arose into her line of astounded sight.

She had seen tree cats in plenty, and Uncle Roth had in the presence chamber of the hold two rugs made from great cat beasts with spotted hides for which he had traded some years back. But this was—

Nancee drew a deep breath, and a little of her hold on the club loosened. Here was one of those great cat people with whom the Horseclans had a treaty-of-assistance. Of that she had heard even before she had come to envy the caravan guards and talked as much as she could with Oonaa, the archer.

"Cat lord—" She spoke in a hoarse whisper. She was no woman of the Clans; this furred death before her had no kincall for her. But what had

Dik done which had given him the power to call such into his service? The Horseclans alone shared shelter with the cats.

"Where is the wagon?" Once again the clear words in her head.

"No wagon." She spoke aloud, but perhaps the cat could understand speech too, for it stared with great green eyes at her, the grayish brindle of its fur seeming to fade into the maze of branches wherein it crouched.

"This one is sore-pawed—this one is hungry—" There was a low throaty growl to underline that. "This one wishes to ride—"

"There is nothing to ride," she returned bitterly, and then, wondering if she could indeed communicate without words which it might not understand, she tried to form the message in her mind, haltingly, as one would speak a language of which one knew but a phrase or two. She pictured the camp as she had seen it last before she had sought the stream. Then deliberately she beamed what she had not seen but what was clear to her mind had happened—the complete killing raid led by Dik.

Again the cat growled, and it pulled back under the willow boughs until she feared it was going. Why she should cling to this one animal which might mean her no good, she could not have said. But she felt that she could not bear to let it go.

"Those will be coming—" She mind-pictured Dik striding confidently toward the willows, satisfied that the easiest part of his massacre and pillage waited before him.

"This one will kill if any two-legs tries to—" The words in her mind faded out, but she was aware of movement against the gravel, of seeing a paw—outsize for even the large animal before her—rise claws curved as if already dug into flesh to tear.

"These hunt cats—" She pictured the hide Dik had had made into a cloak and wore proudly.

The young prairiecat spat and whipped out with that uplifted paw to scrape a fall of leaves from a willow branch.

"This one is of the blood of Dark Slayer. No two-legs can—"

"They can stand at a distance," she interrupted that boastful claim, "and fill you full of arrows. Dik is a master archer." Deliberately, as she had tried earlier to project what she had deemed had happened to their camp, so did she now mind-picture a gray-brown body well covered with quills which snapped wildly from side to side as a wounded animal expired under feathered death.

"So." There was an odd note in that. The cat mask again came farther into view—the yellow eyes only slits, the mouth open enough to show the whole armanent of fangs. Though Nancee knew that the cat was hardly yet out of cubhood, still there was something about it which held her in a kind of awe.

"Would you wait here for this two-legged killer of his kind?" came the quick demand then. "He will fill *you* with his arrows or take a blade to cut you down."

"The cat warrior knows of a better place?" Out of her resigned belief that she faced an already lost battle a small hope arose.

"This way." The swaying of the branches was all which remained to mark the cat's retreat. Because she could think of nothing better, she followed, trying as well as she might to go without disturbing the branches and so betray her path to any who might watch from the hilltop.

However, the screen lasted until she was faced by a stand of grass where a number of bruised stems showed her a new trail. Keeping to her hands and knees, Nancee followed.

In the wall of the hill here there was a break—perhaps some spring storm long ago had eaten away the bank. A tree of greater girth than the willows among which she had taken refuge lay crown downward, its withered and broken tangle of roots uphill. To one side of the trunk there was a scatter of earth and a large hole from which came a musky stench that nearly made her gag.

"The black killer thing is gone," sharp into her mind came the "voice" of the cat. "That one has left a hidden way of its own. Crawl, two-legs, and you will see. I do not think that those you fear can look into the earth itself. Crawl!"

Obediently she crawled forward into the evil-smelling pit in the soil. She found it large enough that she could still keep to hand and knees, but it was dark, and she had only a very faint scrape of claw now and then to let her know she still followed the cat.

There came an abrupt change as ahead she saw daylight, which was dimmed nearly at once by the cat shouldering its way through. So she came, head foremost, into another stand of grass and brush, warned in time to slither belly down under this other natural cover.

Nancee found herself looking down into the small hollow where they had pitched camp. The first hues of sunset were at her back as she skulked behind a bush to peer through.

Three bundles of red-splashed clothing had been rolled aside. Mik, Hari, and Uncle Roth, she was sure, and had no desire to see them closer and prove her identification right. Three men hunkered on their heels after the way of prairie barbarians. They had ripped open the supply bags and were wolfing down the nearly stone-hard rolls of travel meat, chewing with determined force.

Dik was not there. A ripple of foreboding ran up her spine. Only too well she could guess what occupied the man she had come to loathe. Snooping into the willows—hunting—*her!*

There was the pound of a huge hoof on the ground. Even where she lay in hiding she could feel the force of that through the earth. Boldhoof, the one treasure Uncle Roth had held fast to, was impatient. Large and armed as she was with hoof and teeth, the mare was generally even of temperament. Nancee had had those soft lips pluck a round marble of maple sugar from her palm and knew she had nothing to fear from the tall mountain of a horse.

The Northhorses were not unknown here in the southern lands, but those who had them gave them great care. None were bred here, being sold only by tribes who were so jealous of their monopoly that they would not ever offer a stallion to be bought by an outsider.

They would not have gained Boldhoof even, had it not been that her former owner had died of the coughing sickness two months back and Uncle Roth had claimed the animal as burial price. The secret he discovered within a day thereafter he had shared only with Nancee. Though Dik might have discovered it by some spying. Boldhoof was in foal! And should she throw a colt, why then their family fortune could be established as soon as the foal appeared.

Hate was bitter water in Nancee's mouth as she watched the outlaws below. Though they seemed at such ease she was certain that they must have sentries out and perhaps even men on the search with Dik. She counted seven horses—most of them the smaller mounts known to the prairie men. If those were of the Horseclans breed—

She could no longer see anything of the cat, who had gone to earth making itself invisible, its brindled fur one with the ground and the sun-browned grass. Again the girl heard and felt the impatient stamp of Boldhoof. Never had she longed so much for anything before as she wished she could communicate with the huge mare. These rogues had picketed her, but they could not guess the strength beneath that well-groomed hide. Perhaps a single sharp pull would free—

"The evil two-legs!" A flash of warning cut through her own thoughts sharply enough to immoblize her for a moment.

"Sooooo—" That word was drawn out to become the hiss of a serpent.

She turned her head unwillingly, still hoping against hope. Looked up.

Dik had fulfilled his claim as an expert hunter. He stood there, his unsheathed sword gripped in his hand. Nancee knew the meaning of that threat. Dik could use his sword like a throwing knife. She had seen him win a handful of good silver bits doing just that. One swing and she would be pinned to the ground—and he could place that unwieldy spear exactly where he chose.

"Lady of the House of Bradd!" He made the greeting a jeer, and in his eyes she could read exactly what she knew would be there. "You have been overshy. But all is well now. Come to me!" His soft slur of speech ended with a snap like that of a whip.

She could be a fool and defy that order—and lose everything by being mishandled and perhaps even thrown down to those stinking men huddled around the fire. Or one could rise as Nancee did now, her attention on Dik, wary and waiting for his next move.

"Lady of Bradd"—again his leer and the tone of the words was like a blow—"it would seem that you come late to our meeting. But that you do come is as it should be." He spoke without the slur of the frontiersman, the garbling of an underling; he might be some man of name in exile.

"There is no Bradd," she found her voice to say flatly. "As you well know. Roth had no kin land anymore."

"Which is the same as saying that you are also landless—but that you are lordless is a different matter, my lady. The man who takes you will have his rights, as you are heiress now and there is more fighting in the east. Even as we stay here there could be a reversal of all which has happened and you could call yourself duchess and first lady in Bradd."

Her lips twisted in a grimace. "That will never be."

"Ah." He was smiling, a smile which carried with it the chill of deepest winter. "*Never* is a word no true man takes for surety. Come!" Again that snap of order, this time fortified with jerk of the swordblade, beckoning her to him.

She rubbed one wrist against the other, remembering her plan born out of the wildest fear at the riverbank. In that camp there would be other weapons than her own teeth. Again that death lay beyond was nothing to fear—life, on the other hand, was promised enduring horror.

Nancee took two steps farther and then was rocked by the message which flashed into her head:

"Two-legs, why do you what this piece of stinking guts and evil orders you?"

The cat! "Go," she found wit enough to return, watching Dik. If the renegade had any mindspeak the creature from the prairies might already have brought a sad fate upon itself. "Go—this one is a killer-of-all, men and animals both. He would wear your hide with pride. Go before he comes to hunt you!"

"There will be a hunting, yes, a good hunting!" The answer seemed as loud to her as if the prairiecat had shouted it aloud in human-formed words. "Be you ready for that hunting."

She took another short step. There had been no change in that twisted leer with which Dik was regarding her. She was almost sure that he had no mindtouch ability. "Go before he discovers—"

There was no answer—nothing she could touch which suggested that the cat was still within range. So, for all its confidence in battle, it had indeed followed the prudent way she had suggested. But deep in her there was another small taste of death—she was wholly alone.

"Lookit, Ed. Th' boss has him th' ladybird, all nice and easy!" One of the men by the fire had arisen and was staring upslope at them.

"What yuh do now, boss? Bed her and make yurself High Lord—"

"What I do is my concern." Again the arrogance of a high-kin man, and something in the note of that wiped all the gap-toothed smiles from the faces of his followers.

Nancee's chin went up a fraction. She might be wearing clothes stinking from months of travel, her hair hanging in wet tails about her head and shoulders, but the manners of the great hall were hers, and now they provided her with a kind of armor, keeping away the horrors which might still face her here.

She had only one thing to depend upon—Dik would seem to have some ambitions laid back in the war-torn country from which she and Uncle Roth had been fleeing. It was true that if Bradd still held any power the man who wed her could sit in the high seat there. But that anyone would now fasten on such a thought made her weigh Dik's plans the lighter. There was nothing left in the once-rich land which would be worth even a clipped silver piece now. Yet it was still this belief she sensed in the renegade which gave her any kind of a chance.

Without looking back over her shoulder she spoke again:

"Kehlee of the Peaks squats in the ruins of Bradd—unless he has swept the land of everything, even sold our people to slavers. Do you go up against Kehlee's squadron with this army of yours?" From some inner strength she produced that same flat tone which denied him any thought of having imprisoned more than just her body.

"We shall see." He did not sound as if he had any fears of her dismal suggestion being truth. "Harz, over with you and let the lady sit there."

The man directly before her did move, and with a will which suggested that Dik ruled his own following if he did not play overlord in the east. Nancee seated herself with the same sweep of skirts she would have used back in the House of Bradd. Dik had returned his sword to its sheath. Now he made a gesture, and the others of his noisome force shuffled away, allowing him good room to seat himself not too far from his captive.

He now held to her part of a dry and crumbling journey cake, one end of which was covered with thick grease. "Eat!"

She longed to lean forward and throw it into his face, but she ate, the rancid taste giving her queasiness.

"You are wiser than that meat over there." He spoke clearly, as if determined to make her see the very depths into which she had fallen, perhaps thinking so to cow her further as he gestured to the tangled bodies at the other side of the hollow. "I think we shall deal well with one another." Now he reached into a saddlebag and brought out a length of dark dried meat, from which he cut a mouth-shaped piece, flipping it into his open jaws with a turn of the knife.

The knife had been riding in his boottop. Nancee made note of that. Then she heard the heavy stamp of Boldhoof's foot. The Northhorse—if they were lean of loot this outlaw force had at least that bit of luck—there was also what rode in the two panniers. Those had not been loosened from their pack across the mare's broad back before the raiders had struck.

Metal, always good for sale to the skillful smiths of the Horseclans—some of it dug with her own hands when their small party had chanced upon one of the old ruins before they had joined the wagon train. That train was where Dik had enough interest with the wagon boss to get them cut off and left behind, ripe for his taking.

"Two-legs—"

That voice again sounded in her head. There was no change in Dik's expression as he watched her. Dared she believe that she was the only one here that the prairiecat could reach?

She took the chance. "Cat-one, this is death for you. Get away while you can."

Nancee chewed and swallowed. Again she heard a heavy stamp from the picket line. The other mounts were moving uneasily. Then one gave a shrill whinny which brought Dik's head around.

"What's to do with those horses, Mish?"

One of the men who had slouched away from the fire spat over his shoulder.

"Jus' spooked—they's bin doin' that for a while. Tree cat hanging around maybe. Tha's like 'em."

"See to it." Dik did not raise his voice, but there was a bite in it.

He turned back to Nancee. "Tree cat," he repeated slowly as if trying to impress on her the dangers which might be piled mountain-high against anyone in this wild country. "Get one of them on your trail, lady, and you'll know what ill luck really means."

Defiance was on the tip of Nancee's tongue, but she swallowed hasty words. She must let him believe that he had won—at least for now. Perhaps he had, unless she had such courage as that of Mairee.

One of the horses flung up its head and uttered a startling loud neigh. Boldhoof stamped as if in some answer known only to the equine kind.

"Cat-one—" Nancee's thought was sharp. "If this is your doing—"

All the men in the bowl had turned to look at the picket line now. Two had swords out, and a third was fitting an arrow to the string of his bow. Even Dik had half turned his back on her, though she did not believe that she dared move without his seeing.

"Cat-one—these are ready for the kill!" She could not be sure what game the half-grown cub was playing nor why, but she was sure that the prairiecat was behind it all.

"Get it!" Dik's order grated and sent the men into action, though she noted that they moved slowly, watching the brush and the two trees between which the picket line had been anchored.

Nancee measured the distance between her and Dik. His attention was now all for the horse line, and he had drawn his own sword. That knife in his boottop—dared she try for it?

As if the hidden clan cat read her purpose, only half-formed as it was, mind to mind, there came a squall as nerve-racking as any sound she had ever heard. The horses, including Boldhoof, went wild lunging at the ropes. That of the Northhorse parted as if it were made of tapestry thread and the huge mare swung around, shouldering its smaller neighbors apart, leading to the break-free of one of those. At the same time Nancee flung her own light body forward. Her shoulder struck behind Dik's knees, sending the man staggering for a step or two, but not before she had jerked that boot knife free, its hilt fitting into her hand as if it had been made for her alone.

The men pulled back as Boldhoof reared and dropped both hoofs together with a ground-shaking force. While two of the other horses, now free, ran up and away over the edge of the hollow, their fellows flailed out with hooves and jerked their heads against the confinement of the ropes which held them.

"Whar's tha' double-be-damned cat?" shouted the archer, his bow swinging from side to side as he tried to find some target.

They were all looking upward into the trees, endeavoring to sight the menace. Yet, save for the threshing of lower limbs caused by the jerking of the picket line below, there was nothing to be sighted.

Dik had regained his balance and swung around, his eyes narrowed, the intent look of the hunter on his bristle-cheeked face. He took a single stride to where Nancee was regaining her feet, the knife in her hands.

"What kind of damned witchery—" he began, and then his hand flashed out. Before she could dodge or try to defend herself his fist struck her chin, not full on as he had intended, for some providence allowed her to jerk her head back in time, but with force enough to send her spinning backward, the world a whirl of pain and light around her.

She fell right enough, and part of her waited for the second blow she was sure would come. Instead there was a hoarse shout and her dazed head and misty sight could not warn her. There was the heavy smell of horse scent, and with it the odor of raw fear.

Over her loomed a trampling monster. A great head bowed, and jaws opened and closed again on her hunched shoulder. She was dragged upward, though her feet did not quite leave the ground, and so she passed into a darkness through which came only faintly for the second time the yowl of a cat.

Pain in her back and her feet reached into the dark and brought her out again. She was near stifled by the heavy smell of horse sweat, but she forced her eyes open. Yet, she was being drawn along the ground, backward, unable to see where she might be taken. And it was Boldhoof's mouth which had closed upon her, the mare's giant strength seemingly little disturbed by the burden of the slight body she had gathered from the ground.

There was a whistling flight of an arrow, the kind used to frighten game into a stampede during which the stragglers could be picked off. Yet Boldhoof paid no attention to the shaft, which must have passed near by the sound of it.

Nancee was half-conscious—the pain in her shoulder where the great teeth gripped her and the bruising of her body dragged along the ground made her sick—but she held onto the small portion of awareness she had. Surely one of the men back there would use an arrow to better purpose soon—

For the third time the battle cry of a cat rang out, and this time from close to her, from the air, as if some furred warrior had grown wings.

"Two-legs, let the good horse free you and then join me here!"

Somehow that reached her in spite of the pain of her body and the near blankness of her mind brought about by Dik's blow. She was freed suddenly from that crushing of her shoulder, and she slumped, unable to move. Then she could have screamed, perhaps she did, as something tangled fiercely in her hair and pulled up her head. There was a furred body behind her; she caught only a glimpse or two of it as it endeavored to keep its hold in her hair.

Somehow she got to her knees, and that torturing grasp on her hair loosened. She flailed out with one arm, and her hand struck against a stone-firm pillar seemingly covered with damp hide. Grasping at that, she strove to come erect, though she had to lean against the foreleg of the Northhorse to do that.

"Two-legs, there is no time for resting. Get you up!"

Nancee wavered along Boldhoof's side, and her hand hit against one of the panniers which had still beladen the horse. Apparently the raiders had not stripped their prize. That voice in her head provided the energy she must have. As it impressed "Climb" on her, Nancee strove to fight her way up over the pannier onto the broad back. There was a flash of gray-brown and the young prairiecat was there also, crowding against her.

Boldhoof went into a rocking trot and then such a gallop as Nancee would never have expected the heavy animal could produce. She lay on that back, her fingers laced in the belts which held the panniers, while the cat flattened itself beside her.

"The voiceless horses of those have run," it cast into her mind. "This good mountain stepped on two of the bad two-legs—perhaps neither will rise again. This is better than the wagon—but we shall find that, two-legs, and Frog Hunter shall be among the bold ones—with another name—you shall see. I am Rider of the Mountain that runs—"

She managed to raise her head a fraction. There was the flow of air about them; truly Boldhoof was running now. Nancee listened for a sound of pursuit; she was not able as yet to look back. Surely Dik would not let them go so easily!

"Dik—" she said aloud, forgetting the difference now between mindspeech and that from the lips. "He will follow."

There was an odd feeling in her mind. If perhaps the cub laughed so among his peers, that was what she sensed now.

"The loud two-legs was stepped upon by this great mountain."

To be stepped upon by Boldhoof—could she wish a more successful fate for Dik Romlee? Her mind still seemed hazy, but she held onto the fact that they did seem to be free and moving at a wind-raising rate of speed. But how had Boldhoof had the luck to break loose just at that right moment?

"This one called upon the Mountain." There was a burst of pride and satisfaction in the mindtouch from the cat. "The lesser horses were told to run. Run they did. But the Mountain came with Rider!"

She shook her head a little and winched at the resulting flash of pain. That the cats of the clans talked with both man and mount was well known. However, those furred and hoofed ones were familiar from birth with each other and with the humans of the tribes. Boldhoof came from a country where horses were truly dumb beasts.

"Only because two-legs have no speech either," returned the cat crisply. "Ask now what this one thinks."

Tentatively Nancee denied her headache and her uneasiness at being a part of this flight. She tried to reach out to contact Boldhoof.

There was a sensation of pleasure and freedom, of being a mistress of herself—and with it a small, almost humble touch for Nancee. The girl pulled herself up higher and could not help but stare at the large maned head before her, twining her fingers harder into the straps of the panniers. The ears on the head twitched, then slanted directly back as if pointing to her.

She filled her own mind, that part of it she hoped would be a passage to Boldhoof, with thanks and return pleasure.

"Now"—that was the cat cutting in impatiently—"we go to the clan. This Mountain will carry us safely and we can find the trail where there is no reason to hide. Let all see Rider and no more will he be a kitten-cubbling to wagon-ride!"

Nancee laughed shakily. They had forded a river where the water had risen high enough to wet the pannier and Boldhoof's barrel, and the whole of the wide-open country lay before them. To go to the clan—why not? She had no kin—

"Save Rider," the cat cut in sharply.

"And Boldhoof," she agreed. "Two who fight very well and are valiant company. Agreed—let us now seek this clan of yours, Rider of a Moving Mountain!"

THE SILENT ONE
Chilled to the Bone (1991) Mayfair Games

There was a chill wind, the first thrust of fall. Here in the city street there were no leaves to blow, only the urban discards of sticky bits of food wrappers.

The woman who had walked so slowly along was seeking house numbers, and many of those were no longer displayed. Coming at last to the steps of a half basement she saw below a window with a sign which glittered, a sign made of the very product it advertised—large, many-colored beads.

Marta Hartmann looked at the card in her hand and then to the sign. In her worry-beset mind the two had no possible connection. Yet at that moment she was willing to take any chance.

In fact she was down the two steps into the area way, her hand on the latch of the door with a spurt of determination. There was a second sign there—*OPEN.*

Somehow she was not surprised to hear the jangle of a bell when she did just that, a sound which pushed her back some forty years to when she had gone with her grandmother to Miss Worley's yarn shop.

The day outside was gloomy enough but inside here there was the brilliance and light of a treasure house. Beads, indeed! They hung in strands on the walls, and they were heaped in divided trays on the counters. While inside glass-fronted display cases were beads put to use, formed into jewelry, necklaces, bracelets, earrings, a show of what was barbaric wealth of every possible color and shape.

For a moment this display, which was far too extensive to be really seen in detail, even pulled her thoughts away from her errand here. She was drawn without being conscious of it to peer into the nearest case, pulling impatiently—really trifocals were the limit while shopping—at her glasses.

"African trade beads—"

She was startled, her reaction too quick. In fact for a moment she felt a touch of the vertigo which came with stress and which she fought so fiercely.

A woman had come out of the inner room. She was quite unlike what Marta had expected. Not the gypsy-like figure her mind had built from what hung and lay about.

For a long moment Marta simply stared at that tall, dark-suited person who might better be met behind the desk of a vice president of a bank, a most conservative bank. Then her total astonishment found voice:

"Ilse, Ilse Bergen, it *is* you!"

The woman dropped a string of beads on the counter as she looked at Marta as piercingly as she would at one of those globes she had just put down.

"Yes, I am Ilse Bergen but I don't—" Then her voice changed from politeness into warmth. "But it is Marta! Marta Ferris!" Her two hands came out to Marta in the welcome they had always been quick to offer.

Marta's thin lips twisted in a grimace even as she met that grasp. "You didn't really know me, did you, Ilse? Well, I don't wonder. And it isn't Marta Ferris any more—it's Marta Hartmann. Which is why—"

Now that the time had come somehow she had lost the words. Again she closed her eyes as those rows of beads hanging on the wall seemed to swing.

"You—you are—this?" She broke loose from Ilse's hold. The card which had guided her had been crumpled between their palms, now she shoved it at the other. Then she took fast grip on the edge of the nearest counter to steady herself.

"Marta!" The hands were gone, and there was an arm around her shoulders.

"I'll be all right," she managed to mouth, drawing on all her resources as she had so many times during the last weeks of sickness and sometimes sheer panic.

Then she found herself safely away from those dangling strings of beads, seated in a chair, Ilse standing over her with a mug held out and the old imperious look on her face as if she would accept no denials.

"Drink this."

Marta had to hold the mug in both hands she was shaking so, but she obediently sipped something which was neither coffee nor brandy as she had expected, but was warm and spicy and somehow soothing,

"Now." Ilse seated herself on another chair so closely that their knees were almost touching. "Drink that up." She had the crumpled card in her fingers and glanced at it. "Where did you get this?"

Marta swallowed another mouthful of the brew. The shaking was almost gone. She had glanced over the rim of the mug cautiously; she no longer saw spinning walls.

"Esther Walters, she belongs to the quilting circle. She said—" Marta swallowed again. "Only I never thought that Dr. I. Haverling was you!"

"Mrs. Walters—oh." Ilse leaned back a fraction. "Yes, I remember Mrs. Walters. As for the Haverling, Marta, I was married, my husband died some years ago."

"I'm sorry," Marta made what she knew was the weakest of replies to that.

"If Mrs. Walters gave you this," Ilse now flicked the edge of the card with one fingernail, "you must know what she called upon me for."

Marta put the mug on the edge of a table where there were small tools and trays of unstrung beads.

"There was trouble," she said slowly, "about some lost papers—her husband's mother died very suddenly and they could find no record of investments which were very important. She said you were able to—to somehow sense where those were."

"And you did not dismiss what she said as nonsense, as well you might?" Ilse was watching her now very intently.

"No. I—I have read of such things. I do believe that some people are able to—to help when there is no—no reasonable way for the ordinary person to accomplish something."

"I see," Ilse nodded. "And now you have a need for help in such a way?"

She was not going to cry, no, she could not let herself cry! But the tears came in spite of all her efforts, and after those her words spilled out so fast she was sure she was not making sense but she could not control them.

"It's Alexia—There's something wrong. The doctor says she is perfectly well—but mostly I think she believes that I'm the one who should be—be given treatment! But I've seen it happen to her, Ilse, little by little, day by day. She's changed—horribly. And it isn't drugs—that's what I thought at first, you always fear that these days. She just isn't Alexia any more. Most of the time she isn't. But other times—other times she is just as she used to be. I can't let it go on like this anymore!"

"Alexia is?"

"My granddaughter—she's only sixteen, Ilse. And she is all I have left. She was a darling, such a darling!"

She had decided to explore the garden. It had been a show place once. And she went out longer and longer each day. But she no longer talked about what she was doing.

Marta groped blindly in her purse for a wad of tissues and dabbed at her eyes. She did not want to face Ilse—how could she really explain after all? Perhaps it was she who was imagining things.

"Marta, my dear, in what way has Alexia changed? Can you remember when it began?"

Marta drew a deep breath. "I'll try to make some sense." She was giving that promise not only to Ilse but to herself. "Alexia's parents, my son Robert and her mother, were killed in a plane crash when Alexia was three. Jonas was alive then, Jonas Hartmann, my husband. We took Alexia, she was the daughter we had never had and a delight to both of us. I think, I am sure, we made her happy.

"When Jonas died it—it was difficult for both of us. That was three years ago. But we had each other and that was a comfort. Then, about six months ago, Jonas' great grandmother died. She was Lilly Hartmann, the wife of Herwarth Hartmann.

"I don't suppose many people remember about him now. He came over from Germany and made a fortune. They used to call him lucky, almost everything he tried in the way of business turned out well. He was also a very proud man, one who always insisted that his family in Germany had been of consequence at one time and it was his constant ambition to return the family to what he considered its rightful place. Back in about 1910, after he had made several millions, he took Lilly and his son Albert to Germany. He insisted that they visit an old castle there in which he believed the family had once lived. In fact he bought a kind of summer house, which was still partly intact, had it torn down, and all the stones numbered so it could be brought back here and rebuilt.

"His pride almost ruined the family—he spent at least a million dollars building a huge mansion and then filled it with art works. He never knew it, but he was cheated on a lot of those purchases. Anyway he tried to make Albert into his idea of a proper heir and it didn't work.

"Albert ran away from home in his teens. He went out west and went into mining, married the daughter of a farmer and refused to have anything to do with his family. There was something behind it all which he never told anyone.

"Herwarth Hartmann died and Lilly lived on and on—she was a hundred and one when she died. And for about fifty years, her last ones, she had lived as a recluse in that big house, most of it was closed up. The money, what was left of it, was a trust which passed to Jonas and so to Alexia and me. That, and that big useless house.

"When the lawyers got in touch with us we came here to see about settling the estate. Mainly we came—well, because we wanted to get away from our home for awhile—I thought it might be good for both of us—I did."

Marta wiped her eyes again. Why couldn't she stop this stupid crying?

"It seemed to be good for Alexia. She was interested in the old house, and we spent a lot of time with appraisers. It was almost like a treasure hunt—we even found a forgotten wall safe with some very charming Victorian jewelry in it which I promised to Alexia. And after that she went hunting on her own for things. I never saw her so excited.

"Then—then she changed. She had decided to explore the garden. It had been a showplace once. And she went out longer and longer each day. But she no longer talked about what she was doing. She in fact talked less and less. I wanted her to come into town with me, and she kept saying she had things to do. Then—then she went out at night!

"I found her bed empty, I'd hunt her, I'd wait up. I tried to reason with her that it might be dangerous when I confronted her.

"She—she was so angry. It was not like Alexia at all. We had always been on such good terms. I thought maybe she might be meeting someone. But we were strangers there, we never went to town except together and we had been so busy with the house that we had not tried to meet anyone but the lawyer and the appraisers when they came. I tried to follow her twice—it was as if she just disappeared!

"Then I even asked Mrs. McCarthy, we had gotten her in to help us clear things out. Her mother had been cook for the Hartmanns in the old days and she knew something of the storerooms and the like. She—she said—Alexia— Alexia had been—caught!"

"Caught?" queried Ilse.

"That's what she called it. There—it seemed there were old stories about some children—young people in the past—who acted as strangely as Alexia— some were from the town and had gone exploring on the estate—there were stories, as there always are, about it being haunted. I think there was one little boy who just disappeared, though they searched for weeks. And a girl a little older than Alexia who had been gone for several days and when she was found—she had had some sort of a shock and had to be put in a hospital. There was even a relative of the Hartmanns who had come over from Germany back in the '30s, a young refugee who was going to stay with Lilly as a companion. She hung herself! Though they say it was because she had bad news about her people back home. Oh," Marta squeezed the wad of tissue tighter into a ball. "People talked and there were all kinds of stories. It is silly to listen!"

"Not always," Ilse returned. "Some such rumors have more than just a grain of truth in them. Did Mrs. McCarthy also suggest that these various victims had the same attitude as Alexia?"

"Yes. She said that those from the town, the boy and the girl, took to going off on their own, running away once or twice when their families refused to let them. I believe that the Restons actually locked their son up and he got out by climbing out of a window on the night he disappeared. Ilse—I don't live with *my* Alexia any more, and I am frightened, so frightened—" Her voice trailed off. And then she fumbled in her purse and brought out a small plastic bag.

"Yesterday Alexia was writing something, and I came into the room and spoke to her. She actually screamed and leaned forward over the paper she had been working on as if I were not to see it. Then she crumpled it up and swung around. She was wearing something, a string of beads, around her neck. I'd never seen them before. They had been hanging under her shirt and came out when she moved.

"The string caught on the corner of the desk lid and broke. She—Ilse, she was like a mad thing, scrabbling around on the floor picking up those beads! And she yelled at me—words I did not even believe she knew—horrible words. She grabbed up all the beads—or she thought she had them all—and ran out of the room and up the stairs to lock herself in her bedroom and she refused to answer me. She was a totally different person. After she had gone I found these caught under the fringe of the rug."

She held out the tiny bag and Ilse took it, swinging around a little so that she could lay it still unopened on the work table.

"You alone handled these, Marta, after Alexia's necklace broke—no one else?"

Marta nodded. The other woman worked loose the knotting of the bag top and then drew to her a square of dark cloth, allowing the contents of the bag to roll into view on that surface.

There were two oval beads about a quarter inch in size. At first glance they were dull, certainly not attractive as those in the trays about. Ilse picked up a small tool and with that turned each of the beads around. At a closer inspection they showed very faint signs of having once been carved, time having worn away most of the design.

"These were not found in the house when you were present, Marta?"

"No. Alexia must have found them. She had such fun as she said, treasure hunting, and she did discover all sorts of unusual and pretty things. There were trunks full of old dresses—and, Ilse, even cards of beautiful laces which had never been used—there was one fan of carved ivory she just loved! She was so excited and happy!" Marta closed her eyes—it hurt to remember, oh, how it hurt!

Ilse made a quick move with her index finger, pinning one of the beads to the cloth. A second later she jerked back as if she had touched a live coal. Then very carefully she shook both beads from the cloth onto the palm of her hand, closing her fingers tightly about them, the look on her face was one who determined on a duty which was against great odds.

"Alrauna," she almost spat the word as if clearing her mouth of something foul.

"Alrauna?" Marta said. "What—?"

"There is another name for it—mandrake. It is very old, connected strongly to old evils. There are many tales and legends about it. These were carved of mandrake, and for no good purpose!"

"But where could Alexia get them? She always showed me everything—" Marta's voice trailed off.

"Apparently she did not this time." Use's own eyes closed. She still held her hand gripped tightly about the beads. Then she dropped them and twitched the cloth about them.

"We must take steps and very soon, Marta. This is of the most importance. I must see this house—"

"Alexia—there is trouble for her?"

"The fears which brought you here, Marta, are very well founded. Alexia is in grave danger, and not only peril of body. No, do not ask me to explain now—for I cannot be sure myself what awaits us at this strange house of yours. But the sooner we reach it the better."

Time seemed against them, Marta thought. There was a frustrating wait for the commuters' train. Ilse had stuffed into an overnight bag a book which was so old that pages had loosened from the binding. This she read, and then put aside with a sudden gesture as if she had found some information sadly needed.

She turned to Marta then, but she did not speak of what might lie before them but rather of earlier days when they had both been in school. She recalled this and that incident from the past in a soothing voice which drew Marta, impatient at first, into shared memories as if that very tone of that voice carried with it some deep comfort. She could not put Alexia out of mind, still there was a kind of strength issuing from her companion which calmed and steadied her.

They picked up Marta's car from the station lot and drove quickly through the small town, cutting off from the main highway on a winding secondary road. Here fall was all bright color and it had life of a sort which braced one. Another turn into a drive, the entrance of which was nearly completely curtained by the growth of untended bushes, brought them by a narrow and rutted way up a low hilltop to confront the masterpiece Herwarth Hartmann had established to honor his family line.

There were towers, and stretches of ivy-covered stone walls in which the windows were sometimes completely curtained with the twining vines. Wild asters and ironweed in its imperial purple had edged in from fields to take over formal flower beds of which only the faintest traces were left.

Marta led the way to a deep recessed doorway; there was carving running around it and a shield of arms prominently displayed.

"We—we thought it was fun," she said slowly as she set key to the lock. "It all looked so—so stagey, almost like one of the gaudy covers on a paperback novel. We joked about it. Only now—now—I am afraid!" And she pushed the door open as if indeed she would rather it remained closed.

They came into a wide hall into which descended a staircase at the foot of which a statue of a nearly life-sized nymph held aloft a torch. A feeble light issued from that, enough to abate some of the thick gloom which was in such contrast to the bright fall colors of the day without. There was a very small measure of light also which entered down from a two-story ceiling where there was a round opening enclosing glass of yellow, red, and a purple faded to violet.

"The fears which brought you here, Marta, are very well founded. Alexia is in grave danger, and not only peril of body."

The air about was chill, and Marta beckoned her guest on into a side room where a fire smoldered on the hearth. She went at once to poke at it in a futile manner while Ilse stood in the middle of the room surveying the ranks of dark furniture, seemingly ranked to discourage visitors.

She pivoted slowly, her head up, almost like a hound testing for a scent. Then she said with authority:

"Old, tired, but there is nothing overt here to alarm."

"You think that there is something wrong—here?" Marta slipped the poker back into the stand and now she gazed swiftly from side to side at the shadows.

"One cannot overlook anything. But," Ilse opened her purse and took out the rolled up piece of cloth containing the beads.

For a single moment she allowed the beads to again nestle in her cupped hand, at the same time once more gazing about as if she expected to find some change in the room or its atmosphere. Then she said with decision:

"No, the trouble is not here, Marta. There is no response. We shall have to look elsewhere—"

"All through the house." Marta straightened. As if having some action in which she could have a part gave her more control. "But let us have some coffee first, and Mrs. McCarthy's cookies. In the kitchen—we really have made the kitchen our own—"

She set off briskly. It might have been that she wanted to delay discovery; that she was clinging fiercely to the everyday as a defense.

The kitchen indeed was a sharp change from the rest of the house. It was very large, and there was a bay window at one side in which glass racks had been hung to support a number of pots, each containing greenery. Ilse went directly to the display. She pinched off a small leaf here, another there, raising each in turn for a prolonged sniff.

"An ambitious herb garden," she commented, "and perhaps a very useful one for us now. Verlain, garlic, angelica. Who is the master gardener who is able to coax along such a collection as this?"

"Lilly Hartmann—I think she began it. She had an old cook who was supposed to be what Mrs. McCarthy says her mother called a 'yarb woman.' Mrs. McCarthy knows something about it. And takes care now. I've promised her the whole collection when she wants it. I believe that her son is building her a small greenhouse." She twisted off a leaf herself. "Rose geranium, at least this one I know. Now—coffee."

There was a round table near the herb-embowered window and they sat down together, a plate of cookies between them. Marta had just poured the coffee when the back door opened and a girl wearing a parka as bright as an autumn-touched maple leaf burst in.

She was tall, but in spite of the bulk of her clothes, looked too slender. Her hair had been cropped in a boyish style and one lock curved down over her forehead as a very pale blond scallop. Her eyes seemed very large and were of a cool shade of gray, almost like silver with a thin frost overlaid. At the sight of Ilse she stopped so short that the door she had opened so quickly smacked her, nearly propelling her into the room.

"Alexia!" Marta set down the coffee pot. "Do come and meet a very old friend of mine. Ilse and I went to school together when we were just about your age. I ran into her quite by accident and she is to be our guest for a day or so. She—she knows quite a lot about beads and is willing to help us appraise those bead purses you found in the chest drawer." The words were coming too fast, Marta knew, but she felt at that moment they were truly inspired. "Oh, this is my granddaughter, Alexia, Ilse. And this is Dr. Haverling, Alexia."

"Doctor?" There was certainly no welcome to be heard in that cool young voice.

Ilse smiled. "Not of medicine, no. I am a doctor of philosophy—my degree was not medical at all. Marta tells me that you have been finding treasure troves all about this great house."

She had set her hand down on the folded cloth which again enshrouded the beads, pressing the palm flat. Her gaze was measuring Alexia intently.

The girl shrugged. "Oh, there's a lot of stuff stuck away. Most of it's just junk." She came farther into the room in an odd sidling manner as if she must continue to face Ilse. And there was certainly animosity in both her voice and the expression of her face where a pallor underlaid the tan of summer.

"Come, my dear," Marta cut in hastily. "There are some of Mrs. McCarthy's brownies and some of the chocolate drink you like—You must be chilled through—"

Alexia gave an impatient shrug. "I'm all right, Gran. I just went for a walk. I'm not hungry anyway." She had slid on toward the door when Ilse spoke:

"Kind, wer gab Dir das geschenk?"

German, Marta thought bewildered. Her own was rusty now, but what did Ilse mean by asking "Who gave you the gift, child?" And Alexia did not even know German.

Yet the girl shook her head as if to shake out some thought before she said quite plainly:

"Sie—Sie gab es hir."

She gave it! What was it and who was she? But Ilse was already asking that:

"Sie, wer ist Sie?"

Alexia's two hands had gone to the collar of the parka, and now she twisted them into the material of that as if she wanted to choke off the words something was making her say:

"*Die Schweigende!*"

Marta sat down abruptly and Alexia whirled about and was gone again through the back door. Her grandmother looked helplessly to Ilse—

"What did she mean—the Silent One? And—Alexia does not speak German!"

Ilse's hand still lay heavy on the beads.

"There are powers which can make us do many things. The Silent One—" she repeated thoughtfully. Then with a pull at the cloth about the beads she uncovered them again. This time she emptied them into one palm and folded the other over them. She leaned back in her chair and closed her eyes while Marta watched her helplessly. Ilse's lips seemed to thin, her mouth became set. There was building purpose, a grim purpose about her.

Marta shivered. She never thought she was psychic in any way, yet at that moment there seemed to be closing around her a feeling as if she were caught in some dark place, that invisible walls were fast building. She wanted to fling out her arms to push them off, and that panic which had threatened her for days was breaking through all the bonds she had held against it.

"Ilse!" She could not stop that call which was in its way a cry for help.

The other woman opened her eyes. "Yes." She said that word not as if in answer to Marta but rather as if some sum she had proposed for herself had been solved. "You spoke of a building which Mr. Hartmann had brought from Germany, the blocks marked so it could be erected again here in the proper way?"

"Yes. It is in the garden, but it is not a real building—it is very small. They said it was the only part of the castle which he thought could be moved, the only part which was not a complete ruin."

Ilse's purse was closer to a tote than a conventional bag. She had opened it while Marta spoke, and now she took out a pair of small bottles, two blue candles, and a small pot of silver, its lid and sides pierced with an intricate design.

Leaving these on the table top, she arose and went to the herbs, examining them carefully, harvesting a single leaf there and a twiglet bearing several here. These she brought back to the table and laid them out carefully. Marta watched uncomprehendingly.

"We fight trouble as best we can," Ilse said. "This is an old trouble. If I am not mistaken, this evil was brought with the Anchorite's call from Germany."

"Anchorite's call?" Marta repeated.

"It is of the old church." Ilse was busy placing in the pierced pot a powder from a box, and then laid on top of that some of the herb leaves. "We can believe that the castle had a chapel. It was sometimes done in the old days when a man or woman who was considered sinful would be in a manner walled up in a special cell built against the wall of a church or chapel. They were allowed a window on the world but no door, and the window was intended for them to watch the sacred mass.

"For some of these anchorites this was an enforced penance, for others a free choice. The great mystic of old England, Julian of Norwich, was a voluntary anchorite, and there has been much recorded concerning her influence over those who came to her window for aid. She was a woman of great spiritual power. However, this imprisonment might also be a punishment—perhaps sometimes unjustly enforced—and that is what I believe has extended its poison into Alexia's life now.

"A woman unjustly relegated to something which was near a living death would, over the remaining lifetime granted her, build up certain despair, hatred, evil rage. This would produce in those sensitive to influences a residue of all that poor creature felt and knew. That portion of the first personality who experienced such great rage and hate could continue to be a poison, even after the physical death."

Ilse touched the beads. "These are a focus for such a personality. They are part of a rosary, a rosary used in petitions, not to any comforting or truly spiritual power, but rather to one of darkness and evil. If what I have read is true, there must be a cleansing. This will not be an easy thing, but it is my hope that the fact that the place of one time imprisonment no longer rests on the ground where the evil was first rooted will be an aid."

Marta leaned forward, putting both her hands on the table. "What can I do?" she asked. Belief had come, the real world she had known might refuse that belief, but she felt she was no longer a part of that world.

"We shall do this." Ilse was busy with those things she had brought with her, and as her fingers sped from one to another she began to explain, carefully and sometimes repetitiously, making very sure Marta understood as well as she might.

The twilight had closed in early. Leaves drifted across the path, crackled thickly underfoot. Marta swung the torch beam at the drifts of leaves. The long un-pruned shrubs were nearly tall enough to top her head, and in places they were matted into what was close to a wall.

However, immediately before her a way had been recently raggedly chopped, with half-cut twigs and branches left dangling.

At the center of the open space they had entered stood a small building. It was in the form of a tower, as if someone had fancied building a miniature castle out of legend but had not gone beyond this.

Save for the sound of the leaves crackling under their feet there was silence. They were already out of sight of the house, swallowed up by these thickets which to Marta had become far too dark, too thick, too shadowed—

The slashing of undergrowth was more apparent the farther they went. There was something ruthless, cruel about it. Marta strove to control her thoughts—she had lost, she felt, all touch with the life she had always known. She was allowing herself to be swept along into a dark fantasy.

The torchlight bore ahead into open land. Now the silence was broken, not by any rustle of leaf but sounds which might come from sullen, throat deep muttering.

Ilse's hand fell on her arm, Marta started, looked around. Her companion motioned her to wait, and then went down on one knee. The candles were brought out, housed as they had hastily been in old wooden sticks Marta had discovered in the kitchen cupboard. Then came the silver brazier and one of the small flasks Ilse had shown her earlier. Marta fumbled in her pocket for matches. But she had more attention for what lay before them than she had for what Ilse was doing.

At the center of the open space they had entered stood a small building. It was in the form of a tower as if someone had fancied to build a miniature castle out of legend but had gone no farther than this. The height was about a story, and facing them directly was an opening, narrow but tall enough to be considered a door.

Through this issued a pale light which showed that, if there had ever been a closing for that aperture, it was long gone. While the light was somehow sickly, unpleasant, certainly it did not burn as clearly as the candles Ilse had just induced into flame.

Marta stooped and picked up one of those as she had been instructed. Ilse gestured to the torch and, reluctantly, very reluctantly, Marta switched that off. Its fuller light had seemed in a measure to be a weapon against what they must face. Though, even with all of the coaching, she could not yet be sure of what that might truly be.

A thin tendril of smoke arose from the brazier which swung from a chain Ilse had looped about her right wrist. She held in that same hand a flask of some dark glass, while Marta took up the remaining candle.

That penetrating mumble had ceased. Yet Marta was aware of a pressure of silence itself. She straightened, her back stiff, as she moved resolutely forward, Ilse beside her.

The wan light from the doorway did not flicker as did the candleshine, nor was it, Marta believed, from any torch. She had all she could do to restrain herself from calling Alexia, sure as she was that the girl was in this place.

They were at the door now, but it was so narrow that only one might enter at a time, and from it issued air as chill as if they were preparing to walk into some huge freezer. Ilse took the lead and Marta was ashamed that deep in her she was glad of that.

There was a single circular room within, stone walled with nothing to soften or veil those gaunt walls. A bench was part of one wall and opposite that, placed higher so that a person of ordinary height could just see out of it, was a square opening, beyond which was darkness.

Before the bench, facing the wall without an opening, knelt Alexia. There was a string of beads, clasped between her hands, and one by one they slid through her fingers. As each was held in turn she whispered. Her voice was like the hiss of something which was not human. Her eyes were closed and her head was flung up and a little back so that her face was fully exposed. The hood of her parka lay back on her thin shoulders, pulling with it her hair so that there was no softening to her set features. Marta gave a small gasp— Alexia—Alexia was praying!

Ilse motioned a command and Marta hurriedly followed the orders she had been given. She set down her candle on the bench before which the girl knelt. Ilse was placing hers at the same time at Alexia's right. The girl made no move. Now the hissing had stopped, but her lips still moved, as if her prayer was inaudible.

Ilse made one more preparation. She swung the brazier directly before Alexia and that trail of smoke arising from it bent directly outward toward the girl's face.

Then Ilse spoke, and the words she used were not German, nor in any other language that Marta could understand. They were uttered with a note of command, of demand—as if forming a question which must be answered.

Alexia's facial muscles seemed to twist, to form for an instant the features of a stranger. But her eyes did not open. Instead, from the grimace of her mouth, there came a screech which no one could not mistake as rage.

So threatening was that voice which was not Alexia's (could never be

Alexia's, Marta protested inwardly) that she herself shrank back against the wall of the tower, while the feeling of cold increased, laying an icy touch upon her flesh.

Again Ilse spoke. Then her right hand rose and she pointed first to the right hand candle and then to the left. The flames at their crests elongated, thinned out, and crossed, directly before Alexia's face. Back and forth Ilse led other shining threads from the candles all the time speaking with authority, her words somehow rising and outreaching the screech which continued to break from the girl.

Now Alexia's head and shoulders were enmeshed in a web of the candle beams. For the first time she moved. The string of beads flailed out as she tried to use it as a weapon against those ties of light. She twisted and turned, once half arising from her knees only to fall back again. Her face was a mask of hate and anger, all of what had been Alexia seemed to have utterly vanished.

Still chanting Ilse unstoppered the bottle and she poured from it a liquid which was as colorless as water, catching it in the palm of her right hand.

She was standing directly behind Alexia now, and the girl was twisting wildly, crying out sounds which might have been uttered by a trapped animal.

Ilse's hand went out, passing easily through the network woven from the candle beams. She tipped her palm so that the liquid it contained fell directly on Alexia's head.

"Alexia Hartmann you are." For the first time Ilse used words Marta could understand. "Annarhilde you are not. Go, you who are not, to the place awaiting you. For I name this child rightfully by her name, Alexia, and I do so by that Power of Light in which no darkness can abide!"

There was one last shriek from Alexia and her body crumpled to the floor. The candle weaving vanished, but the scent from the brazier puffed out, seeming thin as the smoke was, feeble as the flame within, to drive away the cold. For that was gone, and with it the wan light, so that only the candles remained.

Marta flung herself forward, her arms about Alexia, enwrapping her with the same determination that the candle beams had shown. The girl stirred and her eyes opened for the first time.

"Gran?" She spoke as she had as a small child when some nightmare had released its grip on her at the coming of loving care.

"Alexia, dear heart, it's all right."

"I—there was someone—" the girl said uncertainly.

"That one is gone, nor shall she return." Ilse picked up the brazier chain.

With it she also took up the candle which appeared to blaze high enough to light the room. Now it caught and held on one block in the wall, one immediately above that square which opened on the outer world. There had been a carving there, a deep one, and it had been crudely defaced, the stone chipped and gouged as if done by poor tools over a period of time.

"The All Seeing Eye," Ilse said. "She could not bear its watching. Hatred brought her here, and because that she had been taught to revere had failed her, she sought other powers. She faces other judgment now, but there will be remembered what she once was and what unrightful punishment was dealt her then. Alexia—"

"Yes."

"In days to come pray for one who suffered much and who took then a wrong path. *Die Schweigende.*"

"The Silent One—" the girl repeated softly.

"It—it is all over?" Marta found her voice.

"Here and now it is over, dear friend. I would say that this place which has seen so much despair, sorrow, and darkness of soul should be destroyed. Though I do not believe that it will ever harbor again that which sheltered in it."

"Yes—oh, yes."

Ilse stooped and picked up the chain of beads which had fallen out of Alexia's hold. She put it with the two others she had carried from the house. Placing them together on the cloth in which she had wound them, she set the packet on the bench and put the flame of her candle to the edge. Fire flashed as if it was tinder or soaked in oil. She opened the brazier now and let what remained of its smoldering contents fall on the small blaze.

The sweet odor of herbs and spices flowed about them, leaving ashes as powdery as dust. Ilse regarded those approvingly.

"Such things are not for our world. Better so."

She blew out the candles and Marta switched on the torch to lead them out into the autumn night where all shadows were harmless.

THE NABOB'S GIFT

Hallows Eve: Tales of Love and the Supernatural (1992) Walker

"It makes me feel as if I am a lobster patty passed around on a tray at a ball supper!"

The Honorable Sara Langston gave a vicious jerk to the fringe of her heaviest wool shawl. She had spoken aloud, though there was no one to hear her.

There was no flame on the hearth of the state drawing room, making it as dull and cold as the world beyond the terrace windows, where a boisterous wind plastered damp leaves to the balustrade. But within her, rage was hot enough to balance the chill.

Not a "suitable alliance," rather an odious connection. So she had not "taken" during her first Season, nor the second, nor the third. So she was a gawk of a female with no pretense to presence nor style, as Mama had not scrupled to declare for these three years past. She had long ago accepted the difficulties of her position, eldest daughter but not Mama's own child—Louisa was that. And Papa being well into dun territory.

Now, when there seemed a chance that Lord Mortlake would come up to scratch and offer for Louisa, as Sara had been forcibly told this hour past, Sara must be agreeably surprised, everlastingly grateful that a tolerable soul was ready to take her.

She had been faced with this for more than a year, but time and distance had been welcome barriers; now both had been swept away. Even in the beginning it had been gothic—betrothed to a man she had never seen. Then, six months past, the respite which had sent Mama into a spasm—that her promised groom had been removed by a tiger—a tiger no less!

Sara bit her lip. There was something so out of reason in all this that she could believe she had fallen into some utterly nonsensical novel. Though Jasper Rowland had been removed from her life before he had ever entered it, now her parents did not scruple to agree with Amos Rowland, the returning Nabob—so deep in the pocket as to rival a duke, or so they reported—that she wed his second son Julian.

The two of them, Mama had announced, were on their way from London with Papa this very moment. It was insufferable, barbarous, and there was nothing she could do about it. Amos Rowland wanted a quality bride, and Papa wanted a bride-price to pull him out of dun territory.

Sara knew that instead of a dowry (any such funds would be passed along to Louisa now) favors and cash would flow the other way. The Rowlands were mushrooms. Little better than cits. It was a ramshackle part she was to play, and there was no way of squeaking out of it. A female really had no other shift with the whole of the family against her.

"Sara! Sara! Mama wants you. You'd better not show her that Friday face. Only fancy you will be setting us all in a stare—such a tale for the town!" Louisa teetered in the doorway. She was small, a mere twit of a girl, but her hair was lustrous and dark and she was pretty in a fashion designed to fade early. She had had two offers last Season, and now Mama was sure she had young Mortlake firmly attached.

Also she was spiteful, small-minded, suffered easily from an irritation of the nerves if denied her own way. Mama doted on her, and she had known almost from her cradle how to work Papa.

Sara did not risk the luxury of a reply; she could not trust her tongue. Louisa was wearing that sly smile which suggested it would be ill-advised to show any temper.

Mama, the second Lady Beners, was ensconced in her sitting room by a well-tended fire. She was as small as Louisa and might once have been considered passably pretty. Her situation through the years, as she had to witness the squandering of her fortune by a profligate husband she had never found likable, and those countless incivilities and many reproaches over the nonarrival of a male heir, had stiffened her temper and soured her with grievances. Her forehead, well ridged with wrinkles, showed under the wide ruffles of an elaborate cap, for Lady Beners did not believe in surrendering any town bronze to country living: her wardrobe was kept as much to the first start of fashion as she was able to hold it.

"I trust, girl"—her voice was both deep and ominous—"you have come to your proper senses, and we shall not be assaulted by any more rubbishy notions. This is a highly suitable alliance. Young Rowland is heir to a goodly estate, and we have it on excellent authority that his father is prepared to settle a sizeable sum on him at his marriage. You shall certainly not want for anything. Since Mr. Rowland wishes you both to move in the first society, everything will be done hamdsomely.

"He has already informed your father that he is bringing some fine jewelry from India for his son's bride. Beners has agreed that we may go to London and select bride clothes convenable with your station. I have already sent word to Madam Estelle that she is to look out for all that is fitting. It is plain that Mr. Rowland quite dotes on Julian, and since he is now the only son you may expect a very superior establishment."

Sara let the words flow. Did her misery show in her face? Lady Beners's eyes narrowed.

"I will not abide impertinence from you. Any young female who has shown herself to be such a loss during *three* Seasons must welcome with joy this exceedingly fortunate turn of affairs! Is that not true, Sara?"

She must get away soon or betray feelings that would lead Lady Beners to the pleasure of a thundering scold.

"Oh, there is no dealing with you, you wretched, ungrateful girl! Go to your room and recollect well when you get there that such a manner is highly ill-advised. We expect our guests to arrive at dusk. I told Martha to lay out the lilac crepe—mind you—do not come down with that mulish face. You will be all that is amiable and genteel."

"Yes, Mama," Sara responded colorlessly. Louisa, standing behind her mother's shoulder, smiled maliciously as Sara went out.

At least she had her own bedchamber to be private in. In the dusk two candles stood aflame on the dressing table. Across the bed lay the lilac gown considered suitable for the sacrifice about to be offered up.

Sara dropped on the bench to survey her reflection. No pretense to any beauty. Far from a diamond of the first water or an Incomparable. She had a clear skin, but it was not pink and white, more like dark ivory. Her hair had been tortured by Martha into the closest imitation of a modish coiffure as could be achieved. It was dark brown, and the frizzing and stiffening it had received left it lusterless. The strands were so fine that the ends loosened easily, and she was apt to look windblown within a half hour of reaching a ballroom. Her jawline was too firm for a female, her mouth certainly too large. The nose was passable in that it was straight and not obtrusive. Her eyes were large, seemed sometimes brown and sometimes green.

She lacked presence, which allowed her to sink quickly into the mass of any gathering, even though, for a female, she was overtall. The style of dress Lady Beners deemed suitable for the occasion never became her—she cast a baneful eye now at the lilac.

Even though this proposed parti had been in India all his life and this was his first venture into Society, it would not take him long to realize that his father was set to match him to an antidote. For all the material advantages her stepmother insisted on, Sara could see nothing ahead but everything that was evil—she faced a very dismal future.

"Miss Sara." Martha bustled in. She was a comfortable woman of country origin who had come to Highmount with Sara's mother upon her marriage and had taken charge of the child when her mother had died at her daughter's birth. "Now don't you be downhearted. The pie ain't made 'til the hen is caught." Her fingers were busy with the small buttons of Sara's frock.

Sara laughed hollowly. "This hen is caught, Martha, and the pie is waiting." She moved in chemise and petticoat to the window. The drapes had been drawn across what was really a door onto a balcony running along this side of the house. Sara pulled the flower-patterned folds apart to look out.

Below stretched the formal garden reaching to a line of limes. Behind that arose abruptly the feature of the landscape that gave the estate its name—a steep hill. In spite of the fast-failing light she could sight, crowning that, those queer old stones that the country people disliked. There were stories about those—

"Miss Sara." Martha took the curtain out of her grasp. "'Tis unchancy to go a-lookin' at th' Tall Men—'specially at this time o' the year."

Sara laughed a little more strongly this time. "Martha, I have just seen something more unchancy than those old stones—our guests arriving."

They had formed a procession, her father's curricle, followed by two coaches, all stirring up the gravel of the drive. Sara surrendered to Martha's ministrations, already sure that no amount of use of the curling iron could do anything for her hair, and regarding the lilac with increasing loathing as the maid got her into it, tugging laces and ribbons to their best showing.

"Might be latest fashion," Martha mumbled as she stood back to survey the result of her labors, "but that ain't your color, Miss Sara. It just don't—"

"Suit," returned Sara flatly. Even by the soft candlelight her skin looked more yellowish, and her figure gaunter because of the cut of the skirt. "It's not the dress, Martha. I'm just not meant to be the fine lady. Well, I might as well get on with this idiotish affair."

She allowed Martha to drape an embroidered shawl about her shoulders, and picked up a silver filigreed fan. Once in the chilly corridor she was thankful that in this weather one was allowed the meager comfort of a flannel petticoat and long sleeves with an evening toilet.

A murmur of voices issued from the drawing room where a fire had been laid, and a sufficient number of candles gave clear view of the assembled company.

Lady Beners, in imperial glory of deep-purple velvet, displaying diamonds at wrists and throat and from pins set in her befeathered turban, looked better clad for a London dine out. Her back was board stiff, and she was smiling with well-lessoned pleasure at a gentleman before her.

He still wore traveling dress, all superfine to be sure. However, though his tailor must have wrought with anxious care, he was not a credit to those endeavors. The skin of his face was sun darkened and his hair had retreated to a last stand in a fringe at ear level. His nose was more akin to a snout turning up at the tip, and small eyes added to his porcine aspect.

Lord Beners had taken position by the hearth. But Louisa, standing behind her mother, was engaged in a rapt contemplation of the last member of their company—a young man who *was* a tribute to his tailor.

Sara was as near struck as Louisa. She had met during her unproductive three Seasons many of the Nonpareils. Here was one who could even have fixed female attention had he appeared arm in arm with Lord Byron.

True, he was browned as might be expected from his years in India, but his features had none of the coarseness betrayed by those of his sire. He possessed a straight nose that accorded perfectly with a well-defined mouth, and eyes almost large and lustrous enough to be those of a female.

Sara's uneasiness became a heavier burden; the difficulty of the situation seemed nearly past bearing. That such a paragon would welcome their alliance could not be accepted unless one was completely crackbrained.

Still, he was all correct when they were made known to each other. His father's survey of her person was far more measuring. There was little past greetings said, and then the gentlemen withdrew to array themselves for dinner. No sooner had the door closed behind them than Lady Beners attacked.

"No more whims out of you, miss. The young man is all which is presentable. We are well on our way. My lord has settled matters and there is to be no dillydallying on the wedding date. We shall give a ball on the thirty-first to introduce them properly to the county. The old man is not quite the thing, but he will buy Harewood and restore that—which will be all that is proper. The son is pretty mannered—"

"He's wonderful!" Louisa interrupted. "The handsomest man I've ever seen."

Lady Beners snorted. "Not for you, girl. A pretty face and money in the pocket, yes. But you are going to be 'my lady' when you leave the altar.'"

Sara felt sick. Luckily that very queasiness seemed to raise a veil between her and the outer world during the endless evening. Thanks be, Julian did not seek her out for any special attentions. His father was quite open with remarks concerning his purchase and restoration of Harewood, the only mansion in the countryside which could rival Highmount.

At last Sara was able to creep away. Her agitation of the nerves was in no way lessened when, as she came into the hallway leading to her chamber, she heard loud voices.

"'Tis so! Th' Black Man—he peered through th' window—all nasty—"

Dottie, the chambermaid, was confronting Martha at the door to Sara's room, which was open.

"What is it?"

"Ahhh—" Dottie's voice shrilled up to a scream; she pulled her apron up over her head as if seeking some hiding place and blundered down the hall. Hibbitts himself came out of the chamber, followed by one of the footmen bearing a poker. The butler's face was flushed red.

"Such a to-do—th' gel's nub-cracked. Oh, Miss Sara—Dottie is as flighty as a feather. There be naught on th' balcony, nobody a-looking in." He gave a stiff pull to the edges of his waistcoat. "Be sure she'll not put us to such a stir again!"

Attended by his still poker-armed guard, he passed on after the fleeing Dottie with a ponderous tread. Sara looked inquiringly to Martha.

"Naught to do, Miss Sara. Th' stupid lass has taken a fidget—saying as how there was someone all in black walking the balcony—looking in at your window, where she didn't need to pull back th' curtains in th' first place. A flighty piece she is—"

"I know." Sara went on into the room. "The Black Man—this is the time of year that he is generally seen. All those stories they tell—"

"Stories," Martha burst out. "Foolishness! We'll have Black Men sproutin' from every bush if Dottie spreads th' word—which she is not likely to do once Mrs. Parley gets her tongue on her."

The housekeeper's scolds were famous. Almost Sara could feel sorry for the girl. But the matter soon slipped from her mind; she had too many troubles of her own.

Yes, she thought as she tossed and turned, unable to quiet her thoughts enough to sleep, it was truly a pity that the Black Man was story only. She could do well with the aid of the local boggle, if she could summon him up and put him to haunting the Rowlands, giving them such a disgust of the place that they would take off and out of her life.

Lacking the boggle she had to resign herself during the next few days to playing the part Lady Beners set her. Julian Rowland was perfectly correct in his addresses, but luckily the men were out in the day seeking sport. He had not attempted any display of false affection, and for that Sara was thankful.

Martha informed her that, accepted as the Rowlands were by their host and hostesses, the small staff which traveled with them was not faring as well. Those were natives of India—heathens one and all—and greatly distrusted belowstairs.

"'The sooner those be away th' better," Martha grumbled. "Hibbitts has said as how he is not used to such an' if he has to take much more he'll be lookin' out for another place."

Sara only half heard the words; she was looking at the small casket sitting on the dressing table. It was a marvel of workmanship in precious metal, the patterns on sides and lid strange—and somehow disturbing.

This had been delivered to her only an hour since, with a note from Julian Rowland saying this was brought especially for her and asking that she wear it the next night for the formal announcement of their betrothal.

When she lifted the lid she stared wide-eyed. Martha had come up behind, drawn by curiosity.

"Miss Sara, whatever are those? It gives me a spasm to look at them!"

"They give me worse than a spasm—certainly they are not in the common way!"

On the velvet cushion within lay what were undoubtedly a pair of bracelets, together with necklet. The weak autumn sunlight brought forth sparks of lights from the begemmed setting, but what that so bedazzled was also plain to see.

"Claws!" Sara jerked back her hand. "Tiger claws!"

"Miss Sara—those couldn't be—surely—" Martha's face was a mask of horror.

"No! No one could conceive of such a grossness. But how could he, with his own brother killed by a tiger?"

"They do have some nasty ways o' reckonin' in them foreign parts. Maybe he thinks as how you should be glad th' beast's dead an' shows it so."

"I won't do it."

"Don't fret yourself, Miss Sara—" Martha had begun when Sara spoke aloud some thoughts that had been gathering strength during the past few days.

"They never have spoken of Jasper—why? It's as if he never was at all."

"You be thinkin' of th' other young man, Miss Sara? Now that you speak it so—why, they did not even have proper mournin' clothes with them! They was probably fitted out in London, but it's queer that they have never said naught about him."

"One cannot ask—" Sara returned. She put out a hand and pushed the lid down on the casket. "I'll not wear these, Martha. It would be unfitting."

She endured another evening, but the men, tired with their day's outing, were not inclined to much conversation and her mother claimed most of her attention—outward attention—discussing the rigors of preparing for the coming ball.

When she dragged back to her room she wanted nothing more than sleep—a sleep that would carry her well over the next day and night, or even longer.

Martha got her to bed and she wriggled back among the pillows, the homey scent of lavender from the bed linen somehow a comfort, if a very small one.

There was a small bedside light on the side table and a sliver of moonlight lanced through between the curtains, which were not firmly closed. Sara sighed and closed her eyes.

She must have slept a little; she did not know what it was that had brought her awake. There was light by the dressing table, not that of any nightlight. This was of a yellowish-green color, and it brightened even as she watched.

Then a darker core appeared within that pillar of light. There was a figure that gained substance steadily as Sara watched, the chill of fear rising in her. It was a woman who stood there, and she was now wholly solid, giving the appearance of one truly alive.

Her garments swirled about her with a glitter of metallic threads, and she was girdled with a belt of flashing gems, red, green, and orange-fire yellow.

Both wrists were banded with numerous bracelets, which built towers over her brown flesh nearly to her elbows.

A collar of necklaces descended over her breasts, and there were long dangles of jewels from her ears. Though a triangle of veil had been pulled partly over her head, that did not hide the black hair parted in the middle and smoothed back to a knot against the neck.

Sara could see the stranger's face plainly reflected in the mirror, rendered fully visible by that noxious light. Between her black brows there was a red mark, and across her cheeks spread patterns of filigree as if gold leaf had been pasted to the flesh. In one nostril there was set a diamond as imposing as any Lady Beners prided herself on owning.

The light had deepened, sharper than candle glow, as the woman's hands grasped at the casket. With a click, the lid of the coffer was flung back and the long fingers scrabbled in the interior. When those hands were withdrawn they appeared curiously misshapen, as if the fingers had been folded inward. Between them protruded the claws of the bracelets, as might the tiger from which those had been taken extend them from the pads of its paws.

A dream? To wake—move—to wake! Sara struggled against a force she had never felt before.

The woman whirled, a movement that set the wide draperies of her skirt in motion. Her lips were drawn back to display teeth, very white against her dark skin. But her eyes were more of a threat. The drooping lids were fully raised, and it seemed there were no pupils, rather yellow-green spots of fire.

Sara tried to scream, the only answer to her efforts a hoarse croak. She threw herself backward across the wide bed as the woman moved with an odd stalking tread toward her. If she could only reach the door—

There was something in that advance, a kind of relish of Sara's terror, as if that were some refinement of pleasure for this woman out of nowhere.

Sara fell over the edge of the bed, grabbed wildly at the covers, and pulled herself up. She gave one look. The woman had changed course; she was heading also for the door, striving to cut off the escape of her prey. But Sara had to risk it.

She threw herself toward the only promise of safety she could see—hands outstretched.

There was a blow between her shoulders. She felt her nightgown being ripped from her, the scouring of painful scratches down her shoulders and back. That somehow restored Sara's voice and she screamed at last, shriek upon shriek.

Though that attack had nearly brought her to her knees, she hurled herself ahead with all the strength she could summon and felt the door at last beneath the scrape of her nails. Frantically she sought the latch.

Once more she screamed. The panel yielded, but there was a jerk at the tattered remnants of her gown and she was dragged from her feet, unable even to throw herself through the opening into the hall beyond.

She rolled and then somehow felt the wall behind her back, was able to look up at that terror hunting her. The woman was half crouched, raising one of those paw-seeming hands to her mouth, and was delicately tonguing the tips of the claws, her eyes holding steady on Sara.

Blood. This—this thing had drawn blood—her own blood—and was tasting it!

Again Sara screamed. There were other sounds that she could hardly hear through the fog of horror enwrapping her—voices, feet in the corridor. Louder still than those came a smash at the balcony window as the curtain shook, a shower of glass fragments falling from behind them into the room.

Those same curtains were swept aside, allowing a dark figure to burst through. Sara saw a gleam of metal in a black-gloved hand—the barrel of a pistol. Now the light caught the newcomer full-on. She gave a small whimpering cry.

Dark hair was swept back from his forehead. His features were lean, harsh lined, and from temple to chin on one side of his face ran the line of a deep scar. He did not look at her at all; his attention was all for the woman.

She apparently had not heard his entrance, or else believed she had nothing to fear from him. Her body had drawn together in an odd way, and Sara sensed that she was about to leap straight for her selected victim.

The door Sara had fought to reach was thrown wide open. There were people there. Who, how many, the girl could not have told. She felt that she dare not take her eyes from the woman.

It was the man from the window who spoke first, but not in any tongue intelligible to Sara. She saw the woman snarl and her body shift with an unbelievable speed to one side so she could face the other.

He spoke again emphatically, as one giving an order.

There came a cry from the doorway—

"You are dead—damn you—dead—dead!"

As if those words were a lash laid about her shoulders, the woman whirled again, this time turning not toward Sara but to the doorway and those who had forced their way in. She sprang with all the ease and speed of a great hunting cat, the clawed paws out.

Sara had not screamed. The cry now sounded deeper, but filled with no less horror than her earlier ones had been. The man raised his pistol and shot, the sound of the weapon seeming to finish that cry.

Sara watched with unbelieving eyes. The woman-thing, which had been crouched above a still-quivering body, threw up her head and mouthed a yowl. She strove to rise but instead half fell to one side to fully reveal a bleeding body.

Then the pawed thing twisted, turned, seeming to dissolve into the air. The light that had cloaked it was gone, as if snuffed out like a candle. The man from the window stepped forward. Catching up a scarf Sara had left on a chair, he used that to cover his fingers as he picked up from the floor the pair of bracelets that were evilly afire in the light from the corridor.

On the floor the body of the victim twitched, then was still. Sara shuddered, so faint and sick she could not move. Where that once so handsome face had been was blood. Blood still spurted from the torn throat. And on his knees by that tortured thing was Amos Rowland, his face a mask of horror.

"Devil—" he spat at the man from the window.

"Evil sent returns to evil," that other said. "That is the law. He should have known it well, since he imbibed it with his mother's milk. Her race has strange knowledge. The fate that he would have fostered on me, or was that of your devising—father?" He uttered that last word as he would an oath. "You wished much for him—did you let those wishes outrun caution and humanity?"

"What—what—?" Sara heard her father's voice, shaken as if he could not believe what he had witnessed.

The man bowed. "Lord Beners, it is an ill thing to bring a family quarrel under another's roof. I am Jasper Rowland. As my father's eldest son, I was not his favorite after he took another wife—an Indian lady of very ancient blood, though that line was, by legend, somewhat tarnished. I was—perhaps this seems beyond belief—made the target for a certain ritual curse." He still held the pistol, but his hand went up to touch the barrel of that to the ribbon of scar.

"My brother had another reason to dislike me." He no longer regarded father and son on the floor. "He was also enamored of a native woman, one said to possess these unknown powers. It was to her that he must have applied for a remedy for my existence. But unfortunately he was not constant in his attachment to her, and seemingly she prepared an answer to being cast off.

"These"—he held the bracelets farther into the light—"were to be a luck gift. Unfortunately, it was not said what kind of luck. They are better here—"

With one quick jerk of wrist, Jasper Rowland sent the bracelets spinning into the coals of the fire still dimly aglow on the hearth. There was a flash of that same yellow-green—a billow of stench-laden smoke.

Jasper Rowland laughed. "Well rid," he commented. "But there was an innocent pulled into this embroilment, and for that there can be little excuse." Another of his quick movements had brought him to Sara and he was kneeling beside her with no attention for those others, drawing her gently forward, his strength of arm somehow comforting.

"Can there be forgiveness for this?" he asked seemingly of the company at large, but it was Sara who answered him.

"You saved me—do you ask forgiveness for that?" She did not know the reason for this strange feeling. The many happenings of the past few moments had seemed to be so out of nature that she could not really believe they had occurred. But of this much she was sure: Jasper Rowland she wanted to know the better, and that would come in time.

NINE THREADS OF GOLD
After the King (1992) TOR

The way along the upper sea cliff had always been the secondary road into the Hold. Erosion had left only a narrow thread of a trail, laced with ice from the touch of storm-driven waves.

It was midafternoon but there was no sun, the sullen grayness of the sky all of a piece with the cracked rock underfoot. The wayfarer leaned under the leash of a frost wind, digging the point of a staff into such crevices as would give her strength to hold when the full blasts struck.

The traveler paused, to face inland and stare at a tall pillar of rock ending in a jagged fragment pointing skyward like a broken talon. Then the staff swung up and, for a second, there was a play of bluish glimmer about that spear of rock, which vanished in a breath as if the next gust of wind had blown out a taper.

Now the path turned abruptly away from the sea. Here the footing was smoother, the way wider, as if the land had preserved more than the wave-beaten cliffs allowed. It followed for a space the edge of a valley, narrow as an arrow-point at the sea tip, widening inland. The stream that bisected the valley ran toward the sea, but where it narrowed abruptly stood a building, towered, narrow of window, twined with a second structure, a bridge connecting them, allowing the stream full passage between.

In contrast to the gray stone of the cliffs the blocks that formed the walls of those two structures were a dull green, as if painted by moss growth undisturbed by a long flow of years.

The traveler paused at the head of a steep-set stairway descending from the cliff trail, for a searching survey of what lay below. There were no signs of life. Those slits of windows were lightless, blind black eyes. The fields beyond lay fallow and now thick with tough grass.

"Sooo—" The wayfarer considered the scene. In her mind one picture fitted over another. The land she surveyed was spread with an overcoating of another season, another time. And life in many forms was there.

She gathered her cloak closer at her throat and started to pick a careful way down the stair. The clouds at last broke, as they had threatened to do all that day. Rain began as a sullen drizzle, coating those narrow steps dangerously.

However, she did not halt again until she reached what had once been a wider and better-traveled way leading inward from the sea. In spite of the rain she stopped again, peering very intently at the building. Holding her staff a little free from the pavement, she swung it back and forth. No, she had not mistaken that tug. But a warning was as good as a coat of armor might be—sometimes.

Such a long time—

Seasons sped into each other in her thoughts, and she did not draw on any one memory.

The road had been well set long ago, but now its pavement was akilter from the push of thick-stemmed shrubs, gray and leafless at this season. It still led straight to an arch giving on the nearer end of the bridge that united the two buildings. Down below, the stream gurgled sullenly, but the birds that had haunted the cliffs had been left behind, and there was no other sound—save now and then a roll of distant thunder. She stepped out on the bridge, her staff still held free of the pavement, and the lower end pointed a little forward. If only a small portion of what she suspected was the truth, there was that which must be warded against.

Now the archway leading to the courtyard of the larger building was an open gape. Suddenly her staff swung forward at knee level.

There was a flash of blue flame, a speeding of sparks both to right and left as she took a single step into the courtyard.

"Here entered no darkness—" She spoke that sentence aloud as if it were a charm—or password—at the same time pushing back the hood that had concealed her face, so displaying a countenance like a statue meant to honor a Queen or Goddess long forgot. While the hair wound tightly about her head was silver, there were no marks of age on her, only that calm which comes to one who has seen much, weighed much, known the pull of duty.

"Come—" Her staff moved in a small beckoning.

The two who first advanced into the open moved warily and plainly showed that they were coming against their will. There was a boy, his bony frame loosely covered with a patchwork of badly cured skins cobbled together. Both his hands were so tight on the smaller end of a club that the knuckles showed, nearly piercing the skin. But the girl was not far behind him, and she weighed in her two hands a lump of stone, jagged and large enough to be a good threat.

There was also movement from the wall behind, wherein that gate was, though the traveler made no attempt to turn or even look over her shoulder. Another boy, near as thin as the taut bowstring arming the weapon he carried, and a girl, with a dagger in hand, sprang from some perch above. A second boy, also with bow in hand, joined them. The three sidled around the stranger, their weapons at ready, their faces showing that they were not ignorant of the lash of fear nor the use of the arms they carried.

Five—

"The others of you?" The traveler made a question of that.

Those arose out of hiding, as if the fact that she asked drew them into sight. Two boys, twins, so alike that one might be the shadow of the other, each armed with a spear of wood, the points of which had been hardened by careful fire charring and rubbing. Another girl, who had no weapon, carried a younger child balanced on her hip.

Nine. In so much—

Yet this was not what she had expected. The traveler looked intently from one gaunt face to the next. No, not what she had expected. But in a time of need a weaver must make do with the best there is to hand.

It was the eldest of the boys, he who had leaped first from the wall, who gave challenge. He was of an age to have been a squire, and he wore a much too large and rusty coat of mail, a belt with an empty sword scabbard bound about it to hold it to his body.

"Who are you?" His demand was sharp and there were traces of the old high tongue in the inflection of his speech. "How came you here?"

"She came the sea path—" It was the girl who had lain in hiding with him on the upper wall who spoke then, and her dagger remained unsheathed.

However, it was the younger one who carried the baby who spoke, her gaze holding full upon the traveler:

"Do you not see, Hurten, she is one of *Them*."

They stood in a semicircle around the woman. She could taste fear, yes, but also with that something else, the grim determination that had brought them to this ancient refuge, kept them alive when others had died. They would be stout for the weaving, these nine threads distilled from a broken and ravaged land.

"I am a seeker," the woman answered. "If I must answer to a name let it be Lethe."

"One of *Them*," repeated she who played nursemaid.

The boy Hurten laughed. "Alana, *They* are long gone. You see tales in all about you. Lethe—" He hesitated, and then with now more than a touch of the courtly tongue, "Lady, there is nothing here—" Still holding bow, he spread his hands wide apart, as if to encompass all that lay about him. "We mean no harm. We can spare you a place by a fire, a measure of food, a roof against the storm—little more. We have long been but wayfarers also."

Lethe raised her head so that the folds of her hood slid even farther back.

"For your courtesy of roof and hearth, I give thanks. For the goodwill that prompted such offers, may that be returned to you a hundredfold."

Alana had allowed the small boy in her arms to wriggle to the ground. Now, before she could seize him back in a protective hold, he trotted forward, one hand outstretched to catch full hold on Lethe's cloak, supporting himself as he looked up into her face.

"Maman?" But even as he asked that his small face twisted and he let out a cry. "No—maman—no, maman!"

Alana swooped to catch him up again and Lethe spoke to her softly:

"This one is of your blood kin?"

The girl nodded. "Robar, my brother. He . . . doesn't understand, Lady. We were with a pilgrim party. The demons caught us by a bridge. Maman, she told me to jump and she threw Robar down to me. We hid in the reeds. He—he didn't see her again."

"But you did?"

For a moment there was stark horror in Alana's eyes. Her lips formed a word she did not appear to have the strength to voice. Lethe's staff raised; the point of it touched ever so lightly on the little girl's tangle of hair.

"Fade," the woman said, "let memory fade, child. There will come a balancing in good time. Now," she spoke to Hurten, "young sir, I am right ready to make acquaintance of this promised fire and roof of yours."

It would seem that any suspicion they had held was already eased. The weapons were no longer tightly in hand, though the children still surrounded her in a body as she walked ahead, well knowing where she was bound, through the doorway that led into the great presence chamber.

Outside the day was fast darkening into twilight; herein there was light of a sort. Globes set in the walls gave off a faint glimmer as if that which energized them was close to the end of its power. What this dim radiance showed was shadow-cloaked decay.

Once there had been strips of weaving along the walls. Now there were webs of dwindling threads from which all but the faintest of patterns had been lost. There was a dais on which had stood an impressive line of chairs, tall-backed, carven. Most of those had been hacked apart and, as they passed, the children each went forward and picked up an armload of the broken wood, even small Robar taking up one chunk, as if this were a duty to which all of them were sworn.

They passed beyond a carven screen through another door and down a hall until they came into another chamber, which gave evidence of being a camping place. Here was a mighty cavern of a fireplace wherein was hung a pot nearly large enough to engulf Robar himself, and about it other tools of cookery.

A long table, some stools, had survived. Near the hearth to one side was a line of pallets fashioned from the remains of cloaks, patched with small skins, and apparently lumpily stuffed with what might be leaves or grass.

There was a fire on the hearth, and to that one of the twins added wood from the pile where they had dumped their loads, while the other stirred the sullen glow within to greater life.

Hurten, having rid himself of his load, turned, hesitated, and then said gruffly:

"We keep sentinel. It is my duty hour." And was gone.

"There have been others—those you must watch for?" Lethe asked.

"None since the coming of Truas and Tristy." The oldest girl nodded toward the twins. "They came over mountain three tens ago. But the demons had wrought evil down by the sea—earlier. There was a village there once."

"Yes," Lethe agreed, "there was once a village."

"It had been taken long ago," the boy who had borne the club volunteered. "We—we are all from over mountain, Lusta and I—I'm Tyffan, Hilder's son, of Fourth Bend. We were in the fields with Uncle Stansals. He bid us into th' wood when there was smoke from th' village over hill. But"—the boy's fists clenched and there was a grim set to his young jaw—"he did not come back. We had heard of th' demons an' what they did to villages, still we waited in hiding. No one came."

The girl Lusta looked into the heart of the now bravely burning fire. "We wanted to go back—but we saw th' demons riding an' we knew we could never make it."

Truas, tending the fire, looked over his shoulder. "We're shepherds and were out after a stray. They saw us but we knew th' rock trails better. At least those devils cannot fly!"

"Hurten was shield-bearer for Lord Vergan," the oldest girl spoke up. "He was hit on the head and left for dead in the pass battle. I am Marsila and he"— she pointed to the younger boy who had been on the wall—"is my brother, Orffa. Our father was marshal of the Outermost Tower. We were hunting when they came and so were cut off—"

"How came you together?" Lethe asked.

Marsila glanced around as if for the first time she herself had faced that question.

"Lady, we met by chance. Alana and Robar, they fled to Bors Wood and there met with Lusta and Tyffan. And Orffa and I, we found Hurten and stayed with him until his head was healed, then we, too, took the wood road. There was, we hoped, a chance that Skylan or Varon might have held—only, when we met the others, Alana said the demons had swept between to cut us off."

"You decided then to come over the mountain? Why?" Lethe must know— already she sought the beginning of the pattern she had sensed. There was one or she, the weaver, would not have been summoned.

It was Lusta who answered in a low voice, her head down as if she must confess some fault. "The dreams, Lady. Always the same dream an' each time I saw clearer."

"Lusta's gran was *Wise*," Tyffan broke in. "All of Fourth Bend thought she had part of the gift, too. Lusta dreamed us here."

Marsila smiled and put her arm around the younger girl's shoulders. "Not many have the *Wise* gifts now, but we had records of such at the Tower and—well—we had no other place to go, so why not trust a dream?"

Her face became bleak again. "At least the demons did not try the mountains then. When we found this place we knew that fortune favored us a little. There is farm stock running wild in the valley, even some patches of grain we are harvesting, and fruit. Also—this place, it seemed somehow as if we were meant to shelter here."

"Dreams led!" Lethe moved to Lusta and, as she had with Alana, touched the girl's head with her staff. There was a spark of blue. Lethe smiled.

"Dreamer, you have wrought well. Good will follow in a way now past your understanding."

Then she drew back to survey them all, her gaze resting for a long moment on each face. So this was indeed the beginning.

"Truly," she spoke, "this is the place for such as you."

These were from very different beddings, these seedlings, yet their roots were the same. That had been clear to her from their first sighting. Their hair, tangled, unkempt, was of the same pale silver blond, their eyes shared the same clear sword-blade gray. Yes, the old stock had survived after all, though the seed might have been wide flung.

Lethe shifted the bag she had carried from her shoulder to the top of the table. She loosed the string and reached within, drawing forth a packet of dried meat, another of herbs.

There was already something steaming in the great pot; she was certain that they had not lost the chance for a day's hunting. Now she shook forth her own offerings and added them to that. They watched her closely.

"Traveler's fare, but it may add to your store as is the custom," she told them.

Marsila had watched her very closely. Now, in spite of the fact that she wore breeches patched with small skins, she made the curtsy of a daughter of a House in formal acknowledgment.

"If this be your kin, hold our thanks for shelter." Still there was a measure of questioning in her eyes.

However, it was Alana who spoke, and she did so almost with accusation. "You are one of *Them*, so this *is* your place."

"What do you know of *Them*, child?" Lethe had shrugged off her cloak. Her breeches and jerkin were of a dull green not unlike the walls about her.

"They had strange powers," Alana answered. She reached out and drew Robar to her. "Powers which gave them rule. None could stand against them—like the demons!"

Lethe had taken a ladle from a hook in the hearth wall. Now she looked directly at the small girl. "Powers to take rule like the demons—that is what they say of us now?"

For a long moment Alana was silent and then she flushed. "*They—They* did not hunt people—*They* did not . . . kill—"

"*They* were guardians!" Marsila broke in. "When *They* were in the land there could be no death there."

"Why did *They* go?" One of the twins sat back on his heels.

"When *They* had strong keeps like this, if *They* ruled th' land, what did *They* do?"

Lethe stirred the pot. She did not look around.

"The land is old, many have been rooted here. When years pass another blood comes to masterage."

For the first time Orffa spoke: "So this is the time for demons to rule, is that what you tell us?" There was a fierce challenge in his voice and he was scowling.

"Demons?" Lethe looked to the fire and the steaming pot. "Yes, to this land at this hour, they are demons."

Marsila moved closer. "How else can we see them? Tell me that, once guardian!"

Lethe sighed. "No way else." She turned to face the children. Children? Save for Robar, there was little childlike in those faces ringing her in. They had seen much, and none of it good. But that was the working of the Way, the spinning of the weaver's threads. Standing in shadow behind each was the faint promise of what might be.

"Why have you come? Will others follow you?" demanded Orffa.

"I have come because I was summoned. I alone." She gave them the truth. "The kinblood have passed to another place, only it would seem that I am tied to this day."

"That is magic." Tyffan pointed to her staff where she had laid it across the table. "But you're one against many. Those raiders hold th' land from Far River to th' Sea, from Smore Mount Mouth to Deep Yen."

Lethe looked directly at him. His mop of hair reached barely above her shoulder, but his sturdy legs were planted a little apart, and he stood with his fist-curled hands on his hips as if in defiance.

"You speak as one who knows," she commented.

To her mild surprise he grinned. "Not claimin' magic, mistress, that. You find us here now, that's not sayin' as how we is always here. We has our ways o' learnin'. What chances over mountain—and it ain't by dreams."

Lethe pursed her lips. Looking at him she could believe in what he hinted. This one had stated that he was land-born, land-trained; and the young learned swiftly when there was need.

"So you have used your eyes and ears to good purpose." He nodded briskly.

"Well enough. And what have you learned with your non-magic?"

Orffa pushed past the younger boy. "Enough," he snapped.

"And the demons have not disturbed you here?" she asked.

"There was a scouting company," Marsila answered. "They followed the sea road inward but there came a sudden rockfall which closed that. At night they camped near that . . ."

Tyffan grinned widely and the twins echoed his expression.

"They didn't like what they heard nor saw. We didn't either, but then we guessed as how it weren't meant for th' likes of us. They ran—an' some o' them went into th' river. Hurten, he brought down one with an arrow—he's a champion shot—an' we bashed a couple with rocks. Wanted to get their weapons, but river took 'em an' we didn't dare go after 'em. They ain't been this way since."

"It wasn't us, not all of it," Marsila said slowly. "There was something there—we felt it but it did not try to get us—only them."

Lusta held to the other girl's arm. "The rocks made shadow things," she said.

"So the old guards hold somewhat," Lethe commented. "But those were never meant to stand against any who meant no harm. This"—she gestured with her hand—"was once a place of peace under the sign of Earth and Air, Flame, and Water.

"Now," she pointed to the pot, "shall we eat? Bodies need food, even as minds need knowledge."

But her thoughts were caught in another pattern. Here was a mixture which only danger could have, and had, cemented—delvers, shepherds, soldier and lordly blood all come by chance together and seemingly already united. Chance? No, she thought she dared already believe not.

They brought bowls and marshalled in line. Some had battered metal, time-darkened, which they must have found here; there were cups shaped of bark pinned together with pegs. Lethe tendered the ladle to Marsila and watched the girl dip careful portions to each. One over she set aside and Lethe took it up.

"For your sentinel? Let this be my service."

Before any protested she headed out of the great kitchen. The dark had deepened despite the globe light, but she walked with the sure step of one who well knew the way, just as, once without, she climbed easily to the wall top.

"No need for that." She had heard rather than seen the draw of a belt knife, could picture well the spare young body half acrouch. "Your supper, sentinel, also your relief."

Shadow moved out of shadows. In her left hand the staff diffused a pale radiance. Though Hurten reached for the bowl, the dagger was still drawn. However, Lethe took no notice of his wariness. Instead she had swept the staff along the outer edge of the parapet that sheltered them a little from the incoming sea wind.

"So are guards set, Hurten. I promise you that there need be no watch on duty this night. And there is much we all have to talk of . . ."

She could sense the edge of the resentment that was rightfully his. What leadership this group had known in the arts of war must have come from him.

"Shield Chief," deliberately Lethe used the old tongue, "there is a time for the blooding of blades and a time for planning, that those blades may be better sharpened for the blooding."

"By Oak, by Stream, by Storm, by Fire—" The words came in the old tongue—

Lethe nodded, though he might not be able to see that gesture of approval in the gloom.

"By Sword and Staff, by Horn, by Crown." The old words came so easily in this place, though it was another time when they were common here. "So warrior, you have at least trod a stride or two down that path?"

"My lord was of the House of Uye. When we were given our swords as men he held by the old oaths."

Swords as men! she thought. These must be dire days when boys were counted men. But only dire days could have drawn her here.

"Then you know that this is a place of peace."

She heard the faint snick of the dagger being sent once more into sheath.

"Lady, in this land there is no longer any place of peace." His words were stark and harsh.

"To that we shall take council. Come—"

Hurten hesitated, still unwilling to admit that the watch he had taken on himself might no longer be necessary. But she had already started back as if she thought there could be no questioning, and he followed.

They found the rest around the fire. Orffa and Marsila both looked up in question as Hurten came in, but Lethe was quick to explain:

"There is a guard, and one which will keep the watch well. For now there is that which we must discuss among ourselves." Deliberately she chose her words to ally herself at once with these chosen for a purpose she could not question.

"Time may change but not the seasons." Lethe had waited until they had cleaned their bowls. "The sea winds herald ill coming. There was once some command over wind and weather in this place, but that was long ago. We shall need that for day and night"—she pointed to the fire—"and food—"

"We have been gathering," Marsila answered sharply as if some action of hers had been called into question. "We have a storeroom."

Lethe nodded. "That I do not question. Save that if the dire storms hit, as well they may, there shall be needed every scrap of food, every stick of wood. Herb-craft also, for there are the illnesses which come with weather changes, and some of those are severe."

There was movement at the other side of the table. Alana carried a nearly asleep Robar to one of the fireside pallets.

Hurten leaned forward.

"What are we to you?" His voice was a little hoarse. "We are not of your breed. No." He glanced briefly at the others. "Nor are we even of one House or blood ties ourselves. We make no claim of vassalage rights—"

"Why did you come here?" Marsila planted one elbow on the table and rested her chin upon her hand. "There has been no tale of your kind among us since the High Queen Fothuna died, leaving no daughter for the rule, and all the land fell apart, with quarrels between lordlings and War Ladies. And that was a legend length of years ago. We have none of the old power. Lusta, yes. Twice she dreamed us out of fell dangers—but our race was and is wise in our own way only. Thus we ask, why do you come to speak as a chatelaine here?"

"And I ask again, what do you want with us?" Hurten repeated.

He was frowning, and that frown was echoed by a stronger scowl drawing together Orffa's straight brows. The impish humor that had looked ever ready to curve Tyffan's lips was gone, and the twins were blank-faced.

Lusta's tongue showed a pink tip between her lips but she did not speak, and Alana's hands clasped together tightly on the table top before her.

"You, in a manner, called me. No"—Lethe shook her head, aware of the denial already on Hurten's lips—"I do not say that you knew of me. But in those days of far legend Marsila has mentioned there were gaes laid, and this was mine: that I was tied to Kar-of-the-River—this keep in which we shelter. And so I fulfill now that set upon me. I did not know until I came hither what I would find. As to what you mean to me—that we both must learn. For I must in right tell you this, that you are bound even as I—"

Hurten's hand balled into a fist. He moved as if to stand. He was of no temper to play with words, as Lethe saw, yet what more could she tell him yet?

It was Orffa who got to his feet and moved behind the older boy, as a liege man would back-cover his lord. But of him Hurten took no notice as he said:

"Lady, we are not those for your binding."

Lethe sighed. Patience, ever patience. A weaver must be sure that no knotting despoiled her threads. It was Marsila who put an end to it.

"The hour grows late." She had pulled Alana closer beside her, and the child leaned heavily against her shoulder. "With the morrow there will be time enough for questions."

It seemed that even Hurten was willing to surrender to that. So the fire was set for long burning and they took their places on the pallets within its warmth, Lethe lying down upon a cushion of her cloak—though she did not sleep. For her kind needed little of such rest. Instead, behind closed eyelids, she rebuilt what now closed her in as she had seen it last in other days. Out of the past she summoned others who moved as shades where they had once been true life.

A sound broke through her half-dream. She opened her eyes. One of those on the pallets had sat up, shrugged aside a covering of skins. The fire flickered to show a face—

Lusta, the dreamer!

Lethe's keen sight was not deadened by the gloom. The girl's eyes were closed. Nor did she open them as her head swung around as if in answer to some summons. On hands and knees, eyes still shut, she crawled away from the hearth into inner darkness, and then got to her feet. Lethe allowed her a small start and followed after.

Down the hall into the great presence chamber. The globe light was gone, it was totally dark here, yet Lusta went with the confidence of one who saw perfectly. Lethe followed. To break the girl's trance—no—that was a dangerous folly. She must know what drove Lusta into the night.

They came forth from the hall into the open of the courtyard. Up the stairs Lusta went without a stumble. A moon shone warily between moving clouds, and to Lethe this was light enough. Lusta had sought out the very perch where Hurten had earlier made his sentry post.

She turned slowly, facing outward, and then her hand went out to the parapet and her fingers tapped along it. Sparks flew as if she used a wand of iron instead of her own flesh.

Lethe's head went back. Her nostrils flared as if to catch some faint scent. She was already up the stairs. Now she moved forward, and, standing behind Lusta, put out her own two hands, touching fingers lightly to both the girl's temples.

The woman's lips flattened into something closer than a snarl. This—but she had not thought that the new invaders were so knowledgeable. Or were they only symptoms of an older and fouler plague?

She applied pressure, flesh to flesh, and forced will upon dream. Lusta's own hands paused in their tapping. Then she cried out sharply and crumpled as if all life had been withdrawn in a matter of a breath or two.

Lethe did not kneel at once beside her; rather she now turned all attention to the danger at hand. Where Lusta had wrought a breaking spell, she relaid the guard, this time reinforcing it with will enough to leave her feeling nearly as drained as the unconscious girl at her feet.

It was not well—what she had done would alert that other power that had already made this first move. Yet Lusta taken over, with a gift she had not been trained to protect, was a key which must not be used.

Lethe crouched down to gather the girl into her arms, pulling her cloak about the both of them. Lusta's face was as chill as if she had been brought out of a snowbank, but both of her hands, which Lethe took into one of hers, were warm, near fire-hot. That which the girl had not finished projecting into the break spell was turned back upon her, eating in. She moaned and twisted in the woman's hold.

"Lusta!" There came a call from below, then the scrape of boots on stone.

Tyffan came in a scrambling run. "Lusta!" He went down on his knees beside the two of them. "What—"

"She is safe—for now." Under Lethe's touch the fire had cooled from the girl's hands. "Tyffan, you say she dreamed you here?"

"What is wrong with her?" He paid no attention to that question.

"She has been possessed." Lethe gave him the truth. "Perhaps even her dreaming you here was by another's purpose. This night that which held her in bond used her to attack the guards."

Tyffan stared at the woman. "But Lusta would not—"

"No!" Lethe assured him quickly. "She would not have brought harm to you willingly. But she was not taught to guard her gift, and that laid her open to—"

"The demons!" But how—"

"We do not know by whom or why she was sent to do this," Lethe said quickly. "But she has overused her strength, and we must get her into warmth now."

Hurten and Orffa met them at the door of the presence chamber, and Tyffan gave them a confused answer as to what had happened as Lethe hurried the girl, who was on her feet but barely so, into the warmth of the kitchen place.

She oversaw the brewing up of an herbal potion and stood over Lusta until the girl drank it to the dregs. Lusta seemed but half awake, dazed, mumbling, and unaware of where she was or what had happened. Lethe saw her back to the pallet and then faced the others.

"You asked me earlier what I wanted of you," she said directly. "That I do not yet fully know. But it may also be that another power brought you here and is prepared to make use of you." And she explained what Lusta had been led to do.

"Lusta is not a demon!" Tyffan near shouted.

It was Marsila who answered him. "She is *Wise*. That is a power. Lusta would never use it for any but good. In truth"—now she spoke to Lethe—"she never used it by her will; the dreams came to her without her seeking or bidding."

"We speak of power as a gift," Lethe said. "It may also be a burden, even a curse, if it is not used with control. I do not think that Lusta was given any aid in learning what she could do."

Tyffan stirred. "She—she didn't know as how it meant anything." He looked toward where the girl lay. "Her mam, she died when Lusta was just a mite. M' mam, she was closest kin an' took her. But we had no *Wise* for a long time. T'wasn't 'til after th' demons came that she dreamed—or at least told her dreams. But she's no demon—ask Hurten—ask Truas and Tristy. She dreamed us together!"

"The demons," Lethe returned. "Have you heard that they have some form of the Wisdom among them?"

The children looked to one another and then Marsila shook her head.

"They came like—like storm clouds—and there was no standing against them. There were so many and they seemed to appear without any warning. But my father said we fared so badly in the field against them because the lords and War Ladies had been cut adrift from any one leader. Each fought for their own holds, and one by one those Holds fell. There was no High Queen. It was almost as if we were all blinded—"

Hurten nodded. "My lord—he tried to send for help to the Hold of Iskar, and the lord there told him no because he feared those of Eldan more than the demons. He told the messenger that the rumors of demons were put about to frighten timid Hold-keepers. That was before Iskar was taken in two days and left but bloodied stone. There, it is true"—he spoke thoughtfully now, almost as if he were examining memory and seeing a new pattern in it—"that the Holders did not come together. And what they gave as reasons were mainly wariness of their own neighbors. Was that—could that have been some power of the demons?"

His hand had gone once more to the hilt of his dagger and he stared at Lethe as if he would have the truth even at a point of steel.

"It could be so."

It was Alana who came a step or so closer and looked up into Lethe's face.

"Lady, why would the demons want us who are here in this place—unless to kill us as"—she hesitated a second and the old fear came flooding back into her firelit eyes—"they did all the others? Lusta dreamed us here—but there were no demons waiting."

"This was waiting, and perhaps your entrance here would open doors for them or something else." Lethe was searching—her senses weighing first the children and then the very walls about them. No, there had been no tampering save that she had caught this night. There was no taint of dark in this company.

"What lies here then?" flared Hurten. "The demons came upon us from the north; they are not of our kind. Perhaps"—his eyes narrowed—"they are of yours—Lady." And there was little goodwill in the title he gave her.

"Before your demons," she answered him, "there were other powers abroad. Some were always of the Dark. Open your mind, youth: is this such a place as welcomes the Dire Shadows?"

For a moment there was a silence. Hurten's frown did not fade. Then tentatively his right hand arose between them and the fingers moved in a gesture that brought a sigh of relief from Lethe.

"Bite of iron, warrior." She held out her own hand. He hesitated, then drew his dagger. She deliberately touched the end of the blade, withstanding a stab of flame pain that was true fire. When she took her hand away and turned it over, she held it well into the light.

There was an angry red blotch on her pale skin. She endured the pain for a space, that they might see, and then willed healing into the skin.

"Cold iron." Hurten looked down at his own weapon as if it possessed a potential unknown to him.

"The demons," Orffa broke in, "can die but from edge and point. Only the First Ones—" He drew a deep breath.

"Only those of the Right-Hand Path," Marsila interrupted her brother, "cannot hold iron."

"And our wards still held here," Lethe pointed out. "Still there must be that which would put an end to weaving by destroying loom and weaver."

"You speak of weaving," Marsila said then. "You are the weaver?"

"So it has been set upon me."

"It remains." Hurten turned to the earlier problem. "Lusta led us here, by whose will?"

"Who can tell that?" Lethe spoke wearily, for again the truth burdened her down.

"Will—will she be possessed again?" Marsila approached Lusta with caution. The younger girl appeared deep in sleep, unaware of all about her now.

"I have set guards," Lethe answered. "For now those will hold."

None of them questioned that—as if they avoided voicing doubts. Hurten settled by the fire, but not to sleep. Instead he brought from a belt pouch a whetstone, and with this he set about giving edge to his dagger, working as one who must occupy himself with even so small a preparation against trouble to come. Marsila dragged her pallet up beside Lusta's, just as Tyffan barricaded the girl on the other side.

Hurten's belt with its empty scabbard—without a sword—

Without a sword, that symbol of manhood for his race. Lethe once more closed her eyes, but her thoughts were awake. A sword—she resisted, having the feeling that she was being pushed too swiftly into decisions. It was not for her to deal with weapons as this land now knew them, but neither could she deny to others the safety a blade could offer. However, this could wait until tomorrow. Hurten had stopped the push of the whetstone, returned it to his pouch, was stretching out to sleep.

Lethe lengthened the narrowest edge of thought as a field commander would dispatch a trained scout. The guards were firm, nothing tried them. Lusta? The girl was so deep in slumber that no invader could reach her. Safe? Were any of them safe?

Lusta had offered a gate to some old power—what of the other children? Lethe shrank from what she must do—this was something that could only be justified by dire danger. Did they face that?

She made her decision and began the search. Alana, one arm thrown about her little brother in constant protection—nothing there.

The shepherd twins? A hazy dream picture, partly shared, of a fair morning in home heights. Tyffan—dark shadows acreep—the beginning of a nightmare in which he struggled to reach a farmhouse where Lusta awaited him. That she could banish, and she did.

Marsila—fall woodlands in brilliant color, a sun-warmed morning—rightness and loving memory. Her brother—deep sleep as untroubled as Lusta's. Hurten—the sentry on the wall, a pressing need to hold off some threat that had not yet shown itself—a need the greater because he had no weapon. She had been right—this one needed the talisman of a blade.

Lethe searched memory. She had read them and there was no taint here. So assured, she could await the coming day.

They broke their morning fast with a rough mush of wild grain only made palatable by a handful of dried berries. Lethe waited until they were done before she spoke.

"You have two bows, two daggers among you—that is not enough."

Hurten laughed angrily. "The truth, Lady. But here there is no forge, nor are any of us smiths. Is there an enemy we can hope to plunder?"

"Come—"

Lethe led them back to the presence chamber, all, even Robar, trailing her. She came to face the wall behind the dais. There hung one of the time-ravished lengths of weaving. This was no tapestry like the others, rather the remains of what might once have been a banner.

So hard had time treated what lay here! However, she was not saddened, rather stirred by the need to be about her task. The chairs that had once stood against the wall were debris. But the long table there was intact, save it was covered with dust and splinters of wood.

She swept out with her staff, and the litter was lifted and blown away by a strong puff of breeze. Lethe pointed now to the frail banner.

With the staff she drew a careful outline around what hung there while she hummed—a faint drone of sound, like the sigh of wind in a wood. On the wall the banner moved. Dust motes shifted down, but none of the frail fabric parted. As a single piece it was loosed while her staff moved back and forth as might that of a shepherd guiding a flock around some danger. Down came the length of ancient weaving, to lie full-length on the table.

"Do not touch it!" she ordered. "That time is not yet. We have other needs."

Once more her staff moved, now pointing directly to the wall the banner had curtained. She spoke aloud in command, words that had not been uttered since the days of deep legend.

Cracks appeared between stones, lines formed a doorway. That opened.

"Come!" Lethe waved them on.

The staff itself gave forth the light here, bringing answering gleams from racks, from shelves for storage. Here were weapons. She heard a cry from Hurten as he pushed forward, his hand out to the hilt of a sword. He stood looking down at it in joyful wonder. The others ventured farther in, eyeing what was there as if they did not quite dare touch. Then Orffa took up a sword, and Tyffan, after glancing to Lethe as if she might forbid it even now, closed hand upon the haft of a double-bladed axe.

A moment later Hurten turned accusingly to the woman. "What folly is this? No true steel—" He had been running his hand along the blade of his choice.

She laughed. "Cold iron is not to be found here, young warrior. These are forged of battle silver, but none the less sharp and strong."

For a moment it seemed as if he might dispute that, then he nodded. "To each people their own secrets. This balances well at least." He swung it in a practice thrust.

"No—no—Robar!"

Alana was engaged in a tug of war with her brother. Face red with rising anger, he was struggling to get full hold on a dagger near long enough to be deemed a short sword.

"Want—want—now! Robar wants—!"

Alana seemed unable to break his grip. Truas caught the little boy by the shoulders from behind.

"Here now, young'un, that's naught to play with. Give it to Alana an'—" He had turned his head to view the racks of weapons but was plainly baffled as to what might be offered as a counter to Robar's first choice.

"Want!" Robar howled and then aimed a kick at his sister that struck home before Truas could pull him out of reach.

"Robar—no—!" There was an expression of fear on Alana's face. "Give it to Alana, please!"

As the boy fought and wriggled to free himself, Alana pried his fingers loose one by one. His screaming was enough to bring all the others to the battle. Once his sister had forced one hand open, Robar swung that up and drew his nails down her cheek. She cried out and jerked back, her eyes wide, staring at her brother as if she had never seen him before.

Marsila pushed her aside, but it was Hurten who took command:

"Give him to me!" And when Truas had surrendered the still wildly fighting boy into his hold he added, "Get that thing away from him!"

In spite of having to ward off kicks, which, to Lethe, appeared too well aimed to be allied with blind rage, Truas was able to capture the dagger. Then Hurten carried the still struggling child out of the room.

Alana's whole body was shaking. Tears diluted the blood from the scratches on her cheeks.

"He—he never did that before. Oh, Robar!" She pushed aside Marsila and ran after Hurten and her brother.

There was a subdued quiet. Lethe stooped to pick up the disputed weapon. To both her eyes and her inner touch it was no more than it appeared to be. For a moment a wisp of thought had troubled her. But the scene could have risen simply from the fact that an over-guarded and indulged child—for Alana's care was easy to see—had wanted a choice like the other boys. He was passing out of babyhood and perhaps had been unconsciously resentful of Alana's protectiveness for some time.

The others made their choices quickly. Marsila chose four bows and matching quivers of silver-tipped arrows, gathering them into an unwieldy bundle. Lusta and the others selected daggers, testing the points on fingertips. But for major weapons the twins wanted short-shafted javelins, taking a trio of these apiece. Tyffan held to the axe, Orffa the sword with a belt and sheath to go with it.

Lethe was interested in their choices. Each must have chosen those arms with which they felt the most comfortable. She replaced the dagger Robar had clung to in the rack, and followed the company out. Behind her the door closed and once more disappeared.

Marsila laid the bows down on the table, taking care not to disturb the banner. She motioned to Lusta and Orffa, and they each chose one. Then she selected hers, leaving the other.

"Hurten's"—she nodded to that—"a far better one than he has, and one to serve him well."

Alana sat by the pallet when they reentered the kitchen. Robar lay there curled in upon himself sniffling. As the others drew near his sister pulled at his shoulder.

"Robar?" Her voice both admonished and encouraged.

He sat up. The anger had gone out of his eyes. Instead tears marked his cheeks.

"Sorry—Robar's sorry." His voice was hardly above a whisper.

Alana smiled. "It's true, he is sorry."

Marsila went closer. "Very well, Robar. But being sorry does not take away the scratches on your sister's cheek, now does it?"

He smeared both hands across his face. "Robar's sorry," he repeated woefully. Alana caught him in a tight hug.

"Of course, Alana knows. Robar's really sorry."

Tyffan, fingering the new axe, had seemed to pay little attention. Now he said:

"It is a fair day out. Maybe there will be a beast in the grasslands—easy to be downed with new bows."

"Of course!" Hurten appeared with the bow Marsila had left for him. "Get us perhaps that yearling bull calf we saw two days ago."

Lethe watched them scatter to what must have been the occupations they had settled to since they had come to the keep. In the day there was no fear of the outlands.

Even Robar shared in the gathering of supplies, disputing with a number of angry squirrels for the harvest of fallen nuts, while his sister and Tristy beat the tree branches to bring more down.

Lusta was using her new dagger to cut ragged stands of wild grain still slippery from yesterday's storm. Her harvesting sent grain-eating birds flying, and she turned to her bow. Though it was apparent she was no well-trained archer, she did not always miss.

Lethe left the scene of labor and followed the river, pausing now and then to stand, staff in hand, spying out toward the hills in her own fashion. But if Lusta had nearly opened a door to something of the Dark last night, it was not to be sensed now.

Though her warning sense kept guard, her main thoughts turned to what had drawn her here and why. These children seedlings, threads—hers would be the planting, the weaving. She tightened hold on her staff. After all the years to have once more a purpose!

Lethe returned to the keep at midday to stand again in the presence chamber, looking down at the ghostly banner. Her fingers moved as they might, without direction but from long habit. Slowly she turned to survey the huge chamber. Where there was desolation—yes, there would be life again.

In the kitchen was truly the bustle of life. Hurten had indeed brought down the bull calf and roughly butchered it. And now it lay bundled in its own spotted hide; containers of bark, even large leaves pinned together with thorns, were full of the last of the berries, nuts, edible roots, all of which Lusta was sorting with the help of Alana; while Marsila had brought in a string of ducks.

Hurten appeared again with the twins, and this time they had not plundered the moldering furniture in the other rooms, but had good loads of wood, storm gleanings—though these must be set to dry.

They shared the work as if they had done this many times before, and Lethe nodded. Already these were bonded after their own fashion; her task would be the lighter.

Through her self-congratulation broke a cry of fear. Alana had pulled away from the table.

"Robar—where is Robar? Tyffan, did he follow you again? Where is he?"

"Never saw him." There was an odd note in the older boy's voice. "What do you mean, followed me?" He was so quickly angry, as if he had been accused of some wrongdoing.

Lethe tensed. Now there was something awakening here, hostile to the accord that had lulled her.

Orffa was also showing signs of anger. "Little pest, always creeping around where he shouldn't be," he muttered.

Alana was confronting Tyffan. There was fear but anger also in the words she flung at him.

"When you passed us you said you were going to the pond. You know how he loves to go there."

Tyffan shook his head. "He wasn't with me, I tell you."

She turned then on Orffa. "You were hunting up on the hill, you must have seen him."

"I never saw the brat. He's always in some trouble or other. Best tie him to you and be done with it, trader trash!"

"Mind your mouth!" Marsila snapped at her brother. "If Robar did go to the pool—"

Alana let out a keening cry and darted for the doorway, Marsila but a step or so behind her. A crash sounded from the table: Lusta had dropped one of the metal bowls. Hurten caught Orffa by the shoulder and jerked him around to face him.

"That pool is deep, Orffa. Also, there are no 'trader trash' here. Keep that tongue of yours clean!"

Orffa's face was scarlet as he jerked free from the other's grip.

"I never saw the brat!"

Lethe shivered. She had been a sentry—surely she would have sensed evil in the valley this morning if it had lain in waiting there. The contentment that had been here only moments earlier was shattered as if she had willed it away herself.

Lusta? Her gift; that was understandable. Robar? Lethe had sensed no power in him, but he was so young a child that at his age he would have very few natural defenses. Robar—!

Not the pool, no. What was wanted for Robar was not danger for him, but through him. And what was wanted must lie within these walls.

"Fool!" Hurten snarled at Orffa. The younger boy's hand flew to his sword hilt. Now the twins moved in and Tyffan was rounding the table to join them. Lusta stood with her hands pressed to her whitened cheeks.

"Keep your tongue to yourself!" Orffa cried. "Do not try to play the high lord with me! I do not know where the brat went—"

"He came here," Truas said. "Saw him on the bridge."

Orffa showed teeth. "Why didn't you speak up before, thickhead—or were you so gagged with the dirty wool you couldn't?"

"Here now," Tristy answered before his brother. He still held the bloody knife he had been using on Hurten's kill. "What's gotten into you, Orffa?"

"Orffa?" He made a near threat of his own name. "Who are you to name me so familiarly, beast-keeper? I am of the blood of Ruran who was lord—"

"Stop!" Lethe's staff was between the boys. Her eyes had narrowed as she looked from one furious scowl to another. "You saw Robar come here? Then let us find him." Either the tone of her voice or some effect of the staff brought them together again—temporarily.

"We'll search—" Hurten agreed.

"Perhaps there is no need to go far." Lethe beckoned to Lusta and asked, "Which of those boxes of nuts there did Robar fill?"

Lusta shivered, and her hands whipped behind her back. "No! No!" She turned her head from side to side, like a small trapped animal gnawed by fear.

"Yes!" There was no escaping that order.

Lusta's right arm moved outward, her fingers hooked like claws. She was staring down at the array of the morning's harvest with fear-rounded eyes. Her hand swung, steadied over one of those containers.

Instantly Lethe raised the staff and touched the crude basket.

She had their full attention now, their quarreling forgotten. Her grip on the staff was loose enough to allow it play, swing of its own accord. She followed that direction, the others close behind her.

Back into the presence chamber—to the wall of the hidden room. She had been a fool to underestimate this other power. That early scene with Robar in there—why had she been so blind?

She strove within her to trace, to know—

"There must be all of you here. Find Marsila—Alana—"

Lethe did not look to see if she had been obeyed, but she heard the shuffle of badly worn boots across the hall.

"Lady." Lusta had crept to her side. "Lady I am afraid—I cannot—I do not know what you would have me do."

"Nor do I know yet what has to be done, child. As for can and cannot, Lusta, that will wait upon what we learn."

She fought within her to set aside all the lives about her, to think only in terms of her weapon—no blade nor axe, spear nor bow, only what was her own. As she wove life, so now she must weave another sort of web, one to be both defense and trap.

"Robar! Please." There was a tug at her arm. "Is Robar truly here?" Lethe looked around quickly—not only Alana was here, but all the rest.

She began a chant, the words issuing stiffly from her lips as if it were so long since they had been used that they had grown as rusty as untended armor. Once more the concealed door opened.

Around them the globe lights dimmed as if their radiance was being sucked out of them.

Lethe threw out her arm to catch Alana, who would have darted before her.

"Robar!" his sister screamed, and then her voice was muffled, for which Lethe was briefly grateful.

The light of the staff flared. In the armory a shadow sprang forth from shadows—and the light caught on a bared blade.

Lethe's weapon swung down between her body and that intended blow. Robar crouched. His face was not that of a child. That which had entered him had molded his features, was blazing from his eyes.

The staff swung, pointed. Sparks formed into a tongue of light, but that was fended, curled back, before it touched the child.

"Join!" Lethe's other hand moved as her voice rose above the insane shrieks from the small figure before her. Spittle flecked from his lips. Dread intelligence stared grimly and grotesquely from his eyes.

"Join!" Her free hand was gripped, she felt the surge of energy, then came a second and a third—that which had first brought them together was still in force.

The staff warmed. The thread of solid light from it was still held away from Robar, but the space was less and less.

"You are Robar!" Lethe called upon the power that lay in names. "You are one with this company. You are Robar!"

Small lips twisted into a sneer.

"Fratch!"

Lethe was prepared. That challenger name did not surprise her. As there were the weavers among the kin, so there had been destroyers. But time was long, and that which destroyed never grew without feeding. Had it been the invaders who had fed this one awake again?

"You are Robar!"

She sought the Touch, to seek out, to shift one personality from another. The light spear was now less than a finger-width from the grimacing child.

"Robar!" That was meant as a call, a summoning. At the same time she drew deeper on the energy fed her by the others.

The light touched the child's forehead. His features writhed and he howled, a cry no human could have uttered. Then—it was as if something that had been confined in too small a prisoning burst forth.

Robar fell like a crumpled twist of harvest grain. Above his body wavered a mist into which bored the spear of light. Then the mist spiraled downward upon itself until it was but a gray blot which the blue bolt licked into nothingness.

"Robar!" Alana threw herself at her brother, pulling him close, twisting her own body around him as if to wall him from all harm.

"What—what happened, Lady?" Tyffan asked hoarsely.

"That was a shadow, of something which should have died long ago." Lethe tried to take a step and tottered.

Strong young arms closed about her as Hurten and Marsila moved in. "A shadow of a will. First it tried to fasten onto Lusta, for her gift offered it power. Then it turned to Robar because he was too young to have those safeguards which come through living. Fratch—Styreon who was"—she addressed the empty air—"you were ever greedy for that which was not yours—nor shall it ever be!"

They went out of the armory, Orffa carrying Robar, who lay limp in his arms, Alana seemingly content to have it so. Marsila and Hurten kept their hold on Lethe, the end of her staff dragging on the floor, though she still kept it within her grasp.

Here was the table on which lay the banner. What was to be done was clear now, and the sooner done the better. Lethe spoke to Lusta:

"This is a beginning. Sister, take your dagger, that which is of the great forging, and not made of fatal iron, and cut from the head of each of these comrade-kin of yours a lock."

They asked no questions, and submitted to Lusta's knife. For the first time Lethe set aside her staff. From her belt purse she brought forth a large needle, which glistened gold in the light. This she threaded with a strand of hair and set about weaving it into the webbing as one would darn a very old and precious thing. So she did again and again as they watched. And with each new strand she repeated aloud the name of him or her to which it had belonged, forming so a chant.

Thus Lethe wrought in moments lifted out of time, for none spoke nor moved, only watched. When she was done they looked upon a length of silver-gold on which faint patterns formed, changed, reformed, growing ever the stronger.

Lethe withdrew her needle. "One is combined of many, even as you united in your flight out of death, as you gave me of your strength to free Robar—you are indeed one.

"But from that one weaving there will come much which is to be welcomed—and time will welcome it and you."

It is told that in the fell days when the Ka-sati had laid totally waste the land and those of the barbarian blood would raise a temple to the Eternal Darkness, there came a company out of the northern hills, riding under a banner bearing nine stripes of gold. Those who bore it were of the blood of legends. What they wrought was to the glory of earth and sky, flood and flame—the darkness being utterly blinded by their light.

A VERY DICKENSY CHRISTMAS
The Magic of Christmas (1992) Penguin/Roc

"It is to be," Mrs. Hotchkiss stated with the inflexibility of one who refused to accept opposition from either mankind or the weather, "a regular old-fashioned Southern Christmas—very Dickensy."

"Dickens was English," Sara said in her mind. She kept her lips firmly closed, however.

"Laurel Hall is perfect, of course"—Mrs. Hotchkiss would have seen to it speedily if her guidebook enshrined Maryland manor house, three times lauded for its super-fine bed and breakfast rating, was not—"if we can just have snow." She paused, suggesting that she would put in an order for that with a higher authority. "Then Jed will bring out the sleigh."

"Of course, the drag hunt will meet here on Boxing Day—"

Sara so forgot herself as to murmur inquiringly "Boxing Day?"

"Yes." Mrs. Hotchkiss brought her hand firmly down on a section of the Christmas issue of the *London Illustrated News*. It was opened to a well-worn page listing the delights of spending a Christmas in a country mansion. "Boxing Day, the day after Christmas, is time for a fox hunt. We have arranged for a special meeting of the Rex Hall Hounds—it is only drag hunting, but they say the huntsman who lays the trail is very good, and last season's hunt was most exciting—quite the leading local event of the winter. So this year

Willard Grayson, he's master, has agreed to assemble the hunt here." Her eyes shown with that glare of a collector finding some treasure in a trash heap.

"Of course, we weren't open to the public before—not," she declared firmly, "that we are open to the general public now The guest list has been very carefully selected—we even have an acceptance from Ambassador Willard and his family. That is why we must have the ghosts." She stared over Sara's shoulder into the wide entrance hall. "Mrs. Willard is very interested in local history; she particularly mentioned the ghosts, her secretary said, when she finally decided they would come. It must be very carefully arranged. Jed will pick you up at the bus stop and bring you in the side way. The west wing has always been kept for only family, and you will have a room there. You must make very sure that you are not seen by any of the guests; it will spoil everything if you are. You will arrive the afternoon of Christmas Eve. Your first appearance will be that night at five minutes after midnight. You will walk along the upper hall where it is part balcony, with your partner. Both of you will stand at the top of the stairs.

"The lighting will be candlelight, and Lorenz has set up a most ingenious veil-like hanging through which you will pass and so return unseen to your own quarters." Mrs. Hotchkiss transferred her attention to Sara completely for the first time. It was a critical and very piercing pair of eyes the girl now faced.

"You'll do." The tone suggested that that should he modified by "barely." "You will try on the dress the minute you get here so Miss Evans can see if it fits. Remember, your meals will be served in your room, and you are not to be seen by any guest."

Sara nodded. It was an odd job, to be a Christmas ghost in order to project the proper atmosphere for Mrs. Hotchkiss's new essay into bed and breakfasting. But it was odd enough to be interesting, and she certainly had no other plans for the Christmas season. That was a time for family parties, and her family had ceased to exist two years back when a plane met a mountaintop on a foggy morning.

She had managed to keep busy at a number of things, the latest being helping out in Rose Wright's vintage dress shop as a model—there was always a demand for someone able to wear fashions which fitted a very slender waist. That was where she had encountered Mrs. Hotchkiss and been swept into this venture of ghosting.

Who was her fellow ghost? Some actor out of a job, she supposed. And an efficient one, as her temporary employer would have known just where to find the proper type.

There was the story to fall back on, faultlessly typed out by Mrs. Hotchkiss's secretary and now in Sara's bag. Young daughter of the house, falling in love with a boy who chose to go south for the fighting during the Civil War. His return at Christmas to see her, his being betrayed and shot in the garden; girl dies of lingering sorrow and perhaps regret—maybe she had urged him into that visit. Very sentimental and properly ghostly.

Mrs. Hotchkiss's belief in the power of suggestion was well-served. When Sara disembarked from the bus from Baltimore in the late morning of the day before Christmas, there was already a satisfactory sifting of snow on the ground and a promising fall continuing in air. She saw, as they left the small town, a country well-veiled in the season's white, with splashes of color marking those houses where the inhabitants had thought to add to the Christmas feeling with displays of their own imagination.

Her driver was not a talkative man, and Sara was content just to enjoy the country. For the first time she felt a timid stirring of what might even be termed "the Christmas spirit."

Laurel Hall was duly impressive. She had a good look at massive door wreaths and impressive formal swags of pine and holly as they passed the main part of the house and swung on around the side. It was larger than she had thought—having the look of a lesser cousin of one of the English manors she had seen pictured. It was old, but it had been well kept up, and was impressive enough to front a card.

Sara was greeted by Mrs. Hotchkiss's secretary, who looked rather harried, and shown to her room with a speed which gave her little time to look around. As she went, Miss Evans continued to impress upon her charge the need for keeping strictly to her quarters and remaining unseen. Her surroundings, however, were as impressive as the house of which they were a part. This wing of Laurel Hall had never been subjected to the impious invasion of bed and breakfasters, no matter how lofty those might be, but had rather been kept "for the family." But it was rather overwhelming to one used to a studio apartment over a garage.

The bed was huge and curtained. There was even a fireplace where a fire was burning, and there was a table flanked by a chair. But Sara was given little time to list any such amenities.

Miss Evans pointed firmly to the bed and the dress which lay outspread there.

"You're to try it on at once." She was smoothing out the very full skirt. "If there is fitting to be done, Martha will have to do it quickly. She is to maid the

Lee and the Tucker suites and won't have time to do anything later."

Sara shed car coat, sweater, T-shirt, and jeans and stood while Miss Evans tossed the dress over her head. It was not vintage, she was sure of that; a modern copy and a rather shoddy one, such as might be worn in a third-rate production of *Gone With the Wind*. And it certainly did not fit! It slipped down Sara's slight figure and nearly cascaded to the floor if she had not caught it.

"It's hopeless!" Miss Evans's harried expression dug a deeper wrinkle or two. "You will have to see about the other."

She left Sara to disentangle herself from the froth of skirt and went to tug at the rounded top of a big trunk. The tray she discarded quickly, to shake out of crumbling and much creased paper a second dress.

"Oh." Sara's hard-learned knowledge from the shop was quick to awake a protest. "That is fragile." She ran her hand lovingly along the folds of old satin lying across the secretary's arm.

"It's old, all right. Let's see if it fits."

"It won't fit if it's in rags," countered Sara firmly. She possessed herself of the dress and put it on with due care. There was a tall wardrobe at one side of the room, and one of its door mirrors furnished a floor-length view.

The satin was yellowed but must have once been white. There were festoons of ruffles around the very full skirt, caught up at intervals with fat satin roses of a dark red. The bodice was low cut and the sleeves mere puffs of lace with a rose to hold each so.

Sara held out the skirt. "It fits. But I'll have to have something to wear to hold this out—this was meant to be worn over hoops."

Miss Evans looked a little less strained. "Oh, yes, Mrs. Hotchkiss thought of that." She turned back to the bed to pick up a contraption formed of hoops of varying sizes, narrowing toward the waist and held together with a weaving of wide bands. "This was meant for the other dress but ought to go with this all right. You'll have to fix your hair like this." She turned and picked up an octagonal box frame of an 1860s photograph. The picture was yellow—a most serious, even distressed-looking young lady, or else the process of being photographed was in those days painful, no beauty perhaps. Her dark hair was drawn back into a net which was marked on one side by a wreath of small flowers.

Miss Evans was already on her way to the door. She made a gesture at the trunk as she passed it. "Other stuff you may need is in there—gloves, fan—Martha will bring your lunch. The bathroom's through that door. Mrs.

Hotchkiss wrote out instructions, you'll find them on the desk. I've got to run." And she was gone.

A half hour later, when her lunch was brought to her on a tray, Sara was well settled in. The food was good, but the maid who had brought it had some of the same harried air that Miss Evans had shown and had certainly not been talkative. Sara sipped her second cup of coffee and reread the instructions for her part in the evening's entertainment. There was a distinct timetable laid out: she was to be gowned and ready at exactly five minutes to midnight—there was a desk clock ticking away above where the instructions had been laid—her partner in the ghost world would come to her door.

Arm and arm they would walk along to where the hall became the balcony. The lighting below would be limited to candles both in holders and on the stairs. Once there they must turn to face one another. Her partner would bow, she would curtsy. They would then face the stairs but in retreat, not to descend, and find the filmy curtain which would veil them from any audience below. Once so veiled they were to return as quickly as possible to the west wing and safety. It sounded very well staged and somehow, knowing Mrs. Hotchkiss, Sara thought it might turn out just as planned.

She had not expected this restlessness, however. Though she had come prepared with reading matter, she felt caged. There were no sounds to penetrate the thick walls, yet she was certain that the guests were already arriving. Even those arrivals were hidden from the windows on this side of the house. It had continued to snow steadily, and there were corners of drift around the bushes below, matched by even smaller pockets on the window-sills.

The maid who had brought her lunch had stirred up the fire, though the house was not chill. Central heating of a modern period, Sara guessed, and certainly in the west wing which was family quarters. She wondered about the family—of whom did that consist these days? The Seldons, who had held this manor since the time of the second King Charles, were long gone—unless Mrs. Hotchkiss was in some way a descendant. No one had spoken of a Mr. Hotchkiss.

She went back to survey what she had laid out on the bed. The satin slippers from the trunk were too frail to be worn, as were the lace clocked hose, but those would not be seen under the spread of skirt. Her own white panty hose were suitable enough, as were the low-heeled slippers she had brought. There were two much belaced and be-tucked petticoats which were all right, and the fan, with its delicately carved ivory sticks, webbed together with lace, had survived. The short white kid gloves flaked apart at her touch—

but there was a pair of lace mitts which were lying with the dress she could not wear, and those would do.

Sara picked up one of the books she had brought along, a history of costume. However, she did more leafing through it and looking at the illustrations than actually reading. That odd feeling that she was somehow removed from real life as it was being lived at Laurel Hall right now seemed to grow stronger and stronger as the early winter dusk drew in.

She wondered about her partner to be. He was an actor, of course, and to him this would be just another job, a very short one. Would he find it amusing to play the ghost, or boring and something to be quickly put behind him?

For at least the tenth time she picked up the sheet of instructions and read it through, though by this time she could recite it by heart. She had better get dressed early and do some walking about—a good thing the bedroom was so large—so she could discover just how to manage the skirt.

Her dinner, also tray borne, arrived early. Sticking up right between cup and small coffee pot was a note folded three-cornered.

"All will be ready—leave at exactly five minutes to twelve."

More fussing, maybe that was Miss Evans.

Sara ate. The food was very good, and she thought she was being given a share of what was being served downstairs. At least Mrs. Hotchkiss did not stint with that.

At ten she began to dress. Luckily, even if the rest of the hall might be doomed to candles, there was good electric light here and an excellent makeup mirror in the bathroom. She twisted her hair around and wove it up with a ribbon as she had devised in the afternoon, enough like the snood thing the girl in the picture wore to pass. She had even been able to detach three of the red roses from less visible portions of the skirt ruffles to fasten to the side and, after a long and critical inspection of her face, thought she would pass in candlelight. Leaving off any rouge, she had used mainly powder and even in this bad light her skin looked much whiter.

The assumption of the dress over the hoop was a struggle and she could, she knew, have done with the aid of another pair of hands. But it was done at last, and she had actually managed to make secure the last small fastening.

Fan and mitts in hand, she faced the long mirror of the wardrobe and was actually startled. Somehow she did not look like Sara Haines masquerading as a ghost, but like a girl who might once have occupied this room by right of birth and been secure in the heart of a loving family.

She spread her skirts with twists of the wrist which seemed very natural, and she curtsied to that other girl. No, that was not quite right. Try it again. The skirt, all laces and roses, swirled out and this time—yes, that was just the way she must do it!

Now she turned and took short steps down the length of the room. They always spoke of ghosts as gliding. How did one glide? Or was that only a fantasy of writers? Slowly, don't let the hoops swing so—now, try again. Well, maybe not a glide but at least not a stride. For one who habitually wore jeans this was a new art.

Sara opened the fan, eyed an arm chair coquettishly and curtsied. She wished she could stand off and watch herself with a critic's eye. Luckily they were not going to be on display long, her fellow ghost and she. Down the room, watch the hoop for swaying, now turn and curtsy. Sara drew a deep breath. At least the hoop hadn't tilted up. But by candlelight a lot of faults could be hidden and—

There was a tap at her door.

The maid come to see if she needed help? No—her eyes had found the clock—actors would say they were on. She drew herself up and took several deep breaths, one part of her surprised at her uneasiness. There was nothing to this, walk down the hall, let herself be seen, step back through a curtain—one would think she was going to play Lady Macbeth or something of the sort.

Sara opened the door.

He was not tall; he could not have bettered her own five feet six inches by more than three inches at the most. Nor was he dark. Though the hallway was not brightly lighted, the beam from the room behind her easily picked out that unruly mop of hair which was only slightly removed from being a distressing gingery shade. He was not handsome; there were no dark demanding eyes questing for her from either side of an imperious hawk sharp nose—No, the nose was close to snub and he was not smoldering; he was favoring her with close to a conspiratorial grin.

Even his gray uniform did not fit too well. Certainly Mrs. Hotchkiss had *not* had a secondary costume for him to fall back upon. The yellow sash pulled in the jacket in visible wrinkles at his waist. But his black boots shone bravely, and when he swept her a grand bow somehow he seemed at home in those badly tailored clothes.

Sara curtsied. "I'm Sara Haines," she introduced herself a little breathlessly. And now she was very glad she had not been fronted by Rhett Butler or any such heartthrob.

His cheerful grin became an open smile. "Bryce Seldon, at your service."

He stood aside a little and crooked his arm in invitation.

"Bryce Seldon," she repeated. "But that was—"

"Oh, there have been a number of us from time to time along the family tree," he assured her cheerfully.

So that was it! Mrs. Hotchkiss had fastened upon some surviving member of another branch of the family to play her ghostly captain. But of course, that was an excellent solution; he would know far more about their little charade.

"This way?" Sara fitted her mitted hand comfortably into the crook of his elbow. A good many of her doubts had vanished. This was going to be a fun thing—

"This way," he agreed, and led her to the right. She hurried to manage the swing of her skirts, at least he did not have her kind of costume to contend with.

They moved at a sedate pace along the hall, and suddenly lights and sound enveloped them from the left. They had reached that part which became balcony and now they would be visible to anyone watching. Bryce, she found it very easy to think of him so, curbed his stride even more.

Then she heard a gasp, a couple of cries from below, but she kept her head turned a little as if she were regarding with dotish approval the countenance of her escort.

They reached the head of the stairs. Sara loosed her hold on that gray-clad arm and Bryce stepped around to face her. One of her hands went out to him without her even willing it as she sank into the practiced curtsy. Her fingers were taken in a strong grasp and lifted until he could brush them lightly with his lips. Then she was standing again. But he did not release her hand; rather he drew her on, her back to the stairs, and she felt the long strips of the veiling flutter about her. There were sounds from below, but Bryce was hurrying her on now, turning once more to the west wing. They must be out of sight before anyone came exploring, she knew that.

However, he did not just deliver her to the door of the room in which she had spent such boring hours, instead he tucked her hand under his arm firmly again.

"They won't follow." He seemed very sure of that. "Want to do a bit of sightseeing, Sara?"

"Oh, yes!" The excitement which had gripped her ever since she had left her room was holding. They could not join the party, but that did not mean they had to just shut themselves up again.

"Now this"—he had drawn her along as if he were very eager to have her company and was afraid that she might not give it—"is the long gallery, right over the ballroom. Family portraits—" He waved one hand to the wall. There were a few very dim lights along the inner wall to her right, the blankness of draped windows to her left.

Sara had a sudden idea.

"Are we there?" He had not loosed his hold on her, but she pointed with the fan in her other hand to the row of dimly seen pictures.

For a moment he hesitated. Then he chuckled. "Just half and half, as it were," he answered. "I am afraid, lovely lady, I cannot introduce you to your ancestress—of the spirit. For his sins Bryce is remembered with paint and varnish, but not very well. Over here."

He drew her to a position near the door through which they had come. If there had not been one of the low wattage lights near it, she might have seen nothing at all. As it was Sara was startled. Clearly the portrait had not been done by a very competent artist; his subject had the wooden aspect of a primitive, yet the hair—and certainly the nose—

"Common enough looking fellow, isn't he?" commented her escort.

"But—but you do look like him!" she blurted out, and then tried to cover her uncomplimentary error. "It's just the color of the hair—the eyes—"

He was laughing. "And all the rest of it, lovely lady. But the hair's family— you'll find it repeated half a dozen times along here—" He waved a hand to the wall of portraits.

It was then that the music reached them; somehow those thick walls could not drown out the sound. In the ballroom below, they were playing a waltz.

Her companion turned swiftly and made her another of those courtly bows. "My lady, will you do me the very great honor of your hand for this dance—?"

Sara smiled unsteadily. That queer feeling of being still somehow caught up in a play held her again. "Sir," she made answer in a small voice, "I will be most pleased—"

He swung her out almost as if he were afraid she might change her mind. And as she danced, Sara heard him humming. She could never remember any dance which had been like this, which had lifted her out and away from all the world which she knew.

They were close to one of the tall windows when the music stopped. Over her partner's shoulder, Sara thought she could see the brush of falling snow against the windowpane.

"A very Dickensy Christmas—" she murmured as their hands fell apart.

"A what?"

Sara laughed. "That is what Mrs. Hotchkiss said she wanted—a very Dickensy Christmas—with snow, only there's no stagecoach like on a card. I wonder if there is a Scrooge down below some place. If there is, she'll soon rout him out and get him into the proper frame of mind."

"Why did you come?" The question was shot at her so suddenly she found no way of evading it, as she might have done had she been given more time. Instead she found herself talking of the mountain and the plane, the too small apartment in Baltimore which she shared with Ann, who had gone to visit her friend's family in Richmond. Even as she talked, she wondered why she was telling all this to a stranger.

He nodded when she had done. And then she thought it her turn.

"And you—?"

He had turned away from her a fraction and was looking through the window into the night.

"I don't have a roommate bound for Richmond. But our stories do not differ so much. This was something to do and—" Now he turned his head to smile at her. "Sometimes fate plays queer jokes on us, Sara. I find myself highly in favor of Mrs. Hotchkiss's Christmases—as far as they pertain to you and me."

Somewhere along the gallery a clock struck. Sara shivered. That sound might have summoned up the chill which had touched her for a moment. He was holding out his hand.

"Come, Sara, 'tis time for ghostlings to be abed—"

"Tomorrow?" She was slightly breathless.

"Of course," he said, "we have our obligations to fulfill tomorrow evening."

But he did not say anything about meeting her earlier, Sara thought, as she carefully unfastened the gown a little later and saw it laid out in a way to least crush its ruffling. Maybe he had some other job outside—Only as she crawled into the huge bed she wished that she could be sure of that. He did seem to like her—or had until she had spilled out all that about her life. Had she sounded like a whiner? She thumped the pillow and stared up into the drapery of the bed.

Doubts dropped away with the coming of sleep, but they crowded back with the arrival of her breakfast, which awoke her in the morning. The maid plumped the tray down on the table by the fire.

"Merry Christmas, miss. My, you were a real treat last night. I was coming in with the punch cups when you bowed. Oh, it was like a movie, so it was! They were all talking about it after. 'Course we knew as how it wasn't any ghost. But some of them—I think maybe the half believed."

Sara sat up in bed. "Merry Christmas," she echoed the other's greeting automatically. "So it went well?"

The maid nodded enthusiastically. "Madam was very pleased, heard her say so to Miss Evans. Now, I've got to run, there'll be a lot of doings today—"

She was gone as Sara put on her robe and went to wash before sitting down to eat. The breakfast was a hearty one, probably in the proper tradition, too. She found she could not resist the biscuits and jam.

Merry Christmas, she said to herself. But in truth she wanted very much to say that to her companion of the night before. For the first time she felt as if there was a stir of new life somewhere deep within her.

She was restless, longing to go out into the white world beyond for a long walk. It had stopped snowing, but she stepped hurriedly back from the window as two horses came trotting along, a sleigh at their backs, their driver well-bundled up on a small seat behind the low open body of the vehicle in which there were furs and stocking caps and high clear voices she could hear, though not the words. Another of Mrs. Hotchkiss's plans brought to triumphant fruition. The maid had returned for her tray, very much in a hurry, but pausing long enough to say that the big tree was really a sight to be seen and there was to be a special singer of folksongs in for the evening.

Sara had her own plans for the evening, and she had plenty of time to hone and polish them, even if she did spend time with her costume books and begin two of her paperback mysteries and lay them aside for the crime of being dull.

Never had she been so glad to see evening come. She had gobbled her dinner, and it was worth better attention; it was very plain that she was being fed as well as the paying guests. However, it could have been a cold and greasy burger as far as she was concerned, something to be gulped down to keep her going.

Though it was good policy to stick to the wan makeup she had devised the night before, she was not prevented from making the most of what she could use. And she had the small bottle of rose oil some whim had made her tuck into her kit, though the use of perfume had not been important for a long time. Now as she twisted the lid, the odor was strong enough to make her believe that all those crimson garlands on her dress were alive and at the height of their fragrance. She took to pacing the room. When the knock came, she glanced at the clock. He was early, too!

Sara jerked at the door in her impatience. She still had a fraction of fear—

it might not be him.

"Merry Christmas!" They said it together, their voices mingling, Sara's hands quite without her direction going out to him. But he was bowing and holding out to her a small box. It was stained, one end of it cracked half-open, yet there was a twist of ribbon faded to dust color about it.

She stared at it, and him, and at it again, and then very slowly took the box. It seemed very fragile, and the cover broke to bits when she opened it. Inside, on a scrap of time-discolored material, was a heart of onyx patterned with a spray of seed pearl flowers, the same tiny pearls outlining the heart. She caught at a gleam of chain as the box quite fell into scraps.

"It's—it's beautiful!" Sara cupped it in her hand and then swiftly closed the space between them and touched her lips to his.

"Wear it," he said. "It was meant to be worn, you know."

She pressed it into his hand and turned around, pulling up her ribbon-bound hair so he could fasten the chain. Nor was she surprised at the touch of his lips just where he settled the chain.

Then his hands were on her shoulders and he turned her around, smiling his wide smile. "You do a poor little gift great credit, my lady."

Her hand arose again to cup over the heart. "Not poor, not little—I work with old things, remember! This is a very lovely piece and very old. Is it—is it from your family?"

Somehow she wanted so much for him to say yes.

"In a way you might say so." He nodded. "None but I have the right to bestow it, dear one. Shall we fulfill our bargain and then be free again?"

Once more he offered her his arm and they made their stately progress out onto the balcony. There were more voices below tonight, Sara thought. She made her curtsy as grand and graceful as she could, marveling at how, though he looked boyishly clumsy in his ill-fitting uniform, he could be the polished gentleman of past story when he wished.

Then they were back through the curtain, and Sara was not surprised when they came once more into the gallery. Tonight there was no music from below. Her escort went to a small table and fingered a box there—the tinkle of a tune answered and he was back.

"You will grant me the very great honor, my lady?" He held out his hand.

Once more they floated down the gallery.

"You are very, very beautiful, Sara," he said, hardly above a whisper. "Very young and very beautiful."

She smiled. "You are very gallant, sir. Remember, I have looked many times in my mirror. Oh—"

The tinkle of the music had stopped. Another sound had taken its place. Rhythm of a different sort and time. Sara remembered what the maid had said about the folk singer.

Her partner muttered something. Then suddenly his head went up and he was plainly listening.

"I must go," he told her.

"But—when will I see you?" Sara asked.

He was already at the door in three great strides, and she gathered up her skirts to hurry after him. Only when she came out into the hall there was nothing moving in the shadows between the night lights, nothing until Miss Evans came into view.

"Miss Haines! You are out of your room!"

"I was with—"

"You must go back at once! There has been a change of plan. You will have to leave early in the morning as Mrs. Hotchkiss has promised to show the ambassador and Mrs. Willard through the west wing. You must be out of your room before then. You will see Mrs. Hotchkiss in her sitting room at seven. Martha will bring you your breakfast before you go."

Sara trailed back to her room. If they would send her off by seven, then they would send Bryce, too. Her hand cradled the heart. For some reason, though it had been resting against her flesh, it felt cold. She unfastened the clasp and held the pendant out to see the better. There was something odd—a half memory stirring deep in her mind. The back did not feel as smooth as it should. She flipped it over.

There was a tiny oval of glass set in a rounded curve of gold and under that—could it be hair? Sara held it closer to the lamp. The glass was clouded, but surely what it covered was a bit of hair. The Victorians had a liking for such sentimental treasures. She could believe that Bryce might have given her some family piece. The hair aroused a stir of uneasiness, but when she turned the pendant over, the lacy beauty of the pearl flowers enchanted her anew.

Yes, doubtless they would be decanted at the bus station together tomorrow. She would see him again. Later, when Sara went to sleep, the chain was once more clasped around her neck and her hand guarded her treasure.

Did she dream? Afterward she was sure she did, but her quick awakening at the tapping on her door brought her so swiftly out of any dream that memory could not hold it.

She showered and dressed in record time, then ate in gulps of coffee and mouthfuls of toast. Sara gave a last search around the room to make sure she had not forgotten anything. However, more than half her attention was already downstairs, meeting with Bryce, off to the bus stop. Or maybe he had a car and would offer her a ride!

Only when she entered Mrs. Hotchkiss's sitting room, it was to find her employer at her desk dictating to Miss Evans—and there was so sign of her fellow ghost.

"Oh, Miss Haines." Mrs. Hotchkiss paused her dictation nearly in mid-word. "It is good you are so prompt. I wish to tell you that you did splendidly, splendidly. Why, anyone watching you would surely have believed you did have an escort, and it did not matter that that stupid young man did not appear. It all went very well indeed; we intend to repeat it next year. Please consider yourself engaged as of now—"

"There—there was no one—no Bryce?" Somehow Sara forced out the words.

"As you saw, he did not see fit to appear. My dear, what a charming necklace. It looks very old—" Mrs. Hotchkiss was staring at the pendant, and Sara's hand flew to cover it.

"It—it was a Christmas gift," she said. But where had it come from? No Bryce—no partner in the dance—no other—

"Here is your check. I hate to hurry you off like this, my dear, but the Willards have decided they would rather see some of the family treasures in the west wing than attend the hunt. Remember, now, we shall want you again next year. I have no doubts that the story of your charming appearance will spread where it will do the most good and that the Laurel Hall Christmases will become quite sought after entertainment. Now, you must hurry. Jed is waiting at the side door."

Sara held the check in one hand without looking at it. "Yes," she agreed, and then with some force, "I must hurry!"

She did not remember climbing the side stairs, of turning left instead of right. But when she came to a halt in the long gallery, she knew exactly where she was.

Breathless, she looked at that woodenly painted primitive portrait which had so little charm. But there *was* charm, and life, and—

"But you *were* here—you *were*!" she said in what was hardly more than a whisper.

Sara was never afterward sure whether that answer rang in her ears or in her head, but it was sharply confident:

"Indeed, I was, Sara, my sweet lady. Time touched time for a space, you see. There will be next year, darling—a wonderful Dickensy Christmas—just you wait and see!"

NOBLE WARRIOR
Catfantastic (1989) DAW

Emmy squinted at the stitch she had just put in the handkerchief. Ivy had curtained almost half of the window, to leave the room in greenish gloom. Too long, she would have to pick it out. On such a grayish day she wanted a candle. Only even to think of that must be a sin. Miss Wyker was very quick to sniff out sins. Emmy squinted harder. It was awfully easy to sin when one was around Miss Wyker.

Not for the first or not even the hundredth time she puzzled as to why Great-Aunt Amelie had asked Miss Wyker to Hob's Green. Who could be ill without feeling worse to see about that long narrow face with the closed buttonhole of a mouth, and mean little eyes on either side of a long, long nose. Elephant nose! Emmy's hands were still while she thought of elephants, big as Jasper's cottage. Father said that they had great seats large enough to hold several men strapped on their backs and one rode them so to go tiger hunting.

She rubbed her hand across her aching forehead as she thought of father. If he were here, he would send old Wyker packing.

Emmy ran a tongue tip over her lips. She was thirsty—but to leave her task to even get a drink of water might get her into trouble. She gave an impatient jerk and her thread broke. Before she could worry about that, sounds from the graveled drive which ran beyond the window brought her up on her knees to look out. Hardly anyone now used the front entrance drive. This was the trap from the inn, with Jeb. Beside him sat a stranger, a small man with a bushy brown beard.

The trap came to a halt and the small man climbed down from the seat. Jeb handed down a big basket to the man who gave him a short nod before disappearing under the overhang of the doorway. Emmy dropped her sewing on the window seat to run across the room as the knocker sounded. She was cautious about edging open the door of the sitting room to give herself just a crack to see through.

The knocker sounded three times before Jennie the housemaid hurried by, patting down her cap ribbons and looking all a-twitter. It had been so long since anyone had been so bold as to use the knocker. Nobody but Dr. Riggs ever came that way any more, and he only in the morning.

Emmy heard a deep voice, but she could not quite make out the words. Then, as quick as if it were meant as an answer, there sounded a strange cry. Emmy jumped, the door opened a good bit wider than was wise.

At least she could see Jennie show the visitor to the library, where Dr. Riggs was always escorted by Miss Wyker to have a ceremonial glass of claret when his visit to his patient was over. The stranger had taken the covered basket with him.

Jennie went hurrying up the stairs to get Miss Wyker. To speed her along sounded another of those wailing cries.

Emmy pulled the door nearer shut, but her curiosity was fully aroused. Who had come visiting and why? And whatever could be in that basket?

She heard the determined tread of Miss Wyker and saw a stiff back covered with the ugliest of gray dresses also disappear into the parlor. Should she try to cross the hall in hope of seeing more of the visitor? She was so tired of one day being like another—all as gray as Miss Wyker's dress—that this was all very exciting. Before she had quite made up her mind, Jennie came in a hurry, probably called by the bell. She stood just within the library door, and then backed out to head for the morning room where Emmy had been isolated for numberless dull hours of the day since Great-Aunt had taken ill.

"You—Miss Emmy," Jennie was breathless as she usually was when Miss Wyker gave orders. "They want to see you—right now·—over there—" she jerked a thumb toward the library.

Emmy was across the hall and into the room before Jennie had disappeared back down the hall. As she came in, there sounded once more that startling cry. It had come from the big covered basket which was rocking a little back and forth where it stood on the floor.

"This is the child—" Miss Wyker's sharp voice was plainly disapproving.

The brown-bearded man looked down at Emmy. A big grin split that beard in the middle.

"So—you be th' Cap'n's little maid, be you? Must have grown a sight since he was last a-seein' you. Told it as how you was a mite younger."

The Cap'n—that was father. For a moment, forgetting Miss Wyker, Emmy burst out with a question of her own:

"Where is he? Please, did his ship come in? Truly?" There was so much Emmy wanted to say that the words stuck in her throat unable to push out clearly.

"Emmiline—this is Mr. Salbridge—manners, *IF* you please!"

Emmy swallowed and made a bob of a curtsey, one eye on Miss Wyker, knowing that she would be in for a scold when this visitor left.

"Very pleased to make your acquaintance, sir," she parroted the phrase which had been drilled into her.

Mr. Salbridge bowed in return. "Well, now, Miss Emmy, seems like we should be no strangers. Ain't I heard th' Cap'n talk of you by th' hour? Your servant, Miss Emmy. It does a man good to see as how you is doin' well, all shipshape an' tight along the portholes as it were. You probably ain't heard o' me—but I has been a-sailin' with th' Cap'n for a right many years now—would be there on board th' *Majestic* yet, only I had me a bit o' real luck, which gave me a snug purse, an' was minded to come home along of that there windfall. They's none o' us as young as we once was an' me, I got someone as has been a-waiting for me to come home a longish time.

"Th' Cap'n, he gave me a right hearty goodbye, but not afore he asked somethin' o' me an' I'm right proud that he did that. I was to see his little maid an' bring 'er somethin' as was give to him by a princess as heard he had a little daughter to home. He was mighty helpful to her pa, an' she was grateful to him in return, give him somethin' th' which nobody here at home has seen—somethin' as has lived in a palace right a'long of her. Look you here, Miss Emmy, what do you think o' this?"

He knelt awkwardly on one knee to open the basket. For a minute nothing happened. Then there jumped out of that carrier the oddest animal Emmy had ever seen. It looked like a cat, only it was not gray striped. Rather its face, legs, and the lower part of its slender back were of a brown as dark as Mr. Salbridge's beard, while the rest of it was near the color of the thick cream Mrs. Goode skimmed off the milk. And its eyes—its eyes were a bright blue!

It stood by the side of the basket, its head slowly moving as it stared at each of them in turn, Mr. Salbridge, Miss Wyker, who had drawn back a pace or two and was frowning darkly, and the longest at Emmy.

"Miss Emmy, this here's Thragun Neklop, that there means Noble Warrior. He's straight out o' th' king's own palace. They thinks a mighty lot o' those like him thereabouts. No one as is common gets to have these here cats a-livin' in their houses. The Cap'n now, he was favored when they said this one might go to be with his little missy back in his own country. Yes, this here is a very special cat—"

The cat opened its mouth and gave a short, sharp cry which was certainly not like the meow which Emmy expected. Then its head turned so that it looked directly and unblinkingly at Miss Wyker and it hissed, its ears flattening a little. Miss Wyker's frown now knotted all her long face together.

Emmy squatted down so that she was nearly face to face with the furred newcomer.

"Thragun Neklop." She tried to say the strange words carefully. The cat turned its head again, to stare boldly at her. There was no hissing this time.

"That there is a power name, Miss Emmy. His pa was guard o' th' king. Them as lives there, they do not take kindly to dogs—that's their religion like. But cats, them they train to be their guards. An' mighty good they be at that, too, if all th' stories they tell is true."

The cat arose and came to Emmy. She put out her hand, not quite daring to lay a finger on that sleek brown head. The cat sniffed her fingers and then bumped his head against her hand.

"Well, now, that do beat all. Never saw him do that exceptin' to the princess when she said goodbye," commented Mr. Salbridge. "Maybe he thinks as how you're the princess now. Good that'll be. Now—servant, Mistress, servant, Miss Emmy." He made a short bow. "I needs must be gitting along. Have to catch th' York stage."

"Oh," Emmy was on her feet, "please—thank you! And father—is he coming home, too?"

Mr. Salbridge shook his head. "He's got the voyage to make and the *Majestic* warn't due to raise anchor for maybe two months when I left him. He'll be coming through, jus' as soon as he can—"

"It's such a long time to wait—" Emmy said. "But, oh, please, Mr. Salbridge, I do thank you for bringing Thragun Neklop."

"My pleasure, Miss—" The rest of what he might have said was drowned out by another of those strange wails.

Emmy hurried behind Mr. Salbridge who strode for the door. Miss Wyker made no attempt to see him away, as she did the doctor when he came calling. Emmy followed with more eager questions which he answered cheerfully. Yes, the Cap'n was feeling well and doin' well for hisself, too. An' he would be home again before long. He was jus' glad to be of service.

While he climbed back into the rig and drove off down the driveway, Emmy waved vigorously. She was startled by a very harsh piercing cry and she ran back to the library.

Miss Wyker, poker in hand, that deep scowl still on her face, was advancing on Thragun. The cat stood his ground; now that scream dropped to a warning growl. His long slender tail was puffed out to twice its usual size and his ears were flattened to his skull.

"Dirty animal!" Miss Wyker's voice was as angry as Thragun's war cry. "Get in there, you filthy beast!" She poked with the iron and Thragun went into a crouch.

"Thragun!" Emmy ran forward, standing between the war ready cat and Miss Wyker.

"Get that foul thing into the basket—at once, do you hear me?"

Emmy had witnessed Miss Wyker's anger a good many times, but never had she made such a scene as this before.

"Don't hit him!" Emmy caught at the cat. A paw flashed out and drew a red stripe across her hand. But in spite of that the little girl grabbed him up and put him into the basket. "He wasn't doing any harm!" she cried out, braver as she spoke up for Thragun than she had ever been for herself.

In answer Miss Wyker used the poker to flip the lid down on the basket.

"Fasten it!" she ordered, already heading toward the bell pull on the wall.

Emmy's hands shook. She had always been afraid of loud angry voices, and lately she jumped at every sound, especially when she was never sure when Miss Wyker was going to come up behind her with some punishment already in mind. She had done so many things wrong ever since Great-Aunt Amelie had taken ill. Emmy never even saw her any more. Nobody seemed to see much of Lady Ashely now. Miss Wyker was always there at the bedroom door, to take the trays cook sent up with the special beef jelly or a new egg done to the way Great-Aunt Amelie always liked them.

Even at night Jennie was not called to sit with her. Miss Wyker had a trundle bed moved into the room and spent her own night hours there. When Jennie or Meggy came to clean, she was always standing there watching them.

"Yes, m'm?" Jennie now stood in the half open door.

"Take this beast out to the stable at once! I do not want to see it about again!"

"No!" Courage which she not been able to summon for herself brought words to Emmy. "Father sent him—to me. He's Thragun Neklop an' a prince! The man said so!" She caught the handle of the big basket in both hands and held it as tightly as she could.

Miss Wyker, her long face very red, laid the poker across the seat of the nearest chair before taking long strides to stand directly over Emmy. Her hand swept up, to come down across Emmy's cheek, the blow so sudden and stinging that the child staggered backward, involuntarily losing her hold on the basket. Miss Wyker had scolded her many times since the first hour when she had arrived and doffed her helmet of a bonnet to take over rulership of Hob's Green. But until this moment she had never touched Emmy.

"Take that beast out to the stable," Miss Wyker repeated, "and be quick about it. Animals are filthy. They have no place in a well-run household. And you," she rounded on Emmy who was standing staring at her, one hand pressed to her cheek where those long fingers had left visible marking, "go to your room instantly, you impudent girl! You are wholly selfish, unbiddable, lazy, and a handful! Poor Lady Ashely may have been hastened to her bed of illness by your thoughtless impudence! Poor lady, she has had a great deal to burden her these past years but there will be a good many changes made shortly—and your conduct, Miss, will not be the least of those! Go!"

So sharp and loud was that command that it seemed to sweep Emmy out of the room. She hesitated for one moment on the foot of the stairs to watch Jennie's apron strings and the tail of her skirt vanish toward the end of the hall. The maid had taken the basket. What was going to happen to Thragun Neklop? Emmy's tears spilled over the fingers which still nursed the cheek which was beginning to ache as she went up the stairs slowly, one reluctant foot at a time.

There was a strong smell of horses, but there were other scents which were new. Thragun stretched himself belly down in the basket to look through a spread in the wicker weave which had served him for some time now as a window on a very strange and ever-changing world. He saw an expanse of stone paved yard and there was a flutter of pigeons about a trough out of which water was being slopped by a young man whose shirt sleeves were rolled clear to the shoulder. Thragun sniffed—water—never before had he been kept shut up to receive food and water only at the pleasure of another. However if this must be so for some reason he had not yet discovered, then let those who were to minister to him, as was correct, be brought to attention of their duty.

He voiced a call-cry which in his proper home would have brought at least two maids and perhaps a serving slave of the first rank to answer and make proper apologetic submission, letting him out of this strange litter and treating him as Thragun Neklop should be. Was he not second senior of the Princess Suphorn's own household?

The young man turned his head toward the basket. However, he made no attempt to come and act in the proper fashion. This time Thragun gave a truly angry cry to inform this odd looking servant that his superior wanted full attention to his desires. The young man had filled two buckets with water which sloshed back and forth, wetting the yard stones, as he came. Thragun waited, but the slave made no attempt to approach. Instead, inside this place smelling of horses, he was starting to pass Thragun's cage when there was a voice from the general gloom behind.

"Asa, you lunkhead, you messin' with th' Knight agin?" The voice was drowned out then by the shrill squeal of an aroused stallion. Then there were whinneys and the sound of horses moving restlessly.

Asa moved out of the cat's sight even though Thragun turned in the basket and tried to see through another small opening in the wicker. That was too narrow, even though he had been working on it with explorative claws for several days.

He heard two voices making odd noises, some of which he recognized. So did the grooms soothe and tend their charges in the royal stable. Apparently even in this strange land horses were properly cared for. If that much was known, why were cats not properly attended?

Heavy footsteps came toward the basket. Thragun waited. There was more than just hunger and thirst to mark the change in his life now—there was a strange unpleasant feeling. The hair along his spine and his tail lifted a little, his ears flattened.

He was Thragun Neklop—Noble Warrior, acknowledged guardian of a princess. It had been his duty and his pleasure to patrol palace gardens at night's coming, to make sure that nothing dark or threatening dared venture there. Had he not in his first year killed one of the serpent ones who had been about to set fang in the princess' hand when she had reached around the rocks to recover her bracelet? Perhaps he had not sprung on a thief to rip open his throat as had Thai Shan, the mightiest of them all, trusted warrior for the king. But he knew what must be—

"So this 'ere's th' beastie? That there Wyker's got a wicked tongue an' a worse eye, that one! Jennie says that this was brot here special—for Miss Emmy—present from 'er pa. So do we do what that long-nosed witch wants, then what do we say when th' Cap'n comes home an' says where is what 'e sent? An' who, I'm askin', made 'er th' Lady here? My wage is paid by th' Lady Ashely as has been since I was six an' came a-helpin' for m' pa. I takes 'er Ladyship's orders, an' that's th' tight an' right o' it!"

"She's got 'er a thing 'bout cats. Th' moggy to th' kitchen disappeared. It showed claw to that one first time it saw 'er when she came down givin' orders right an' left to Cook 'erself. Then come two days past and moggy was gone. Saw 'er a-talkin' to Rog out in th' garden—him 'as no feeling for beasties. But he 'ad 'im a sixpence down to the Arms that week. An' sixpences don't just grow in that there garden 'e's supposed to be a-planting of."

"So—"

There was a moment of quiet. Thragun's eyes were hardly more than slits, and with his ears so flat he looked almost like one of the big carved stone garden snakes on which he used to sun himself in the old days when all was well with his world.

Something deep in him stirred. Once before he had felt its like and that was when he was shedding the last of his kitten fur to take on the browning of his mask, tail, and four feet. His mother had gathered up her family just at twilight one night—there were the three of them, Rannar, his brother, and Su Li, his sister. They had followed their mother into a far part of the largest garden. There, trees and vines and full formed shrubs had grown so closely together they had formed a wall, and such a one as only the most supple of cats could get through. There was something in the heart of that miniature jungle—a gray stone place fashioned as if two of the Naga Serpents had faced one another before a wall, with another piece of wall above which they supported on their heads. They were very old; there was the green of small growth on their weathered scales.

Mother had seated herself before them, her kittens a little behind her. Then she had called. The sound she made was the sort to stiffen one's back fur, made claws ache to be unsheathed. Something appeared between the serpents, under the roof they supported. Mother had sat in silence. Only they were not alone, cat and kittens. Something had surveyed them with cold eyes and colder thoughts—yet they remained very still and did not run even though they all smelled the fear which was a part of this meeting.

That which had come, and which they had never seen clearly, went. With mother, the kittens scrambled into the freedom of the real garden again. However, from that moment Thragun knew the stench of fear, and that wrongness which is a part of evil to be ever after sensed by those who had met it. Also, he had learned the warning which came before battle to those born to be fighters and protectors.

These two who stood over his basket now did not radiate that smell. But that female in the house did. Thragun knew that it was of her that they spoke now. He had come to this place because his princess had asked him to do so. She had explained to him that there was a great debt lying on her because the man from the far country had saved her father. She had learned that this man had a daughter, and now she wished Thragun to be to that daughter even as he was to her, a noble warrior to be ever her shield and her defense. Knowing that all debts must be paid, Thragun had come, though there were times when he wished only to sit and wail his loneliness to the world.

The man who had taken him by the princess' orders had always sought him out, if he was near, when those times came upon Thragun. He had talked to him, stroked him, spoken of his daughter and the old house where she lived with a kinswoman, waiting for the day when the man's duty would be fully done and he might return himself to be with them. And Thragun understood—to the man, his daughter was a treasure precious above anything in the king's palace.

Now what he felt was that need to be alert before danger, and behind it there was the faint, bitter smell of evil, sly and cunning evil, which could and did slip through the world like one of the serpents-which-were-not-Nagas. He was a warrior and this was the enemy's country through which he must go as silently as wind, as aware as that which hungers greatly. Now he must seem to be as one who had no daggers on the feet, teeth waiting in his jaws. With his mouth he shaped a cry such as a lost kitten might give.

"Like as th' beastie's hungry, Ralf—"

"No one's tellin' me wot is an' isn't right!"

There was a sudden movement and the basket lid swung up. Thragun sat up, his tail top curled properly over his front toes, his unblinking blue eyes regarding the two of them.

The man beside Asa was short and thin and smelled strongly of horse sweat. With his black hair and dark skin he looked almost like one of the stable slaves back in the land where things were done properly. There was none of the evil odor clinging to him, nor to the boy either.

There was a long drawn noise from the man which was not a word, but plainly an exclamation of surprises. He squatted down on his heels, his face not far above Thragun's own.

"Blue eyes," that was the boy. "He don't look like any moggy as I ever saw—"

"Sssssisss—" The man held out his hand and slowly, as if he were dealing with one of his horse charges. "You sure be a different one."

Thragun sniffed at the knuckles of the hand offered him. There were smells in plenty, but none were cold or threatening. He ventured a small sound deep in his throat.

"You be a grand one, ben't you! Asa, get yourself over an' speak up to Missus Cobb. She's already got a hankerin' for moggys an' she'll give you somethin' for this fine fellow."

The boy disappeared. Thragun decided to take a chance. Moving warily, with an eye continually on the man, he jumped out of the basket, still facing the small man.

"Yis—" that almost was a hiss again. "You ain't no common moggy." His eyebrows drew together in a frown. "I thinks as 'ow th' Cap'n, he mustta thought as 'ow you was right for Miss Emmy—she likin' beasties so well. An' th' Cap'n sure ain't goin' to take it calm if you go a-missin'—

Standing up, the man rubbed his bristly chin.

"Trouble is, that ole she-devil up to th' house, she's doin' all th' talkin' these days. We don't get to see our Lady a-tall—jus' tell us, they do—that fine gentlemun o' a doctor, an' Mr. Crisp, th' agent—that our lady can't be bothered by anythin' now she is so bad took.

An' Miss Emmy, she ain't got no chance t' say nothin'. Th' Cap'n so far away an' nobody knows when he's coming back again. It ain't got a good smell 'bout all this, that it ain't. So," he leaned back against the wall of a stall, a proud horse head raised over his shoulder to regard Thragun also.

"Soo—" the man repeated, one hand raised to scratch between the large bright eyes of the horse, "we has us a thin' as needs thinkin' on. Now was you," Thragun congratulated himself that he had indeed found a very sensible man here, "to get out of that there basket an' disappear. How are you goin' to be found—with these 'ere stables as full of holes and 'idey places as a bit o' cheese. An' out there—" he waved one hand toward the open door, "there's a garden an' beyond that, woods—Our lady, she don't allow no huntin' an' them two what wants to answer for her—they ain't changed that—yet. So supposin', Rog, 'e comes along for t' see you an' he finds that there basket busted open an' you gone—might be 'e'd jus' put somethin' in his pocket and say as how 'e did as 'e was told—"

"Now," the man raised his voice and caught up a broom. He aimed a blow at Thragun—well off target and yelled, "Get you out, you mangy critter, we don't want th' likes of you a hanging 'round, no ways we don't."

Thragun leaped effortlessly to the top of a stall partition, but he made no effort to go farther for a moment. Then he walked leisurely along that narrow path to a place from which he could jump again, this time to a cross beam. At the same moment Asa returned, a small bundle in his hand.

"Ralf, what you be about—"

The man rounded on him. "Me? I 'as been a-chasin' a beast what 'as no place 'ere. An' don't you forget that, lad."

Asa laughed, and then darted into the stall where Thragun had made himself comfortable. Flipping open the handkerchief, Asa turned out a chunk of grayish meat, still dripping from the boiling pan, and a wedge of cheese. He hacked the meat into several large chunks with a knife he took from his pocket and crumbled the cheese, leaving the bounty spread out on the napkin well within reach of Thragun. The cat was already licking the meat inquiringly when Asa returned with a cracked cup in which there was water.

"Couldn' get milk," he said as he set the cup down. "Missus Cobb, she's mad as a cow wot's lost 'er calf. Old Pickle-Face is a-giving orders again. No tea for Miss Emmy 'cause she's been a-askin' for th' cat. When Pickle-Face tol' her that the cat was gone for good, she stiffed up an' hit the old besom, then said as how her pa would 'ave th' law on Pickle-Face for gettin' rid o' th' cat. She would not ask pardon, so she's not to 'ave no vittles except dry bread and water 'til she gets down on her two knees an' asks for it."

"I'll be a-thinkin' that little Miss is na going to have so 'ard of it," Ralf said. Thragun snarled. He had somehow got another whiff of that evil smell. Though the words these two stable slaves used to each other were totally foreign, he could pick out thoughts like little flashes of pictures. Not all the temple and palace four-footed guards could do that. But to Thragun it had become increasingly easy over the years.

Asa kicked at a handful of bedding straw and reached for the broom.

"Meggy, she says as how she 'as heard *him* two nights now—"

Ralf stopped, his hand on the latch of the stall, but not yet opening it. His face was suddenly blank. There was a long moment of silence before he spoke.

Thragun raised his head from tearing at a lump of meat. Back in the dusky stall his eyes shone, not blue, but faintly reddish.

"Missus Cobb, she put out a milk bowl last night," Asa continued, his eyes on the floor he was mechanically sweeping.

"Sooo—" Ralf swung the latch of the stall up. "She's one as can sometimes see moren' most. M' granny was like that."

"There's them what says as he ain't 'ere nor never was."

"Look to th' name o' this place, boy. 'Twas *his* they say before any folks came 'ere. They also say as how he brings luck or fetches it away. Lord Jeffery, him as was master 'ere in m' granny's time, he got on th' wrong side o' *him* an' never took no good of life after that. Died young o' a broken neck when his mare stepped in a rabbit 'ole. But his lady, she was from right believin' folks an' they say as how she came down by candlelight an' went to his own stone wi' a plate of sugar cakes an' a cup o' true cream. Begged pardon, she did. After that, all what 'ad been goin' wrong became right again."

"That were a long time ago," said Asa.

"Some things there is, boy, wot'll never change. You get a rightful part o' th' land an' do your duty to it an' them what knew it before you, will do right by you. But if *he* was to come, aye, it would be o' a time like'n this."

He led the horse into the stable yard and Asa fell to cleaning out the stall. Thragun swallowed the last of the food. Not that it was what should be served to Thragun Neklop, but these two had done their best. He washed his whiskers and prepared to explore the stable.

There was a good deal to be examined, sniffed, and stored in memory. Asa and Ralf were in and out on various tasks for the comfort of three horses.

It was very late afternoon before a man came in, Asa with him. He was grinning, wiping his hands on his stained and patched breeches. Thragun's lip curled, but he made no noise. This was evil again—though not as cold and deadly as that he had met when he had confronted that black Khon in the house.

The basket in which he had arrived still sat there, but Asa had dealt with it earlier. There was a break in the bamboo frame door leaving jagged ends pointing outward. Thragun was critical of the work. If he had done that, he would have made a neater job of it.

"Us came back," Asa was saying, "an' there it was. Th' beast. He made his own way out."

The other young man spat. "Think you'd better 'ave a better story when th' Missus asks."

Asa shrugged. "We ain't been hired, me an' Ralf, to take care o' anythin' 'cept th' horses. An' Ralf, 'e ain't really got anythin' to watch except Black Knight. She can't come a-botherin' at us nohow. Why tell 'er? Th' beast's gone, ain't it?"

"An' what if he comes back?" demanded the other.

"Then you gets 'im, don't you? Ain't I seen you throw that there sticker o' yours quicker than Ned Parzon can shoot?"

"Maybe so." The other kicked the basket, sending it against the wall. "You keep your own mouth shut, do you 'ear?"

"I 'ear, Rog, you a-makin' noise enough to fright m' horses." Ralf strode in. "You ain't got no right in 'ere an' you knows it. Now get!"

The younger man scowled and tramped out of the stable. Asa and Ralf stood looking after him.

"That's another who don't 'ave no place 'ere. Were th' Lady herself, she'd see that in a flick o' a horses's tail an' 'ave 'im out on th' road with a flea in his ear, she would. Asa," he looked straight at the boy, "I ain't a-likin' what's goin' on over there—" he nodded toward the house. "She an' that lardy doctor 'ave been puttin' heads together again. Jennie says as how she was tellin' the doctor something about Miss Emmy being hard to manage 'cause she ain't thinkin' straight. They don't know as Jennie was in the little room off th' hall when they was talkin' together. Little Miss—that ain't no one as would take her part was they tryin' to get 'er shut up or something. The old crow, she's always smarmy and soft tongued when any of the Lady's friends come askin'. Oh," he raised his voice into high squeaking note, "Lady Ashely, she's no better, poor dear. I fear we won't see her long. Miss Emmy, oh, th' little dear is so sad feelin'. She is too sad for a child. We cannot get her comforted. Now that there I 'eard when Mrs. Bateman came a-calling. Told Mrs. Bateman as how Miss Emmy couldn't go to no picnic 'cause she was so worried about her aunt. Miss Emmy was up in 'er room where Pickle-Face had sent her to be ashamed of herself because she tried to slip in an' see her aunt that very morning."

"Seems as if someone should know," Asa said.

"Who? Supposin' even Missus Cobb were to get herself over to th' Bateman place an' try to tell them—what 'as she really got to tell? An' Pickle-Face would say as how she is a-lyin'—make it stick, too. There ain't any way as I can see that we can help."

"Ain't right!" exploded Asa.

"Boy, there's a good lot what ain't right in this 'ere world an' not much as can be done to clean it up neither. Come on, we've got to see to that tack."

Thragun's well cultivated guard sense might have been confused by the strange language that these slaves used, but he thought he could fit part of it all together. The little princess to whom *HIS* princess had sent him on his honorable task of protection was under threat from that Khon of full evil. She was now a prisoner somewhere in the house. With a knowledgeable eye he measured the shadows in the stable yard. There was a time of dark fast on its way and dark aided both the evildoer and the guard. His kind, for many lives, had patroled palaces, searched gardens, and knew their own ways of taking care. This was a new place and he knew very little about it. The time was ready not only for him to learn, but to be about what was perhaps more important, defending his new princess. Thragun's jaws opened upon a soundless snarl and his curved and very sharp claws came momentarily out of the fur screening on his toes.

Emmy huddled behind the curtain, both hands pressed against the small panes of the window as she looked down to the terrace. Rog went clumping by, and she scrunched herself into as small a space as possible. Of course, he was not looking in this direction, and, anyway, he was well below her, but she always felt afraid of Rog. Twice he had come out suddenly from dark places in the garden and stood grinning and laughing at her. Also Miss Wyker liked him. He did errands for her. Emmy had seen him take notes and go out the other way—not passing where anyone could see him unless that one was specially watching. He padded heavy-footed along now, and it was near dark. Maybe he was just going back to the hut where he lived—a nasty, evil-smelling place. But the worst of it was those nails hammered into the wall on which hung little bodies, some furred and some feathered—birds and a weasel, and—Emmy rubbed both her wet eyes with her hands.

Her eyes hurt because she had been crying. She tried to see even the edge of the drive to the stable. What had happened out there to Thragun Neklop? Somehow now she thought all a lie, he must be somewhere. She had her own plan, but it might be hours and hours yet before it would be dark enough for her to put it to the test. With her tear-sticky hands she tried again with all her strength to push out one side of the divided panes of the window. Tendrils of ivy waved in the breeze back and forth, but there was no wind enough to make a difference, Emmy thought. This was an idea she had had for some time and she now had a very good reason to try it.

A door away down the hall Jennie tapped, her other hand supporting a tray with a porringer on it. The nutmeg smell was faint, but she could smell it even though the lid was on the small silver bowl to keep its contents warm. Cook had made this special—a smooth, light custard that she said even a newborn babe could take without any hurt. Jennie gave a slight start and looked back over her shoulder. Old houses had many strange noises in the night. But this evening—she drew a deep breath. *HIM*—that patter sound all the way up the stairs behind her—like to scare her into falling or take her death from it. She knocked again and with more force.

The door opened so suddenly that she might have skidded right in had she not caught herself.

"What do you mean? All this clamor when she is asleep! You stupid, clumsy girl!" Miss Wyker's voice was like the hiss of a snake and Jennie cringed. Somehow she got the tray and the porringer between them.

"Please, Cook did think as 'ow the poor lady might find this tasty. She used to be quite fond of it—jus' good milk, and eggs from the brown hen, the best and biggest ever—"

With a snap Miss Wyker had the tray out of her hands and was thrusting before her as if to push Jennie out of the room.

"Cook is impertinent," Miss Wyker scowled, enough, as Jennie said later, to make the flesh fair creep on your bones. "Lady Ashely's food must be carefully selected to match the diet Dr. Riggs has planned. Get back to the kitchen and don't let me see you above the back stairs again or it will be the worse for you." Jennie had backed well into the hall. Now the door was slammed and she quite clearly heard the sound of a key turning in the lock.

For a moment she just stood there and then she gave a quick turn of the head—facing down the hall. Her own face puckered and she put the knuckles of one hand up to cover her mouth as she turned and ran—ran as far and as fast as she could, to get away from that thin high shriek which seemed somehow to echo in her head more than in her ears.

Him! With *him* loose what could a body expect but trouble? Bad trouble. She'd give notice, that she would! There was no one who was going to make her stay here. Her heavy shoes clattered on the uncarpeted backstairs as she sought the kitchen three stories below.

Emmy got to her feet. She had been down on her knees trying to see through the keyhole. These past weeks she had used every method she could to learn things. How long had it been since she had actually seen Great-Aunt

Amelie? Three—maybe four weeks, and then she had only gotten a short peek at her through the door before Miss Wyker had come up and pulled her away, her fingers pinching Emmy sharply to propel the girl toward her bedroom where she had also been locked in. That was another night Emmy might not have had any supper, but Jennie had crept up after dark to bring her some of Cook's sugary rolls and a small plum tart. Emmy had discovered some nights ago that, whether she was being openly punished or not, she was always locked in at night. That was when she first began to explore outside the window. She had awakened from a very queer dream.

Emmy had never remembered any other dream so well. This one was different. It made her go all shivery, and yet not so fearful that she was afraid to try what she had done in her dream. Of course, then there had been someone with her—though she never really saw who it was—just knew that the unseen had watched her with approval and that had made her feel better.

Now she stood in the middle of the room and unfastened the buttons of her dress, shrugging it off, so that its full skirt lay in a circle around her. Next came her two petticoats. Gathering up all these, she threw them in an untidy bundle on the bed. Then, stopping to think, she gathered them up to roll into a thick armload which she shoved under the covers, pulling the pillow around so it just might look like a sleeper spent from crying.

Emmy herself was through crying. She went to the bottom drawer of the bureau and opened it. There was her mother's beautiful shawl which she brought home from India when she had come with Emmy to Great-Aunt Amelie's. There were other things mother brought, too, and Emmy jerked out a package from the very bottom, struggling to pull it open. Then she was looking at what had belonged to her brother she had never seen—to remember. He had died in India, that was why mother brought her here as the bad seasons did make so many die.

For only a moment she hesitated. Mother had kept this suit as one of her treasures. What would she think of Emmy wearing it? No, she would understand! It was important, Emmy did not know how she was sure of that, no one had told her—unless it was the person in her dream whom she had never seen.

She pulled on the trousers, and pushed her chemise into the top of them. They were a little too big and she had to tie them on with a hair ribbon.

So readied, she returned to the window. It was dark enough now, of that she was sure. She climbed on the sill and slipped through, her feet finding the ledge which ran along the wall just below the windows.

Taking the best grip she could on the ivy, Emmy began to edge along that narrow footway.

Thragun slipped like a shadow from one bit of cover to the next. There were lights in some windows and now and then he heard voices. The slaves were gathered in the largest room along the wall. He heard their coarse, rough voices. But he was more intent upon the fact that the walls before him appeared to be covered with a growth of vines. Of course, they were not the thick, properly stemmed ones which provided such excellent highways in the palace and temple gardens. However, he would test just what good footholds they had to offer. There were strange smells in plenty, but he was not to be turned away from his firm purpose now.

Cook stood with both red hands planted firm upon the much scrubbed table, looking across the board at Jennie. Her face was as red as her hands and she made it quite plain just what she was thinking.

"M' lady eatin' only what that puffed pigeon of a doctor tells 'er, is that it? I say it loud and clear, that wry-faced Madam who thinks to cut 'erself a snug place 'ere is goin' to find out that she ain't the mistress. No she ain't!"

"An' just 'ow, Missus, is you goin' to get 'er to listen to you?" Ralf emptied his beer mug and thudded it down on the table.

For a long moment there was no answer. Suddenly Mrs. Cobb straightened up, her weight making her look someone to be taken seriously. She reached out her hand and drew closer a basin of thick brown crockery. Then she turned, without answering the question, and hefted a jug of the same heavy earthenware. From that she poured a stream of milk into the bowl. The milk was so rich and thick one could almost see flakes of butter swimming in it, striving to be free.

The bowl she filled carefully within an inch of the top, then she put down the jug, and, from under the vast sweep of her apron, she brought out a bunch of jingling keys.

Ralfs eyebrows slid up. "Th' keys? 'Ow ever did that Madam let them get outta 'er hands, now?"

Cook's lips curled, but in a sneer not a smile. "Oh, she got our lady's bunch to rattle a little song with, may that which waits at water get 'er for that! But m'lady, she saw long ago as 'ow it was not handy for me to go runnin' to ask for this store and that when I was a-cookin'. Nor was she ever one as begrudged me what I 'ad to 'ave. So I've had m' own keys these five years now."

"An' what are you goin' to do with that?" Ralf pointed to the bowl.

"Ralf Sommers, you ain't as big of a ninny that you 'as to ask that now, are you? This 'ere," she looked around her, "be Hob's Green. An' it didn't get that name for nothin'."

Ralf frowned. *"HIM?* You is goin' to deal with *him*?"

Mrs. Cobb looked down at the bowl as if for a moment uncertain, and then, her mouth firmed, her chin squared. "I be a-doin' nothin' that ain't been done before under this 'ere roof and on this land!"

She walked past Ralf out of the kitchen and down the passage which led to those very dark descending stairs to the vast network of cellars which no one, even in the daytime, willingly visited. Or if one must go, it would be hurried, lantern in hand and looking all whichways as one did it.

At the top of the stairs there was another door in the wall, opening into the kitchen garden, though no one now used that. Mrs. Cobb placed the bowl carefully on the floor. Selecting a key, she forced it into the doorlock and shoved it open a hand's breadth.

She drew back. The way was dark, so much so that she could hardly see the bowl. She cleared her throat and then she recited, as one who draws every word out of some deep closet of memory:

"Hob's Hole—Hob's own.
From th' roasting to th' bone.
Them as sees, shall not look.
Thems is blind, they'll be shook.
Sweep it up an' sweep it down—
Hob shall clear it all around.
So mote this be."

Mrs. Cobb turned with surprising speed for such a heavy woman and swept with a whirl of her wide skirts down the passage until she could bang the kitchen door behind her.

Thragun stayed where he was crouched, watching through the slit of the door she had opened. He sniffed delicately. That which was in the bowl attracted him. Squeezing through the narrow door opening, the cat looked up and down the narrow stone paved way. He sniffed in each direction and listened. Now he was inside the house again and no one had seen him. He smelled the contents of the bowl, ventured a lap or two, and then settled down to drink his fill.

He jumped, squalled, and turned all in almost one movement. The painful thud on his haunch was not to be forgiven. Thragun crouched, reading himself for a spring.

Crouching almost as low, and certainly as angrily as he himself was, a gray-brown creature humped right inside the door. Thragun snarled, and then growled. In spite of the heavy gloom of the passage his night sight was clear enough to show him exactly what had so impudently attacked him by driving a pointed foot into his back.

Thragun growled again. His right front paw moved lightning quick to pay for that blow with rakeing claws. But the paw passed through the creature's arm and shoulder. Its body certainly looked thick and real enough but what he struck at might only be a shadow.

He straightened up. Thewada! So this new place had such shadow walkers and mischief makers as he had been warned about since kittenhood—though he had certainly never seen one himself before.

"A-stealin' of Hob's own bowl, be ye?" The creature straightened up also. It looked like a man but it was very small, hardly taller than Thragun. Its body was fat and round, but the legs and arms were nearly stick thin, and it was covered completely with gray-brown wrappings. Only a wizened face, with ugly squarish mouth and small green eyes like pinheads on either side of a long sharp pointed nose (like the beak of some rapacious bird) were uncovered. However, the skin was so dark it might have been part of that tight clothing.

"This be Hob's place!" The words bit at Thragun. "Forget that, you night walker, and Hob'll see you into a toad, so he will!" He stamped one long thin foot on the floor, followed by the other in an angry dance. Now he pointed his two forefingers at the cat and began to mouth strange words which Thragun could not understand.

Thewada could be mischievous and irritating, Thragun had heard, but for the most part they were lacking in power to do any serious harm. He yawned to show that he was not in the least impressed by the other's show of temper.

"I be Hob!" the dancer screeched. "This be my place, this!" Once more he was stamping hard enough to set his body bouncing.

"I am Thragun Neklop—guard of the princess," returned Thragun with quiet dignity. "You are a thewada and you have no place near the princess—"

Hob's face was no longer brown-gray like his clothes, rather it had turned a dusky color, and if he tried to mouth words they were swallowed up by a voice which wanted more to screech.

"The bowl is yours," Thragun continued. "I ask pardon for sampling it. It is a good drink," he continued as if they were on the best of polite terms. "What is it called?"

His attitude seemed to bewilder Hob. The creature halted his jumping dance and thrust his head forward as if to aid his small eyes in examining this furred one who was not afraid of him as all proper inhabitants of this house should be.

"It be cream—cream for Hob!" He shuffled a little to one side so he was now between Thragun and the bowl. "Cream they gives when they calls. An' truly it is time for Hob to come—there be black evil in this house!"

Thragun stood up, his lash of a tail moved from side to side and his ears flattened a little.

"Thewada, you are speaking true. Evil have I smelled, ever since I have come into this place. And I—I am the guard for the princess. What do you know of this evil and where does it lie?"

Hob had grabbed up the bowl in his two hands and thrown back his head so far on his shoulders that it seemed to be like to roll off. He opened a mouth which seemed as wide as half his face and was pouring the cream steadily into that opening.

"Where," asked the cat again, impatient, "is that evil? I must see it does not come near to the little one I have been sent to guard."

Hob swallowed for the last time, smeared the back of his hand across his mouth and smacked his thin lips. Then he pointed to the ceiling over their heads.

"Aloft now, so it be. She has a black heart, she has, and a heavy hand, that one. What she wants," his scowl began growing heavier as he spoke, "is Hob's house. An' sore will that one be if she gets it! I say that, and I be Hob, Hob!" Once more he stamped on the stone.

"If this place is yours, why do you let that one take it?" Thragun asked. He was staring up at the ceiling, busy thinking how he might get out of here and up aloft as the thewada said it.

"She works black evil," Hob said slowly. "But the law is with her—"

"What is law?" asked Thragun in return. "It is the will of the king. Is he one to share this evil?"

Hob shook his head. "Mighty queer have you got it in your head. The law is of us who have the old magic. Only it will do no harm to that one because she does not believe. There are them who lived here long ago and now walk the halls and strive to set fear in her. But until she believes we can no' drive her out. 'Tis the law—"

"It is not my law—I have only one duty and that is to guard. And guard I will!" Without another look at Hob, Thragun went into action, flashing away down the hall.

Emmy's fingers were pinched and scraped from the holds she kept on the ivy, and she dared not look down, nor back, only to the wall before her as she crept foot width by foot width along the ledge.

She shrank against the wall and hardly dared draw a breath. There was a sound from the next window. The casements banged back against the wall. Then she heard Miss Wyker's voice:

"Miss Emmy, my lady? Alas, I fear that you must be sadly disappointed in her. She is impudent and unfeeling. Why, she has never asked to see you nor how you did."

Emmy began to feel hot in spite of the very cool breeze which rustled the vines around her. Miss Wyker was telling lies about her to Great-Aunt!

"Now, my lady, do you rest a bit and I shall be back presently with the night draught Dr. Riggs has prescribed."

There came an answer, so weak and thin, Emmy could hardly hear it.

"Not tonight, Miss Wyker. I always wake so weak and with an aching head. I felt much better before I began to take that—"

"Now, now, m'lady. The doctor knows best what to give you. You'll be yourself again shortly. I shall be back as soon as I can."

There came the sound of a door closing and Emmy moved, daring to edge faster. Then she was at the open casement to claw and pull her way into the room. There were two candles burning in a small table near the door, but the rest of the room was very gloomy.

"Who—who is there?" Great-Aunt's voice, sounding thin and shivery, came out of all the shadows around the big curtained bed.

"Please," Emmy crossed the end of the room to pick up one of the candles. Going closer to the bed she held it out so she could see Great-Aunt resting back on some pillows, all her pretty white hair hidden away under a night cap, so just thin white face was showing.

The anger which had brought Emmy so swiftly into the room broke free now. "Please, Miss Wyker told you a lie. I did want to see you and I asked and asked, but she said you did not want to be disturbed—that I was too noisy and careless. But it was a lie!"

"Emmy, child, I have wanted to see you, too. Very much. But how did you get here? Surely you did not come through the window."

"I had to," Emmy confessed. "She locked me in my room. And she locks your door, too. See," she crossed the room and tried to open the hall door, but, as she expected, she could not. Turning back to the bed, her eyes caught sight of the tray Jennie had brought with Cook's custard on it.

"Didn't you want this?" She took the tray in one hand and the candle in the other. "Cook made it special—out of the best cream and eggs. She said you always liked it when you were not feeling well before."

"Custard? But, of course, I like Cook's custard. Let me have it, Emmy. Then you sit down and tell me about all this locking of doors and my not wanting to see you."

Lady Ashely ate the custard hungrily, while Emmy's words came pouring out about all the things that had been happening in Hob's Green which she could not understand, ending with the story of how Thragun Neklop had come that very day and how Miss Wyker had acted.

"And father sent him to me—he is a gift from a princess, a real princess. Jennie took him away and I don't know what has happened to him!!" One tear and then another cut into the dust of the vines which had settled on Emmy's round face.

"Emmy, child, can you help me with these pillows, I want to sit up—"

Emmy hurried to pull the pillows together and make a back rest for Great-Aunt.

"Emmy, has Mr. Adkins been here lately?" Emmy was disappointed that Lady Ashely had not mentioned Thragun, but she answered quickly:

"He has come three times. But always Miss Wyker said you were asleep, or it was a day you were feeling poorly, and he went away again." Mr. Adkins was the vicar and Emmy was somewhat shy of him, he was so tall, and he did not smile very much.

"So." Great-Aunt's voice sounded a lot stronger. Emmy, without being told, took the empty bowl on its tray and set it on the chest under the window. "I do not understand, but we must begin to learn—"

"But," Emmy dared to interrupt, "what about Thragun? Jennie said Rog took Cook's kitty away and it never came back."

"Yes, we shall most certainly find out about Thragun and a great many other things, Emmy. Go to my desk over there and find my letter case and pen and ink—bring them here."

However, when Lady Ashely tried to write, her hand trembled and shook and she had to go very slowly. Once she looked up at Emmy and said:

"Child, see that brown bottle over on the mantelpiece? I want you to take that and hide it—perhaps in the big bandbox in the cupboard at the back."

It was when Emmy was returning from that errand that they heard the key turn in the lock. Lady Ashely forced her hand to hold steady for two more words. Then she folded it and wrote Mr. Adkins' name on the fold. Without being told, Emmy seized the letter case with its paper and two pens, one now dribbling ink across the edge of a pillow, and thrust it under the bed, stoppering the small inkwell and sending it after it. Lady Ashely pushed the note toward Emmy and the girl snatched it to tuck into the front of the dusty and torn breeches.

The door opened and Miss Wyker stood there, a lighted candle in her hand. She held that high so that the light reached the bed.

"M'lady," she hissed, "what have you been about? What—"

The light now caught Emmy, and Miss Wyker stopped short. Her face was very white and her eyes were hard and glittered.

"You cruel child! What are you doing here! Shameful, shameful!" Her voice rasped as she put down the candle to bear down on Emmy. She caught one straggling lock of the child's hair and jerked her toward the door. "Be sure you will suffer for this!"

"I think not, Miss Wyker." Lady Ashely did not speak very loudly, but somehow the words cut through. Miss Wyker, in the process of dragging Emmy to the door, looked around, but her expression did not change.

"M'lady, you are taken ill again. This cruel child has upset you. Be sure she will be punished for it—"

"And if I say no?"

"But, m'lady, all know that you are very ill and that you sometimes wander in your wits. Dr. Riggs himself has commented upon how mazed you are at times. You will take his medicine and go peacefully to sleep, and when you wake this will all be a dream. Yes, m'lady, you will be very well looked after, I assure you."

Emmy tried to hold onto a bedpost and then to the back of a chair, but pain from the tugging at her hair made her let go. Great-Aunt was looking at Miss Wyker as if some horrid monster were there. She pressed her fingers to her mouth and Emmy could see that she was frightened, really frightened.

The door to the bedroom was thrown open with a crash and Emmy jerked out into the hall.

"You," Miss Wyker shook her, transferring her hold on Emmy's hair, to bury her fingers in the flesh on the child's shoulders, shaking her back and forth, until Emmy went limp and helpless in her hands. "Down in the cellar for you, my girl. The beetles and rats will give you something else to think about! Come!" Now her fingers sank into the nape of Emmy's neck and she was urged forward at a running pace.

They reached the top of the narrow back staircase the servants used. Up that shot a streak of dark and light fur. It flashed past Emmy. Miss Wyker let go of the child and tried vainly to pull loose from what seemed to be a clutch on her back skirts. Unable to free herself, she tried to turn farther to see what held her so. Something small and dark crouched there.

Then came a battle scream, answered by a cry of fear from Miss Wyker. Now her hands beat the air, trying to reach the demon who clung with punishing claws to her back. She screamed in terror and torment as a paw reached around from behind her head and used claws on a white face which speedily spouted red. Miss Wyker wheeled again, fighting to get her hands on the cat. Then she tottered as that shadow hunched before her now at her feet struck out in turn. The woman plunged side wise with a last cry. Thragun flew through the air in the opposite direction, landing on the hall floor not far from Emmy who had crowded back against the wall, unable even to make the smallest sound.

The cat padded toward her, uttering small cries as if he were talking. That candle which had fallen from Miss Wyker's hand rolled, still alight, down to the stair landing below. Miss Wyker lay there very still. But there was something else, too, something dancing by the side of her body and uttering a high thin whistling sound. Only for a minute had Emmy seen that and then it was gone. Thragun was rubbing back and forth against her legs, purring loudly. Emmy stooped and caught him tight. Though this was hardly a dignified thank you, Noble Warrior allowed it. After all, was he not a guard and one who had done his duty nobly and well, even if a skirt-jerking thewada had had something to do with it? *HIS* princess was safe and that was what counted.

HOB'S POT
Catfantastic II (1991) DAW

In the old days before Papa came home, no one used the big drawing room since Great-Aunt Amelie had stopped entertaining, saying she was too old for company. However, this afternoon it had been turned into a treasure cave and Emmy, sitting on a footstool beside Great-Aunt Amelie's chair, looked around very wide-eyed. There was a picture in one of the books Miss Lansdall had brought when she had come to be Emmy's new governess which looked a little like this wealth of color and strange objects, some amusing and some simply beautiful, like the pendant Great-Aunt Amelie was now holding. There had been a boy called Aladdin who had found such treasure as this that Papa's Hindu servant and both of the footmen were busy unpacking from wicker baskets which looked more like chests, pulling back layers of oiled cloth which had kept the sea air out, before taking carefully from the depths one marvel after another.

"Rrrrrowwww!" A cream and brown shape slipped between two of the chests and stopped to try claws on the invitingly rough side of one.

"Feel right at home, Noble Warrior, is that it?" Papa was laughing. "Well, it is true you've seen some of this before. Does this suit your fancy, perhaps?" Papa picked up from a tabletop a shiny green carved figure. It might have the body of a man wearing a long robe of ceremony but the head was that of a rat!

"Your birth year, Thragun Neklop." Papa laughed again, catching sight of Emmy's bewildered face. "It is true, Emmy. Our Noble Warrior was born in the Year of The Rat. And he will have a very notable series of adventures, too.

"Ali San read the sand table for him and the Princess Suphoron before he left the palace. It's all written out somewhere in my day book, I'll find it for you. The princess wanted to be sure that Thragun was indeed the proper guard for *MY* princess. And here, my dear, is your robe, so you will look as if you belong in a palace."

He reached over Lasha's shoulder and picked out of the trunk a bundle of something which was both blue and green, like the gemmed feathers of Great-Aunt Amelie's pendant. There were scrolls of silver up and down, and when Papa shook it out to show Emmy that it was a coat, she also could see that the silver lines made pictures of flowers and birds and—yes, there was a cat!

"Ohhhhh!" Papa put it around her shoulders and she was smoothing it. Never in her life had she seen anything so wonderful.

"A little big, but you'll grow into it—" Papa did not have a chance to say anything else, for there came a loud snarl and then a series of deep-throated growls from floor level.

Thragun Neklop had left off his scratching to swing around and face a much smaller container of wood very sturdily fastened by a number of loops of rough rope. Slow, stiff-legged, he approached the box until his nose just did not quite touch its side, and there, with flattened ears, he crouched. One paw flashed out in a lightning-stiff strike and the extended claws caught in the rope, jerking the box so it fell toward the cat.

With another yowl he leaped up and away before crouching again, eyes slitted and a war cry rumbling in his throat.

"Here, now," Captain Wexley said, "did you find your rat after all and is he in there?" He reached down and picked up the chest, standing it on the table.

At first, to Emmy, it looked just like any other box, but with Thragun Neklop snarling that way she began to feel more and more uneasy.

Papa was examining it closely. He looked puzzled.

"That's odd. I don't remember this."

"Captain Sahib," Lasha said, "that was of the sending by the rajah. It came just before we sailed and must have been stowed before you could examine it."

"The rajah—" Papa stood very still looking at it. "But he would have no wish to send me a gift, unless," he was smiling again, "he wished to celebrate my leaving. We were always far less than friends. All right, let's see what he thought was due me."

Lasha arose easily from his kneeling position. In his hand he held the knife which usually rode in his sash. "Captain Sahib, the warrior cat warns, let it be my hands that deal with this." He moved swiftly to slash at the rope.

"Some trick, you think?" Papa looked very sober now. "Wait!"

The rope had fallen halfway off the box, but it was still tightly shut. Papa caught it up to carry it into the middle of the room, away from the group by the fire. Thragun Neklop sprang after him, and both the footmen and Lasha drew nearer. Emmy bit her lip. Her splendid new coat slipped from her shoulders as she clasped her hands tightly together. There was something—something very wrong now.

Lasha knelt and forced his knife blade into the crack outlining the lid and then very slowly he eased it up. Thragon Neklop, ears back, sleek tail bushed, watched the action unblinkingly.

Once the lid was off, there was an outward puffing of thick grayish fibers. Lasha stirred with the point of his knife.

"Cotton, Captain Sahib." He went on pulling out the stuff carefully until there showed a colored bundle. It was dark red and it also had a great many cords around it which crossed and crisscrossed like a spider's web. Once more Lasha used his knife on the roundish package. The cords fell away and so did the wrapping.

"A teapot!" Papa laughed. "Nothing but a teapot!"

Thragun Neklop snarled. This was his palace; he was the guard. Such a thing as this had no right here. He could smell vile evil—a Khon, truly a Khon. Evil and with power. It had been asleep—now it was waking.

With a yowl Thragun leaped for the top of the table, ready to send this monstrosity crashing on the floor. Then he stopped, so suddenly that he skidded and his claws tangled in the brocade of the tablecloth so that he nearly lost his balance. Captain Wexley had picked up the-thing-which-was-eye-hidden, and still laughing, held it closer so Emmy and Great-Aunt Amelie could see it better.

A teapot it was, but not like any Emmy had ever thought could exist. At first it seemed to be a monkey such as Papa had drawn a picture of in one of his letters. Then she saw the lid and she jerked back on her seat, her hand going out for a safe hold on a fold of Great-Aunt Amelie's shawl.

For the nasty face of the thing was twisted up as if it were laughing also, but a mean, sly laugh. Two knobby arms were held out, coming together at their wrists to form a double spout which ended in a fringe of bright red claws.

It had red eyes as well as claws, but the rest of it was a dull yellow color like mud. As it squatted between the Captain's hands, Emmy felt it was looking straight at her. But it was Aunt Amelie who protested.

"Richard—that is a nasty thing. Who would ever give cupboard room to such? Certainly no one would USE it!"

The Captain was examining it closely. He caught at the top of the creature's head and lifted it, peering into the body of the pot.

"Nasty perhaps, Aunt Amelie, but it is a treasure of sorts. It is carved of yellow jade—an unusually large piece, I must say, and these," he placed the head back in position and now tapped one of the eyes, "are, unless I am very much mistaken, rubies, the claws are set with the same. It is worth a great deal—" He was frowning again.

"Why would the rajah give such to me?" he said after a pause.

Lasha spoke in a language Thragun could understand if the rest did not. "For no purpose of good, Sahib."

"Precious stones or not," Great-Aunt Amelie sat up straighter in her chair, "I would say that did *not* belong in any Christian home, Richard." Suddenly she shivered and drew her shawl closer about her. "Gift or no, I would get rid of it if I were you."

The Captain gathered up the red cloth which had been wrapped around it. "Very well. When I go to London next Friday, I shall take it. Hubbard has a liking for curiosities and certainly this is curious enough to suit him. I'll pass it to him with my blessing and agreement that he can put it to auction if he thinks best."

He passed the enshrouded teapot to Lasha who put it back into the box, though the cords which had kept it so well fastened were now past use. But he pushed the raw cotton back and hammered the top into place with the hilt of his knife.

Though Papa had other things which might have enchanted Emmy earlier, she kept glancing at the box. Something had spoiled all the fun of unpacking. And Thragun had taken up a post right beside that box as if he were on guard.

He yowled when Hastings, the footman, came to pick it up after they had seen each of the basket chests emptied, his tail moving in a sharp sweep.

"This, sir," Hastings stepped back prudently, one eye on the cat as if he expected to be the goal of any attack, "where does it go?"

"Oh, in the library, I guess. On the side table there for now."

Thragun followed the footman, saw the box put on the table. As soon as the man left the room, he jumped on the bench and leaned forward for a long sniff. His lips curled back in disgust. Khon right enough, though there was a touch of something else. He sat back to think, his tail curled over his paws. There was just a trace of scent left, but one he had smelled before. Once in the time of rains, when the Princess Suphoron had been ill, they had brought to her an old woman who had burned leaves in a brazier by the princess' bed and fanned the smoke across her so that the princess had breathed it in. She had had a violent fit of sneezing which had pleased the old woman who said then that the princess had so expelled the Khon who had entered into her when she had visited an old shrine. For the lesser Khons were sometimes spirit servants of some god or goddess and lingered on in deserted temples long after those they served had departed.

The very faint smell was indeed that of the smoke which had been raised to banish that Khon. Yet it certainly had not banished that which still was snuggly housed within the teapot. Perhaps the smoke had been used to keep the thing in the pot under control until it was completely uncovered.

Thragun snarled and spat at the box. He did not know if the Khon was free to do anything now, he was simply very sure that, as a guardian for Emmy, he must keep alert.

Thragun hunkered down, his legs drawn under him. It was cold here. There had been a fire earlier, but that had been allowed to go out. Though the window draperies were not closed, twilight outside made the room thick with gloom. He could see fairly well. Certainly the box was not opening again by any power of the thing within it, nor could his keen ears pick up any sound. The Captain would take this away—he had said so. Only not at once and Thragun rumbled another small growl at that thought. No good lay ahead for any of them, he was as sure of that as he was that he had a tail to switch in irritation.

However, just to sit and wait upon the pleasure of any Khon was not the way of a Noble Warrior. Thragun never had had a great deal of patience. He preferred things to move into action as soon as possible. They had once before in this house—

Thragun's blue eyes became slits as he remembered the time when Emmy herself had been in a danger, which he had sensed quickly but others apparently had not known. Then Cook had taken a hand in the game—

Cook, and someone else who had a jealous need to keep this house peaceful.

A Khon was a Khon he knew. In his own land there would have been ways of forcing the creature out of cover. Thragun's paws reached out and he pushed the box a little. Somewhat to his surprise, it actually did move a fraction. He snatched that paw back with a yowl of rage. The thing had dared to burn him!

The cat arose and walked slowly around the box, keeping his distance but with his head out as he drew deep sniffs in spite of the disgust that the foulness he could scent was decidedly growing stronger. Hot—fire—but the only fire he should smell now was the faint smoky exhaustion of the last live coals in the fireplace.

However, the heat he sensed did not come from any innocent coals or bits of smoldering wood. What was the Khon trying?

Magic—to fight that which sheltered this thing would take magic. Magic spread from a source like a plant grew from a grounded root. Only here, Thragun Neklop considered the matter carefully; there was no root for HIS magic, nothing to serve him as that pot served the intruder. He needed magic which was at home right here, in this other land. And he knew exactly where to find it.

After a last careful survey of the box, Thragun jumped to the floor and padded purposefully to the door. It was close to tea time, he knew, when these who rightly valued him provided excellent food on his own dish. His tongue curved over his lips and he paused for a moment by the half opened door of the drawing room, scenting the feast waiting within. However, there was a time for one's taking one's ease and enjoying one's rightful food, and there was a time when duty called elsewhere.

Thragun walked on firmly and then, possessed by the need to do something needful, he flashed down the hall. Hastings was coming with a tray, Jennie holding open the door for him. It was easy enough to slip through and get down to the kitchen.

The smells wafted from well-filled tea stands were as nothing compared with the fragrance here. Cook was working at dinner already. As she moved ponderously from table to stove, she caught sight of Thragun.

"Got a bit o' what's right for th' likes of you, my fine gentleman. Give yourself a taste of this. 'Twill only be a foretaste—but Christmas is a-comin' an' you won't be sayin' no to a bite or two of goose then. We have 'im already a-hangin' in the larder."

She dipped something out of a large pan into a bowl.

"Now then, you'll be a-takin' that outside of 'ere—I got me too much to do to go dodgin' you this hour."

She carried the bowl to a second door and set it on the floor, closing the door behind her.

Thragun considered a new problem now. The creature whose help might be well needed had first appeared on a flight of stairs not too far away. There was no way for a cat to transfer this treat to that place. Very delicately he pushed at the bowl and it scraped across the stone flooring. It took three more efforts to get it to the top of the stairs, but there was no way of taking it down. He sat, eyes half closed to consider the point.

There were no secrets in Hob's Green which were unknown to Thragun by now. He always began the night curled up by Emmy. But if she chose to sleep away the more interesting hours, he did not. When the house was quiet, he would go prowling on his own. He had met Hob when Mrs. Cobb, the cook, had set out a bowl of cream to entice the house luck. That had been several months ago when there had been need of all the help one could summon. When another sort of Khon had commanded ill services in this house.

He and Hob had come to an agreement then and had acted together to dispose of she-who-was-black-of-thought. Thragun's lips drew back a little and his fangs showed. Yes, he and Hob had done together what must be done, and most efficiently also.

Since then he had seen Hob once or twice on his midnight trips of discovery. Whether Mrs. Cobb did or did not believe that the fortunate fall of Miss Wyker down the staircase had anything to do with Hob or not, she had since left out a bowl of cream each Saturday night and that was always drained dry in the morning.

However, Hob was not one who yearned for companionship and had not ever sought out Thragun—which was right and proper—a noble guard and a house thewada had really very little to do with one another, as long as the safety of what they were responsible for was not threatened—

Thragun gave a very small growl. His head came higher and he sniffed an earthy, dried grass smell, whiffing up the stairs.

There was the faintest of scuttling sounds and something which might have been a ball of shadow detached itself from the wall on the right-hand side of the stairs. It landed beside the bowl and yellow eyes regarded Thragun slyly. Small but broad flat feet shuffled on the stone and Thragun saw Hob throw up his long thin arms, his fingers clawed as if in threat. Not that that meant anything—it was Hob's first line of defense to try to frighten.

"Hob's Hole—Hob's own—" The voice was high and cracked. "From the roasting to the bone.

Them as sees, shall not look
Them's as blind, they shall be shook,
Sweep it up and sweep it down—
Hob shall clear it all around."

Whether Hob could read thoughts the cat had no way of telling, but certainly he had grasped ideas quickly enough before. So now Thragun wasted no time in coming straight to the point.

"There is a Khon of great evil now under this roof."

Hob had reached out with both hands for the bowl of offering, but he did not lift it from the floor. Instead he turned his head to one side, his face toward the kitchen door and partly from the cat. It was very wrinkled, that face, with eyes far too large, a pair of slits for a nose, and a sharply pointed chin as if he shared a bill with a bird. His eyes, which appeared to give forth a glow of their own, blinked slowly and then swung back to the cat.

Thragun nodded. Hob had forgotten his usual greed, at least long enough to give heed to the cat.

"The master of this household," the cat continued, "has been gifted by an enemy with the source of great evil. Should it escape under this roof, we shall know trouble, and that heavy and soon."

Hob blinked again and then looked down at the bowl. He snatched it up as if Thragun might dispute his ownership and gulped down its contents without even stopping to chew the tender chunks of meat.

Thragun's quiver of tail signaled his impatience. If this were another of his own kind, they would not be wasting time in this fashion. Hob's tongue was out and he held the bowl at an angle where he could run that around the sides to catch the last drop.

Then his voice grated again:

"Hob's Hole!" He stamped one foot to emphasize his claim of ownership.

"Not while the Khon lingers here," the cat answered. "This is a Khon of power and it will take magic well rooted to send him forth again."

The distant sounds of servants' voices reached them and Hob shook his head violently. Thragun knew that refusal to venture far from the portion of the house which the thewada considered its own would hold as long as there was any bustle in the kitchen or the hallways. To impress Hob with the seriousness of this, he must wait until the lower floor of the house was quiet and deserted in the night and he could guide the other to see for himself what kind of darkness had come to trouble them.

Thragun slipped down the hall twice during the evening to see if anything had changed in the library. The box remained as it was. Yet as he marched around it each time, he became more and more uneasy. There was always a bad smell to Khon magic, and to the cat that seemed to grow stronger every time he made that circuit. Yet there was nothing he could do as yet.

He took his night guard position at last on the wide pillow beside Emmy and stretched out purring as he had for every night since he had assumed his rightful position in the household. Emmy stroked him.

"I am glad Papa is home," she said. "Nothing bad can happen when Papa is here—and you!"

Thragun waited until she was asleep and then slipped off the bed and out of the room. He sped at a gallop down hall and stairs. There were still people awake in the house and he could smell the scent of the Captain's cigar from the library. So warned, he crept in with the same care as when he was stalking and took up a position behind one of the long window drapes, hooking it a little aside with one paw so he could watch.

He had no more than taken up his position when the Captain got up and went to the table, pried open the box again, and shook off cotton covering to unveil the enemy, turning the teapot around in his hands and studying it carefully.

"You *are* ugly, aren't you?" Again he lifted the head lid and peered inside. "I don't think anyone would fancy drinking anything which had been brewed in you. The rajah might have had it in mind to frighten us when he sent this. You'd be better off in a case where you'd be locked away from mischief."

He put down the pot on the table beside the box, making no effort to rewrap it. Then he shrugged, ground out his cigar in a copper tray, and made for the door, not giving the thing another look, as if he had forgotten it already.

Thragun growled deep in his throat. Khon magic—now it started. He was certain that the Captain had not unpacked the miserable pot just to look at it—no, he had been moved to do it by some power beyond his own curiosity.

With the Captain gone, and the lamp turned down, the room took on another and more ominous look. Thragun crept from one bit of concealment offered by a piece of furniture to another. The darkness was certainly not complete—growing stronger by the moment was a sickly yellowish light which issued from the misshapen pot.

He sat up and was watching that with such intensity that at first he did not see the thing which scuttled over from the gap which was the fireplace. But the smell of moldy straw awoke him to the fact that he had been joined by Hob.

The thewada of the house came to an abrupt halt. He had to lean far back so that his head was up far enough for him to see the now glowing pot. One broad foot came down with a stamp which narrowly missed Thragun's swinging tail. So, Hob also knew it for what it was. But the cat was not prepared for the next move made by his companion.

Hob leaped, clutched the edge of the table, and drew himself up to approach the pot closer. Thragun moved uneasily, though he thought it prudent not to follow.

"This is a thing of evil." He did not suppress his warning.

Hob reached for the pot which was nearly as large as his own pointed head. In the strange light his wizened face took on a somewhat sinister look. Hob was no quiet spirit when it came to that which aroused any threat of ownership of all within these walls.

Before Thragun could move or protest, he swung the pot around and hurled it straight at the wide hearthstone. There was a loud noise which sounded almost like an exultant cry. The pot, in spite of its substance, shattered and with such force that the many pieces appeared to go on crumbling until there was nothing but dust.

Thragun cried out, bared his fangs, hunched his back. In that moment of breakage something had reached out to touch him—something evil. He held against it.

Hob reached behind him on the table and caught up an object which glistened. He leaped toward the cat. That evil yellowish glow lingered enough to show that what the attacker held was a paper knife, a begemmed dagger also part of the curiosities Captain Wexley had brought home. Thragun moved with the swiftness of his kind when facing danger. However, Hob had already dropped the dagger. He was now dancing, holding the hand which had grasped its hilt to his mouth. From the hearthstone the yellow glow arose and circled the house spirit, clung to his whole body. Then it was gone as if it had sunk into Hob's wrinkled brown skin.

Hob—the Khon had taken possession of Hob!

Thragun could not suppress a yowl. But there was a shrill cry even louder. Hob swung around and jumped back toward the fireplace. A moment later he had scrambled into the opening and was gone. Thragun shook his head from side to side as if someone had flung some blinding dust in his eyes. He was as cold as if his slender body was encased in that white stuff Emmy called snow.

What had Hob done—what had HE done? Whatever was now loose in the house was the worst danger Thragun could imagine.

There was no use trying to track Hob through his own private runways, many of which were only open to a body which could become unsubstantial at its owner's will. Thragun sped from the library, made his way as a pale streak through the dark up the stairway until he reached Emmy's room again. He was thinking fiercely as he went.

Were he back in his own land once more, those who knew of such things would speedily beware of the Khon by instinct alone and would take steps to separate Hob from his new master. But in this country Thragun had no idea of who might be approached.

Mrs. Cobb, who had first made him aware of Hob's existence? Somehow Thragun believed that she would not be able to handle Hob as a Khon. And he knew that most of the other servants were afraid of even mentioning Hob himself. He was a legend within these walls, but also something to be feared.

Thragun headed for his place on Emmy's bed. In all his time he had never seen a one with the old knowledge such as could stand against a Khon.

"No!" Emmy twisted, her face showed fear and she cried out again, even louder, "No!"

Then her eyes opened and she looked at Thragun as if he were the Khon in person.

"It—" she began when there resounded through the house, loud enough to reach them in spite of the thickness of the walls, a heavy crash. Emmy screamed.

"It'll get me—it'll get me!"

"Emmy!" Miss Lansdall had come so quickly from her own bedchamber next door that her dressing gown was half off her shoulders, dragging on the floor. "Emmy—what is—"

She had no chance to finish her question. From behind the half open door of her own room sounded a second crash which certainly was that of broken glass.

Emmy cowered down in the bed and held fast to Thragun in a way he would have speedily resented if conditions were as usual.

Miss Lansdall looked back into her own room. She swayed and nearly dropped the candle she had brought with her.

"No!" she echoed Emmy's cry of a moment earlier. An object hurtled out of the bedroom, to smash against Emmy's door and fall to the floor with a crackle of broken china. There followed a heavy scent of violets. Thragun realized that Miss Lansdall had just been deprived of one of her most prized possessions—something Emmy had always regarded with delight—a slender bottle painted with the violets whose perfume sheltered within.

There came a second crash and again something flew through the air. Miss Lansdall cried out in pain, the candle fell from her grip and hit the carpet, its hot grease spattering, and then flame flickered in the floor covering itself.

Miss Lansdall threw herself forward. Awkwardly she grabbed one-handed for the pitcher of water on the wash-stand and threw it at the beginning blaze. Her other arm hung by her side and in the limited light from the window, Thragun could see a spreading splotch of blood seeping through her dressing gown sleeve.

Emmy screamed again. Now there were answering noises from down the hall.

The gleam of another candle gave better light to the scene. Miss Lansdall had not risen from her knees though the small flame on the carpet was quenched. She nursed her arm against her and her eyes were wide with fear.

Captain Wexley paused a moment at the door, then strode to her.

"What's all this?" he asked sharply, and then, seeing the blood on Miss Lansdall's arm, he looked to his daughter.

"Ring for help, Emmy. Miss Lansdall has been hurt." He helped the governess to a chair and then took up one of Emmy's own petticoats laid out for morning wearing to loop it around the bloody arm.

Miss Lansdall was shaking as she looked up at her employer.

"Sir—it flew at me and—"

Before she could explain further, there came a loud clap of noise as if a door had been opened with such fury that it had struck the wall. That was followed moments later by an explosion.

"What—" Captain Wexley turned as there came a scream and some cries from down the hall. "What in the name of—" he bit off what he was about to say and ended—"is happening."

"My room," Miss Lansdall had reached out her good hand and taken a tight hold of the rich brocade sleeve of the Captain's dressing robe. "Everything—smashed!"

"Captain, sir—!" Lasha came into view, carrying a candelabra with four candles lit. "In your chamber—your pistol—it is in the fireplace and there is much damage—a mirror, your small horse from China—"

Hastings reached them next and then Jennie and Meggy, with quilts pulled around their shoulders. Both of them let out startled cries as there were muffled sounds of more destruction sounding down the length of the hall.

Thragun listened closely. It certainly seemed that the Khon was taking

Hob through a rampage of damage, striking at every room.

Strike at most of the chambers he had. China lay smashed, mirrors were shattered, draperies were pulled from their rods, even small chairs and tables were turned upside down. Miss Lansdall was not the only one who suffered personal attack either. Mrs. Cobb, drawn by the uproar, swore that something had caught her by the ankle so that she lost her footing and pitched down the stairs, doing such harm to one of her ankles she could not get to her feet again unaided.

Emmy and Miss Lansdall, once the deep cut in the governess' arm was bandaged, went to Great-Aunt Amelie, who was sitting up in her huge curtained bed listening to the tale Jennie was pouring out.

She held out her arms to Emmy and motioned Miss Lansdall to sit down in a comfortable chair near the fire which Jennie must have built up again. There was a look of deep concern on her face as she settled Emmy in the warmth of undercovers.

"It is *HIM* for sure, m'lady," Jennie dragged her own blanket tighter around her, but that did not seem able to keep her from shivering. "*HE* has taken a spite 'gainst us. *HE* has!"

Great-Aunt Amelie listened, but for a moment she did not reply. Before she could, Miss Lansdall cried out, for a large piece of burning wood apparently leaped from the fire. Luckily the screen had been set up, but it struck against that with force enough to make it shake.

There was such a howl come down the chimney that Thragun yowled militantly in answer and jumped from the bed to run to the hearthstone. If Hob was planning on more mischief and truly aimed at those here, he would do what he could. Though if he might be able to actually attack Hob he was not sure. A thewada was apt to change into thin air under one's paws, and a Khon's reply might be even worse. This trouble was of his own making. If he had not brought Hob into the affair, the Khon, still fast in his pot, might well have been taken safely out of the house even as Captain Wexley had promised.

There were more crashes and Emmy was crying. Miss Lansdall's face was very white. Jennie had dropped on her knees by the bed, her hand out as if she reached for comfort to Great-Aunt Amelie.

However, Lady Ashley pulled herself even higher on the pillows, and now her expression was one of intent study as if she were trying to remember something of importance.

"The still room," she said as if to herself. "Surely Mrs. Cobb has some in keeping there. Jennie, I will not order you to go there—"

"M'lady," Jennie sat up, "if there is something as will answer *HIM*—" her voice trailed off.

"Rowan," Great-Aunt Amelie said sharply. "Get my robe, Jennie, and my furred slippers. Emmy, you are a brave girl, I know. Remember how you aided *me* when it was necessary. You must come, too."

Emmy's lower lip trembled, but she obediently slipped out of the bed and put on her own slippers.

"My dear," Lady Ashley was speaking now to Miss Lansdall who had started to rise, her face plainly showing that she was about to protest, "I am a very old woman, and there is much which you younger people dismiss as impossible these days. But Hob's Green is a house very much older than I. Some man well-learned in history once told my father that parts of it were standing even before the Norman Lord to which William granted it came here. There are many queer tales. Hob is supposed to be the spirit of the house. Sometimes for generations of time all goes well and there are no disturbances, then again there are happenings which no one can explain. When I was several years younger than Emmy, there was a footman my father dismissed when he found him mistreating one of the village boys who helped with the fruit harvest.

"The man was very angry, but he was too fearful of my father, who was a justice of the peace, to strike at him openly. Instead, he waited for fair time and stole into the house, meaning to steal the silver. When the servants returned from the fair, he was found lying in the hall, his head badly hurt and a leg broken. His story was he had been deliberately tripped on the stair.

"But this present disorder seems to be aimed at us within the house and not some intruders. Thank you, Jennie. Emmy, do you think you can carry that lamp? It is a small one and it gives us better light than a candle.

"No, Jennie, I must do this. We shall not have our home troubled in this fashion. There was an old woman who looked after the hens in my father's time—" Great-Aunt had taken the shawl Jennie handed her as she finished tying the sash of her warm quilted robe and pulled it about her shoulders. "Now just give me my cane and let me steady myself against your shoulder, girl. Emmy, you can go ahead and light our way. And—" she looked over to where Thragun waited by the door, "you may just have a part in this, I think, for they say that cats can sometimes see much more than we do, and I believe that you are such a one. Now—let us go."

"What about the hen woman, Great-Aunt," asked Emmy. She held the lamp in a tight grip and tried to concentrate on what Great-Aunt had started to say rather than think of what might be waiting outside in the hall, or at the bottom of the stairs, or in the dark ways into the kitchen quarters.

"She was what the villagers call a wisewoman, Emmy. Like a cat, she might have seen farther than the rest of us. Mrs. Jordan, who was cook in that day, had a respect for some of her ways and called her in after the footman was hurt. There were strange noises to be heard then, but none of this wanton destruction, at least. The woman brought some sprigs of rowan and put them around. After that, things were quiet again. Rowan is supposed to keep off all dark influences and to close doors against their entrance. From that time on, it was customary to keep some rowan to hand—fresh if possible, dried if there was no other way."

Their descent was slow. Great-Aunt held on to the stair rail with one hand and to Jennie, who kept step with her, with the other, while she pushed her cane through her sash to keep it ready. Thragun flowed down into the dark, once or twice looking back so his eyes were red balls in the reflected light.

Lady Ashley said no more, perhaps saving her breath for her exertions. However, there was noise enough in the house. Emmy heard her father calling for water and smelled what might be singed carpet. Two of the portraits on the walls of the lower hallway had fallen face-down on the floor, spraying fragments of glass from under them.

The clock boomed as they turned toward the kitchen wing and Emmy counted the tolls to five. The night was going. It was already time for the servants to be about. Yet this morning no one had time to think of regular duties.

Even the fire in the big range had not been built up and there were no kettles waiting for early morning tea. Spread across the floor was a clutter of utensils, as well as a welter of knives, forks, ladles, and large stirring spoons. There had been a clear sweep made of the many shelves and storage places.

"Be careful, milady." Jennie kicked, sending some of the debris out of their path. "Now you sit here and tell me what you want."

Great-Aunt was moving more and more slowly and breathing heavily. She let Jennie steer her to Mrs. Cobb's own chair and sat down, resting her head against its tall back. Her eyes closed for a moment and then opened.

"Keys—"

Her voice sounded very weak, hardly above a whisper.

"Yes, milady—" Jennie picked up a crock which was the only thing left on a shelf near the stove and felt behind it, to bring out a set of large old keys.

179

"Luckily Cook leaves the spare ones here of a night when she plans to start early in the morning."

"Still room—rowan—"

Jennie nodded. She had busied herself lighting one of the lanterns waiting to be used for anyone needing to venture out into the stable's yard after nightfall.

For a moment she stood looking at one of the doors which led from the other side of the kitchen. Then she stooped and caught up a toasting fork, its handle long enough to make it a formidable weapon. With this in one hand, the keys and the lantern in the other, she advanced toward the door, Thragun already ahead of her.

The key turned in the lock and they were able to look into a room whose walls were composed of shelves, each of those loaded with jars and bottles. There was a scent of spice, of herbs, a large stock of the small bottled jams and jellies.

Jennie paid no attention to any of those and luckily Hob-Khon had not yet carried his program of breakage this far. The maid hunted out a bunch of leafed stems which had been hanging from the ceiling on a cord and swiftly made her way back to the kitchen, taking time only to lock the door behind her.

She laid her trophy on the well-scrubbed table and Thragun did what he had never dared do here before, jumped up beside it, sniffing inquisitively. He sneezed and raised his head. There was indeed a strong strange odor, but it had nothing of the dark about it.

"*HE* won't come so easy, milady," Jennie observed.

"Probably not, Jennie. But what do they say tempts Hob's famous appetite? Cream, is it not? And surely something quite out of the ordinary to be added on this occasion. Hmmm—"

She looked about as if waiting for a suggestion.

Jennie had gone to fetch the cream. The only other object on the table was a covered bowl. Thragun sniffed that—spices—Great-Aunt Amelie took the cover off.

"Why, it is a Christmas pudding! I thought that Mrs. Cobb had not yet begun to make such! And this one has been steamed ready for the table, though it is cold." Lady Ashley pulled the bowl closer.

"Oh, milady." Jennie was back with another bowl, the contents of which made Thragun's whiskers twitch a fraction. Certainly its contents were more to be desired than this Christmas pudding. "That was sent up from th' village just this evenin'. Thomas brought it in on th' cart from Windall. Cook, she an'

Miss Davis over at th' Jolly Boy has been for years now a-talkin' 'bout which Christmas pudding be the best—them with brandy or them with rum. So this year Miss Davis up an' sent one of hers over for to give us a taste like."

"Bring a plate, Jennie." Great Aunt sat up straighter. "And then turn the pudding out. We'll just see if Hob has a taste for a seasonal dainty."

So the table was set, the bowl of cream, the pudding on a plate. Under Lady Ashley's direction, the bits of rowan were placed around three sides of the offering allowing only the fourth to be open.

"Now we shall have to leave it to Hob. He has no desire to be seen, or so I was always told. Come—"

With Emmy before her with the lamp and Jennie still holding the toasting fork at ready to help her, Lady Ashley went slowly out. They had left Jennie's lantern sitting on the ledge of the cupboard shelf and Thragun remained where he was, on the table well away from the rowan.

With slitted eyes he looked to the fireplace. There had been more noise from the forepart of the house, not muffled by the length of passages and rooms in between. He thought that Hob was still busy at his destruction and that he was doing more than ever to cause all the damage he could as he went.

But after the others had left there was silence. What new mischief was the Khon about?

Out of the fireplace sped a shadow, and Thragun subdued the hiss he had almost voiced. He did not know how the preparations Lady Ashley had made would act. But he sat up on his haunches and with his forepaws made signs in the air, following as best he could his memories of what was done to discourage a Khon in his old home.

It was Hob in form who squatted on the table top, grabbed the bowl of cream in both hands and held it high, drinking its contents in a single slurping gulp. Then he swung about to look at the pudding.

There was a crinkling of Hob's wrinkled face as if he were in pain and his two claw hands at the end of spider-thin arms patted his protruding belly which looked as if he had already swallowed the bowl along with what it held.

Thragun did not hesitate:

"You are Hob, the thewada of this house—"

Hob's head was cocked to one side as if he did hear and understand, but his eyes were all for the pudding.

"Hob's Hole—Hob's own
From the roasting to the bone.
Them as sees, shall not look,

Them as blind, they shall be shook.

Sweep it up and stamp it down—

Hob shall clear it all around.

So Mote this be!"

Hob's one hand went out to the pudding, though his other still rubbed his middle as if to subdue some pain there.

"Hob's Hole alone—Hob shall hold it!"

Thragun snapped at a piece of the rowan in spite of the fact that it scratched his lips. With a jerk of his head as if he were disposing of a rat, he tossed that.

Hob threw up an arm but, by fortune, the rowan sped true, striking against that round ball of a stomach. Nor did it fall away.

With a screech Hob leaped up. One big foot touched rowan and he screeched again. Then he began to shake as if some giant hand had caught him and was determined to subdue all struggles.

Hob's mouth opened to the full extent as if half his jaw had become unhinged. Out from between his small fangs of teeth came a puff of sickly yellow as if somewhere within him there burned a fire and this was smoke. His head, flying back and forth from the violence of that shaking, sent a second puff and both struck full upon the top of the pudding.

Now that shivered and rocked. Thragun, not knowing just why he did it, threw a second sprig of rowan and that touched, not Hob, but the pudding.

There was a howl of dismay and defeat. Hob was loosed from the shaking, to crouch on the table. The pudding was gone. A shimmer of the yellow Hob had been made to disgorge hid it completely. That faded, seeming to sink into the ball of dried fruit and flour.

Hob, his head now in his hands, rocked back and forth. But Thragun pressed closer with a third sprig of rowan which he laid on the top of that ball. Only what stood there now was a teapot—a fine brown teapot, its lid crowned by a sprig of rowan also frozen in time and place.

The cat gave it two long sniffs. He could smell none of the evil that other pot had cloaked itself in. It must be true that the magic of this land was indeed more than even a Khon could fight.

Hob straightened, rubbed his stomach, and there was no longer any sign of pain on his withered face. With a swift bound he reached the fireplace and was gone into his own hidden ways again.

Thragun regarded the teapot critically. It was certainly far more innocent looking than it had been in its other existence, and by what all his senses told him its evil will was firmly and eternally confined. He yawned, feeling all the fatigue of the night, and jumped from the table.

The lantern flickered and went out. But the pudding pot remained to mystify Mrs. Cobb later that morning and many mornings to come.

NOBLE WARRIOR
MEETS WITH A GHOST
Catfantastic III (1994) DAW

Such a noise! Even ten temples' worth of rattle swinging, horn blowing priests at the heights of celebration could not drown out—this! And the smells! Thragun Neklop lifted a fastidious lip enough to show a very sharp fang. This was like the Ninth Hell itself and no proper place for the well conducted, feline or even human. He felt cross-eyed from watching through the narrow slit in his bamboo riding case, yet he dared not let down his guard.

The roar of a dragon sweeping on its helpless prey made him almost cower, but he was Noble Warrior, Princess' own guard. Dragon or no dragon, he faced danger directly and with both blue eyes wide open. The dragon crawled along one side of this infernal place and its side scales opened so that those it had previously devoured were issuing forth apparently unharmed. Would the wonders of this barbarian territory never cease?

Now another crowd was sweeping into those dragon scale doors. And Emmy, his own Princess Emmy, was hurrying along toward this unknown fate. Noble Warrior gave tongue in no uncertain yowl. He saw Emmy's head turn in his direction, but then her father swung her up and into the dragon and—

Noble Warrior's traveling cage swung aloft. He had been picked up. And the scent of this newcomer was unpleasantly familiar though he could not see more than a looming shadow. Emmy—he must be transported to join Emmy. Only that did not happen. The carrying cage rocked as its bearer picked up speed. Not toward the dragon but away from it. They burst out of the noise and confusion of the station into the open. But not the open Noble Warrior knew. There was the smell of horses, that was familiar, but there were other smells, nearly as bad as some in the poor villages at home. And the noise continued.

Noble Warrior threw himself against the front of the cage. He tried to slip one brown paw into the crack about the door, to free himself. But he did not have a chance. The cage was whirled up into the air and came down with a slam which brought another yowl out of him. The cage rocked with the floor under it and Noble Warrior was sure he had been loaded into one of those wagons such as Emmy often traveled in, sometimes taking Noble Warrior, who knew his place and sat statue still by her side while she pointed out various points of interest.

There was still that familiar scent. He could only think of the stable yard at home as the carrier rocked from a kick. Noble Warrior crouched belly to the floor to consider his present plight. He did not believe in the least that Emmy had abandoned him to this fate—whatever it might be. But Emmy was fast in the dragon and he was left to do battle on his own.

Alerting all his senses he tested as well as he could what might lie beyond the walls of the carrier. He could smell horse very strong. And there was also the smell of unwashed human—a human who drank the fire spirit—that groom the Captain had ordered off his land! There were other smells also. And all the while, the noise ebbed, roared, and ebbed.

The wagon came to a halt and there was a beam of light. Once more, Noble Warrior's carrier was swung out into the open and he caught a fleeting glimpse of a soot-stained brick wall and the iron pickets of a fence. Then he was again in drab shadow as the carrier thumped to the floor.

"Here y'be, guvener. Right one an' all."

"So."

Noble Warrior's head swung around. He could not see through the weaving of the bamboo, but the fur along his back ridged and his ears flattened to his skull. But he made no sound—no guardian warned before attack, that was not the way.

Only there was evil here—just as he had sensed it at other times and in other places. Khon? Demon dweller in the shadows? Or more?

He had no time to speculate. Once more his carrier was swept up and off, to be placed on a flat surface again. Now it was surrounded by smells which made him sneeze and shake his head. There came a fumbling with the catch and the doorway to his temporary prison swung open. Noble Warrior made no effort to leave his conveyance. Make sure, instinct warned. Who knew who or what awaited him.

"Here, puss—puss—"

A large hand appeared in his range of sight. The skin was discolored in places almost as if it had been burnt, and on the forefinger was a large ring, the setting of which was the red of a half awakened coal.

Noble Warrior hissed a warning as that ill-omened hand approached. He readied his own paw for a good raking slash.

The hand remained where it was for a long moment and then a second joined it. In the hand was a round ball. There was a sudden squeeze and from the ball issued a puff which caught Noble Warrior straight in the face. He coughed, uttered the beginning of a howl, and subsided to the cushion beneath him.

The hand with the ring reached in to catch him by the scruff of the neck and dragged him out to dangle helplessly in the air while the owner of the hand surveyed his captive. Helpless Noble Warrior was—he could not even summon a growl.

"Soooooo—" The large head opposite him nodded. "Indeed—even as Jasper said—"

The hand loosened its grip and Noble Warrior fell, landing on a table top not far from his carrier. He tried to command his body, to leap for that refuge. But he was as helpless as if he were entangled in a bird hunter's net.

"We shall be friends—"

Noble Warrior managed the weak beginning of a snarl. What he saw was dark, shadowed. It was even as the Great Old Ones of his own kind said; evildoers were always dark shadowed. This one resembled nothing so much as one of the carven Khons set up in warning.

His shoulders were hunched and his head, which looked too large for his body, might not sprout the fangs of a Khon to be sure, but his teeth were yellow and he showed a nasty snaggle of them as he grinned. Pallid, grayish skin was half concealed on a retreating chin by a straggle of fuzzy beard. But the spreading dome of his head was bare save for more fuzz over large ears which showed distinct points. He wore a loose coat or jacket which might have once been white but was now begrimed and stained into a twilight gray. His eyes had retreated into dark caverns under an untidy thatching of brow, but they held a bright glint which Noble Warrior caught. Maybe not a Khon—but certainly one who had willingly chosen the Dark Path.

"We shall be friends—you shall see—" The great head nodded. "Until we are, there shall be precautions taken."

Again the hand swooped and the helpless cat dangled in the air as the man shuffled across the dark room and pushed his captive into a cage, snapping the door behind him with a click, and turning his back as if he had fairly settled the matter.

Noble Warrior lay where he had fallen. There was a stench in this cage, and with it came the dregs of far off fear and pain. He snarled and tried to move. Whatever spell the Khon master had put upon him seemed to be lessening. Now he pulled himself up and sat as one of the Old Blood should.

The light of the room was dim. There were several windows, but they were barred and set very high on the wall, so covered with dust and the webs of long dead spiders that they might have been securely curtained. Over the table where his carrier still stood, there hung a lamp and there were candles posted here and there—a whole line of them on an old desk at one side where there was a pile of age-eaten books. His captor had settled down in a sway-backed chair next to that desk and had one of the books open now, impatiently switching candlesticks around for a better reading light.

There were a number of cabinets lined up under the windows at one wall, the doors of several hung open to show rows of bottles and jars of strange things Noble Warrior could not guess the use for. At the darker end of the room was a single door. That was flanked by two tables which bore—cages! Cages such as the one in which he found himself.

There were other captives—his cat sight was not defeated by the gloom. In one were rats—but such rats—their fur was white or else unwholesomely mottled in color and they scuttled about aimlessly. In the next—

Noble Warrior stiffened. There was no mistaking the scent, overpowered as it might be by the smells of this place, but there was a cat. Not one of his own regal breed, of course, but still another cat. Though its fur was matted and it seemed so lost in despair that it made no effort to cleanse itself, he could see now that it was a female, and had fur unusually long and black.

She was half curled against the bars of her prison, her eyes closed, her position crying out hopelessness and fear.

There came a buzzing sound and the man by the desk shook his head impatiently. "Time—never any time. Devil take Henry—" Leaving his book open, he got rustily to his feet and shuffled to the far door.

As he approached the cages flanking the door, the other cat's head came up a little. Noble Warrior saw its mouth open but without sound. The man brushed by it, paying no attention, while the rats scrambled in a wild dance around their prison.

When the door closed behind their jailor, Noble Warrior raised his voice:

"I am Thragun Neklop of the Royal Guard. Who are you and where is this place? What does this evil one want of us?"

The black cat raised its head and opened golden eyes.

"This is a place of pain, and hunger, and we are forgotten. I was—" the black cat shook its head slowly, "I cannot remember. What I am—what you will be—is one to suffer, suffer as he wills it. And will it he will!"

"I do not understand."

"Oh, you will, my fine would-be fighter, you will—as have the others before you. And probably not to any productive purpose."

Shadow detached itself from shadow, leaped to the same table as supported Noble Warrior's cage, to become substance. Another cat—the largest he had ever seen—this one also black, its ears ragged from ancient battles, its eyes bearing strange red sparks within their greenness.

The newcomer took a couple of strutting steps and then settled down, sitting upright, its tail end wrapped composedly over its forepaws. It looked Noble Warrior over, and the open contempt in that survey brought a snarl to the prisoner's lips, a flattening of ears in warning.

"You are a strange one," the black cat observed. "Yes, I can see why old Marcus was ready to pay a full guinea for you. Supposed to come from foreign parts if I heard their talk right. Maybe this time he will be able to do it—I've heard tell that in foreign parts they have other learning."

"Do what?" demanded Noble Warrior.

"Make a familiar out of you. Old Marcus, he's cracked in the noggin as Henry says. This place," with a slight sweep of his head, the cat indicated what lay about them, "is an old hidy-hole where those before Marcus thought to speak with the Devil and gather black power. Some of them—" the black cat paused, "some of them in the past had the Old Learning—but always on the dark side. There was Sir Justin Clayman—yes, and that Parson turned wizard—Master Loomis. They did things such as would make old Marcus' eyes pop right out of his skull. He tries, but he's far from learning even the first of the lessons. That's why he's trying other ways now, why he wants a familiar. He heard tell of the Princess first—" The cat inclined his head toward the captive on the other side of the room.

"She's a foreigner, too—comes 'cross seas from the Far East. But she's no magic maker and he can't turn her into one. So when he heard tell of another cat as seemed to bring luck to people—well, he made up his mind to gather you in and see if he would fare any better with his plans."

"What about you?" Noble Warrior had followed this garbled account as best he could, translating it into what he knew of old. One who would work with Khons needed an animal as some kind of a helper. Yes, he had heard of the priests of Kali and the serpents they were said to send to gather the souls of those who opposed them.

"Now wouldn't he just like that." The black cat opened his mouth in an unmistakable yawn. "Oh, I could be what he wants right enough. But I've served my time as the saying goes. Sir Justin, he was a right pleasant one to work with. Parson Loomis now, I'll not say the same for that one. No, old Marcus can't get his bonds on me—seeing as how I'm living in another time these days."

Noble Warrior's eyes narrowed. There had been so many strange, dark, and unpleasant emanations in this place that only now he realized that other-space chill.

"You are dead," he said harshly as the fur along his spine quivered.

The black cat's mouth stretched now in a grin. "Just figured it out, have you, new boy? Only you may call it dead—I find my present state most satisfactory. You'd better be worrying about your own. The Princess there," he nodded again to the other prisoner, "she hasn't long to go now. He's decided she's not worth the trouble of feeding her."

Noble Warrior looked at that other captive. She had raised her head a fraction and was eyeing the stranger cat almost pleadingly.

"This herder of Khons is not going to get me to serve him!" Noble Warrior emphasized that with a deep throated growl.

"Keep on believing it, youngster. You'll change your mind quick enough. Not that Marcus can do it, you understand—make you his slave. But it'll be a rare fight and Simpson here will have plenty to watch while it's in the doing."

Noble Warrior edged closer to the door of the cage. He had neat, slender paws and he knew how to use them. The opening of cupboards and doors was no mystery—though the latch on the carrier had been out of his reach. Now he could wriggle past one bar and lay a paw to the fastening here, but in spite of his prying it would not give.

The ghost cat watched him. "Good try," he commented. "Only it is not going to work. You will have to think of some other way—and there isn't any."

Noble Warrior settled back once more. He was thinking again over all that had happened since he had arrived in this dire place.

"That thing—the one the Khon Master used—the one which puffed at me—" He was thinking aloud more than addressing Simpson.

"Got it on the first try, haven't you? Yes, a puff of that and you're as limp as a dead rat. He'll use it, too."

In all his life Thragun Neklop had never asked for help, but he realized that perhaps such a surrender of Warrior pride might serve him best now.

"If the Khon Master did not have that—"

For a long moment Simpson stared back. His eyes changed; deep in their centers that spark of red grew and began to glow.

"You want help, is that it?"

Noble Warrior met those flaming eyes squarely. This visitor from the shades had not helped that other cat prisoner. Would he be moved any quicker to give aid to him?

"She is no fighter." Somehow Noble Warrior was not surprised that this other read his thought. "She could not have defended herself as such a fine young fellow as you might do. So, Marcus has done little save twitter over books he cannot understand and brew stinks enough to take one's breath away."

"Not like those others," Noble Warrior inserted slyly, "the ones who knew your value."

Simpson nodded. "True, very true. I think—" He arose and stretched luxuriously, "that it is time old Marcus be shown his proper place in one world or another."

He was gone, although Thragun Neklop, blinking twice, did not see him leap away. He extended his claws and rasped them across the splintered flooring of the cage.

Properly sharp, yes. If he could only get a chance to use them. Then he looked once more to the other cat. She was huddled in upon herself like a round black mat. If he got out—if he could fight free—what of her?

Then the door beside her cage scraped open and Marcus shuffled back in, a lamp in one hand and a small basket in the other. He set both on the table and, muttering to himself in a voice too low for Noble Warrior to hear, set about assembling a number of other things to join the light and basket he had brought with him.

Once more Noble Warrior blinked. Simpson was in plain sight, sitting on the edge of that table now watching Marcus' actions, disdain to be read in every tilt of whisker. It was plain to Noble Warrior that the old man was completely unaware of the big feline almost within touching distance of the bowls and boxes and small bottles Marcus brought from other shelves and set ready to hand.

At length, having combined a pinch of that, a drop of this from one container or another, the man nodded almost briskly and swept all the clutter away from the major portion of the table top. He then proceeded to draw on the cleared space with thick crayon markings and curlicues in red. In the end he surveyed critically a star between the points of which were scrawled convoluted shapings which made Noble Warrior spit in rage. This was truly demon dealing.

Having surveyed his handiwork with apparent approval, Marcus reached for something Noble Warrior had seen before—that noxious puffer. But Simpson's paw touched that strange weapon first, sending it rolling from the table.

With an exclamation the old man went down on his knees to retrieve what Simpson had rolled under the table. Noble Warrior could not really understand why this would-be demon commander was not aware of the ghost cat.

Beyond Marcus' groping fingers Simpson made a pounce and brought both forefeet down on the rounded end of the weapon. Noble Warrior could not see any puff of dust at this distance, but Simpson withdrew instantly as Marcus' hand closed upon the bulb. With a grunt of satisfaction he got creakingly to his feet, and weapon in hand, came toward Noble Warrior's prison. Steel muscles moved under the shields of fine fur. The training of kittenhood days was very much a part of him now. One human hand fumbled at the latching of the cage and the other advanced with the puffer.

Noble Warrior saw the fingers squeeze on it, but this time there was no dust to clog his nostrils and turn him into a limp fur string. As the cage door swung wide enough, with a battle cry, he leaped straight at that great round head, claws raking deep and true.

Marcus screeched in turn and stumbled back, striving to tear the cat's body from him. There was a rake across his eyes and then Noble Warrior dropped to the floor. The man blundered blindly along the table, sweeping off the contents to shatter on the floor.

Noble Warrior was across the room in two bounds and had gained the table where the other cage was standing. The latch, which had been placed outside the reach of the captive, was easy enough to get at now. He caught it in his teeth, gave a twist, and the door opened.

"Out!" he yowled.

She squeezed by him, moving so slowly he wanted to hurry her along with a nip on the quarters.

"Neatly done," Simpson stood on the floor below. "Come along now. You've given old dog face something to think about—marked him good, you did. But we'd better be out of here before he gets some of those scattered wits back into his head."

With Simpson in the lead, the Princess pattering along behind, and Noble Warrior playing rear guard, they threaded through a hall upstairs and were shown a broken window in a nasty smelling, cupboardlike hole.

For the first time Noble Warrior had to think of what would come next. There was no Emmy to hand—she had been swallowed by the dragon—and her father, the Captain, was also already far away. He was alone—no, the Princess was with him, and in a strange country he did not understand at all.

"Simpson—" he began uncertainly.

"You're on your own now, fighter. Now the Princess—" In this strange light of day they stood in a mean little strip of sour, bare earth. "There's a place for her. There's a little girl down the street and across the square who will welcome her. But that's no place for you. I don't know what they teach kittens in those foreign parts of yours, beside how to be good fighters. But you should have that which will take you home even if you have to make it on your four feet. Look inside yourself, youngster, and find it."

Thragun Neklop looked. And he found. He knew the way—he need only go in that direction and keep on until he got there. Why, that was no problem at all.

"Simpson?"

The cat ghost was fast fading only to a shadow of a shadow.

"Get going, youngster. You've given me a good day. Old Marcus won't be trying to make himself a wizard—at least not for some time—not insulting the shades of Sir Justin and Parson Loomis with his messes. Seems like he met with his match and that was one of us—very fitting. Good journey to you, my young friend, may the mice be many and the road a straight one. Now I'm to see this young lady to her proper place in life. As a good familiar ought."

The Princess hesitated and then wobbled to Noble Warrior and touched noses, before wavering along behind a fast disappearing shred of darkness. Thragun Neklop drew a deep breath and started to seek his own way.

NOBLE WARRIOR, TELLER OF FORTUNES
Catfantastic IV (1996) DAW

Noble Warrior's whiskers twitched as he sulked down the narrow alley. Under his fastidious feet, though he went with all the care he could, the filth on the pavement spattered his paws. He had learned early in this journey that there were plenty of enemies on the prowl. A dog, its coat spotted with mange, had not been quick enough—Noble Warrior had reached the top of a barrel with just a hair's breadth between his tail and those fangs.

He had been driven by pangs of hunger to forage in a pail set beside a door. But he still ran his tongue around his teeth, trying to rid his mouth from the taste of rancid meat scraps.

This was no place for the guard of a princess, and the sooner he was out of it the better. Follow that instinctive direction within him, the ghost cat had advised. At the time—once he realized that he *did* have just such a direction—it had seemed an easy enough thing. But Thragun Neklop had never before had to cross a city of the barbarians, and barbarians certainly these close dwelling creatures seemed to be.

He leaped to the top of a rotting box to rest and try to put in order the events of the past few days. There had been the bamboo cage which was his own private palanquin, and he had meant to ride in it with Emmy, his personal charge, not far away.

Then had come to the place of the dragon where people were swallowed up—Emmy among them—into its fat belly, and his own cage seized and then carried off. Sold he had been like any slave to that stupid meddler in magic—set up to be a familiar, as the ghost cat Simpson had informed him. Only the dolt of a would-be magician had certainly NOT been a match for two cats. Yes, he was certainly willing to give Simpson a full share in that bit of action.

Now he was well away from the house where Marcus had tried to handle what he did not understand, and, with another goal to concentrate on, starting back home.

He was hungry again, but as his head swung toward the other end of the alley, he picked up traces of a scent which made his whiskers twitch—this time in hopeful promise.

He had left Marcus' shell of a house in the very early hours of the day. Dawn had come, and he could hear the stir in the larger streets. Ahead, at the other end of the alley to which his empty stomach urged him, there was a great deal of noise. He picked up the scent of horses, yes, and some of those woolly creatures called sheep which Emmy found so pettable.

Now he shook each paw vigorously, having no wish at that time to lick pad and fur clean, and made for that end of his path.

The noise grew louder. He could easily pick up the snorting and whinnying of horses mixed with hoarse shouts of men. Reaching the end of the alley, he crouched behind a pile of baskets to spy out the land ahead.

There was certainly a lot of coming and going. Carts laden high were being maneuvered to where they could be unloaded. There were so many smells now that he could not sort out the one which had promise. He wanted none of bold journeying across a place where one was apt to come under a horse's hard hoofs without warning. And certainly he had no intention of being sighted by any of the men and the few aproned and beshawled women there.

With the skill of his guard training, Noble Warrior selected a path to the right. Where the whole of this cart-filled place seemed busy, there was an eddy there of less confusion.

This appeared to center around a cart which was unlike the others. Noble Warrior blinked and blinked again. Yes, this cart was certainly NOT of the breed of the others. In fact—yes, it looked almost like a farm hut such as he had often seen in his homeland, mounted on wheels. And it was painted in bright colors. There hung a string of bells suspended across a curtained doorway in the back.

Noble Warrior relaxed a small fraction. They had the proper ideas, those of the strange cart. All knew that bells above a door were powerful charms to keep Khons in their dark places. Could it be that here, so very far from the palace of the Princess Suphron, he had indeed found people of the proper heritage who would recognize him—Thragun Neklop—for what he was—a palace guard of high rank? Yet one never forgot proper caution—not if one wanted to make the most of one's allotted nine lives.

He watched with all the patience of his kind. Set a little to one side on the pavement was a small fire carefully tended by a woman wearing the familiar clinking coin jewelry he knew. Dancing girls dressed so. Over the fire on a tripod was a kettle, and from that wafted the scent which had first reached Noble Warrior. He uttered a small sound deep in his throat without meaning to.

Resolutely he made himself forget about the pot to eye the rest of the company. There were a line of horses a little beyond and men wearing bright headcloths were there, plainly bargaining with the drab-coated people of the city.

The warning bells rang, and a boy about the vanished Emmy's size swung down the two caravan steps to hand something to the woman by the cookpot. He turned away as if to join the company by the horses and then instead—

Instinctively, Noble Warrior crouched small, tensed his body for a spring. He was sure, as if the boy had cried the news aloud, he had been sighted.

He could slide back into the shadow of the baskets, but somehow he did not want to. Things far back in his memory were moving, oddly disturbing his need to remain alert.

There had been a handmaid of the Princess, a slave taken in war. But she had a gift which brought her into the palace and high into favor with the Princess—she could call to her birds and animals, and they came because something within her was akin to them.

Noble Warrior uttered a small protest of sound. There was no hiding from this boy. Nor did a large part of him wish to do so.

The boy had gone down on one knee a short distance away and Noble Warrior knew he was in full sight of the child. Yet the boy made no effort to approach closer, no gesture which suggested any threat.

"Gatto—?" He spoke the word with rising inflection, and Noble Warrior recognized it as a question.

He arose from his crouch, and sat up proudly, the tip of his tail curled across his fore feet, his large blue eyes meeting the brown ones of the boy.

"Jankos?" the woman by the fire called.

Swiftly the boy made a gesture to be left alone. Now he dared move forward until he could reach out and touch Noble Warrior, while the cat allowed such a liberty.

Noble Warrior sniffed delicately at the knuckles of the turned-over fist held out to him. He did not move as the fingers slowly opened and touched the top of his head between his ears in the knowledgeable way of one used to dealing with cat people.

"Jankos!" The woman had come away from her fire tending to approach. But she suddenly stopped as Noble Warrior stood up, took two steps forward, and uttered the cry he used for a friendly greeting.

"It is a cat, Mammam, but such a cat! Look, he has eyes like the sky!"

The woman joined Jankos, and Noble Warrior sniffed at her full skirt. No, she was not an under-skin friend like the boy, but she offered no harm either. Now she got down on her knees to inspect the cat more closely.

"You are right, Jankos. This is no cat such as one sees hereabouts." She was half frowning as she studied Noble Warrior. "He is of great worth by guess, there will be those seeking him—perhaps even a reward."

"Are you hungry, Gatto?" she added, and crooked a finger which brought Noble Warrior willingly into the open and closer to that kettle with the intriguing smells.

Jankos disappeared quickly once more into the wagon and then was back with a bowl into which the woman ladled a portion of the stew she had been tending.

Noble Warrior settled himself on guard by that, waiting for the contents to cool enough for him to investigate them more closely.

The woman sat down on the steps leading up to the curtained, bell-hung doorway, and continued to study the cat. Cats there were in plenty in this land, as well as overseas from which her family had come some years ago. However, never one such as this one. It was as if this find were a blooded horse turned out by mistake with a farmer's draft horse. She raised her voice:

"Pettros, come you here."

One of the men by the horses turned his head with an impatient look on his face but, as she made a vigorous gesture, he came.

"Look you what Jankos has found."

It was the man's turn to squat on his heels and view Noble Warrior who had at last decided that the stew was ready to be tongue tasted.

"From where did you take him," the man turned a thunderous frown on the boy.

"From no place. He came by himself. See, he is very hungry—he has been lost—"

The man rubbed his broad hand across his jaw. The woman broke in:

"By the looks of him he has not been on his own too long, Pettros. Perhaps there will be a reward."

The man shrugged. "He is strange, yes, but there are cats a-many and who offers a reward for such? A horse now, even a donkey, or a good hound—but a cat—I think not. If you wish him, Jankos, bring him along. We have near finished the trading and it is time to hit the road." He got up and went back to the horses and those about them.

Noble Warrior finished the bowl and even was reduced to giving it several last licks. He did not object when Jankos settled down beside him and stroked his sable brown head, scratching in just the right places behind the ears.

This was not his Princess, nor his Emmy, but the boy was suitable as a companion, and Noble Warrior climbed up into the wagon as horses were hitched to it. He sat just before the curtain and watched the man finish off the contents of the kettle and stamp out the small fire. The woman had already edged past him into the interior of the wagon, but Jankos joined him on the top step, his hand still smoothing in well-trained fashion, which brought a rumble of purr from Noble Warrior.

That something deep in him which was his only direction homeward seemed soothed also, and somehow he was sure he was headed in the right direction.

There were, Noble Warrior discovered as they trundled along, three of these wagons. They did not ride as smoothly as the carriage he had shared with Emmy, but they each had their own store of the most enticing smells. There were other children beside Jankos also, but Noble Warrior held aloof from their coaxing, keeping close to his first friend.

At least they were getting away from the place of noise and bad smells, and at last Noble Warrior felt secure enough to curl up on the blanket bed to which Jankos introduced him and got to sleep, relaxing for the first time since his terrors when he had seen the smoke breathing dragon swallow Emmy and he had been stolen away.

Once he had had a refreshing sleep, he did some exploring. No one shooed him away or yelled at him. He spent some time sitting under a cage swinging with the movements of the cart in which hunched a bird, brightly feathered. Noble Warrior sniffed and sniffed again.

He had seen tame birds many times and knew that they were not to be troubled by guard cats. But there was something wrong with this one—it was sick. And the woman fussed over it, trying to get it to eat and drink, folding it closely in her arms from time to time, making soft chirruping sounds as if it could understand her.

They did not keep to the main highways in their traveling, but rather took lanes and often forest tracks. Yet all the time Noble Warrior felt the pull of his instinct. Home *WAS* in this direction.

On the fourth morning the bird had fallen from its perch and lay a crumpled mass of feathers on the floor of the cage. Noble Warrior watched the woman dig a resting place for its small body in the softer earth of a ditch side. There were tear marks on her brown cheeks.

"No Thother," she said when she returned to the wagon. "He served us well, always seemed to know just which card to pick. Remember the gentleman who gave a gold piece—hunted us up after the race and said Thother had picked the winner for him. We shall not see such a clever feathered one again."

That night, when they halted, she brought out a small folding table and set it up as straight as she could on the ground, a lamp stationed at its side. Then she produced a long bag which glinted in the subdued light as if made from one of Princess Suphron's fine robes.

Out of that she shook a number of flat sticks of a dull yellowish color. Noble Warrior's ears flattened a little.

This woman was going to play some of the tricks he had seen used to amuse the women of the court. Much of the past faded from his mind—he was back in a garden beside a pool where a woman, much older and more raggedly dressed than this one, went through the same gestures.

He jumped to the second caravan step, whiskers twitching. Was this woman also one of power whom even the treacherous Khons would answer?

Each stick was marked on one side—the other was plain of any pattern. She gathered them all up again, holding the plain sides uppermost, and tossed them once more.

For a long time she just sat there. Noble Warrior grew impatient. This was not the way matters should go at all. He gave a snort, leaned closer. With a dark paw flipped one of the pieces over.

There was a sharp exclamation from the woman. She snatched up the stick he had moved and examined the pattern on it—then she looked beyond it at Noble Warrior himself as if she had never seen him before.

"Mammam—" Jankos had pushed past the door curtain.

"Quiet!" Her voice carried the snap of an order. "I must—I must think!" She set her elbows on the table and steadied her head on the support of her hands. With a breath which was almost a whistle she again gathered up the sticks, the eyes focusing on Noble Warrior holding a new wariness.

For the second time she tossed them loosely and then leaned back, her attention centered on the cat.

She—she wanted—He put out a paw which hovered over three sticks and then flipped up and over the middle one, settling back to watch her reaction.

He knew the danger of the Great Dark—one learned that as a kitten hardly before one's eyes were open—but this was no harmful curse play.

The woman did not pick up the stick he had chosen, just leaned forward to see it the better as it lay on the table. Jankos crowded closer and now Pettros loomed on the other side.

"This—this one—" The woman's voice began as a half whisper and then arose louder. "This one—" She flung out her hands as if she could not find the words for more of an explanation. Now the man leaned the closer.

"A far journey—" he said slowly.

"Gatto can SEE—just like Thother!" Jankos grabbed up a handful of the sticks and tossed them so that a number fell just in front of Noble Warrior's waiting paws. He bent his head and sniffed—the old knowledge. Yes, it still was with him. He flipped another of the sticks.

"Trouble—" the woman shook her head. But Noble warrior was not yet through; he had already curved a claw around a second stick so that once in the air, it fell across the first. Then he sat back satisfied.

"Gain!" it was Pettros who cried out that word. "Trouble and then gain! Maritza, this is no cat—he is a treasure for us. Do you not see?"

She drew a deep breath. "I see," she answered slowly. With the upraised fingers of one hand she made a sign in the air.

Thus Noble Warrior became indeed one who chose futures. Where Thother had before picked sticks from the bundles people held out, he waited until they were tossed and then turned one, sometimes two, or even three. It was dabbling in things beyond the curtain of this world, that was true. But he was of the breed who knew both worlds. Had he not dealt with Hob on his arrival in this land, soothing the spirit of the house no man could see? Had he not identified the evil Khon sent to destroy Emmy and her father, and finished that nasty spirit off? Had he not talked with ghosts and managed to defeat a would-be follower of the black arts?

Thus they traveled from one village to another. Always, Noble Warrior was assured by instinct in the right way for him. Maritza made him a velvet collar marked with glittering spangles which he wore when he was on duty at the table. Sometimes he thought that she was a little afraid of him for some reason. But the villagers who came to have their fortunes told were certainly in awe and there were a number of coins to ring in the bag Jankos carried when he escorted Noble Warrior back to the caravan.

It was when they came to the fair that there was a shadow sensed by the cat. Something tickled his innermost thoughts as might a wisp of a dream. It was of the dark—not intensely, threateningly so, as had been the Khon, but it was here and he had no wish to seek it out.

Others had come to see what might be offered by the dealers. There was a girl with a thin, sharp-nosed face, a mouth which was a line of discontent and peevishness, dressed like Emmy when she went to some place of importance.

When she came up to the table, the villagers gave way and none of them showed any smiles.

She flounced herself down on the stool opposite Maritza and looked at Noble Warrior with a sly smirk.

"A fortune-telling cat! La, what will it be next, I wonder. A horse to sing opera, a pig to dance? All right, Gypsy, let this animal of yours tell my fortune!"

Noble Warrior's blue eyes stared into hers which seemed unable to meet his squarely. The faint whiff of the dark which had disturbed him since early morning was now like a full puff of rising incense in his face.

She was not a Khon, no. Nor was she of some very ancient evil of this land. But in her there was darkness and danger—not for herself but for others.

Catching up a handful of the sticks, she threw them straight at the cat. One caught in his collar and swung there. But the rest hit the tabletop. He was aware that Maritza had drawn back a little, that Jankos was on the move to come between this girl and Noble Warrior.

For a long instant Noble Warrior simply stared at the girl. She gave a spiteful giggle.

"No fortune for me then, cat. As I thought, it is all a hum—gypsy trickery."

Noble Warrior's right paw swept out. He did not linger to make any choice, he simply snapped one of the sticks into the air and it flew much as the one she had shot at him through the air to land flatly before her.

The pattern on that stick was red and black and curled in a tight series of circles. He heard Maritza gasp.

"Well, what is the meaning?" The girl tapped the stick with one fingernail.

"Lady—" Noble Warrior saw Maritza stiffen. Pettros had come up behind her. Now his hand had reached out to close protectingly on her shoulder. "Lady, you must watch yourself—your thoughts—well—there is danger—"

The girl's giggle became a crow of unpleasant laughter. "What, no dark haired knight to court me? Your cat is not very polite, Gypsy. You should teach him better manners."

She stood up abruptly. Jankos made no attempt to offer her the money bag, nor did she show any sign of dropping in a coin.

"Gypsies," she said as she turned away. "There are those hereabout who have little liking for your kind. I would advise you to be on the road before sundown—well away from here."

Her wide skirts swept around in a swirl and she went off. Maritza's hand came up to cover her husband's where it rested on her shoulder.

"The evil," she said in a voice which was close to a whisper, "is not against her—it is *in* that one, Pettros—she is the danger."

"She is the stepdaughter of the squire," he answered. "A word from her and—" he shrugged. "Best that we take her advice and get on the road—now."

As they trundled off, Noble Warrior, in his favorite place on the driver's seat of the wagon, was no longer concerned. The dark-thoughted one was gone, but there was something else—His head was held high and he tried with all his might to locate that trace. Yes! It was growing much stronger. Home—he was nearly home!

But the track they followed took a winding turn away from the right direction. Noble Warrior jumped from his vantage point and flashed into the woods making a thick wall on that side of the road.

He sped on, leaping here a downed tree, there weaving a way around some mossy stones. There was the sound of water ahead. But there was another sound also—the crying of a child.

Noble Warrior's speed slackened. He was being pulled in two directions, but the crying won. Emmy? Could it be Emmy? No, the voice was too young for her.

He came out on the bank of the small stream. There was a child there right enough, much younger than Emmy. His face, swollen from crying, had also been harshly scratched by briars in one place, and he rocked back and forth in his pain and fear, his clothing muddied and torn.

Noble Warrior advanced with his usual caution when facing the unknown. The child let out a wail and then suddenly caught sight of the cat. His mouth fell a little open.

"K–k–kitty?" he stammered.

Plainly, Noble Warrior decided, this kitten had been lost. Where was his mother that she allowed him to stray so?

"Lissy—Lissy branged you—k–k–kitty? She told Toddie wait, there would be a 'prise. You the 'prise, k–k–kitty?"

He held out a badly scratched and mud grimed hand. "Where Lissy— Toddie go home!" His face was puckering again for further crying.

Noble Warrior advanced until the small hand fell on his head. It was sticky on his fur, but he resigned himself to that. For a moment he stood and let the child pat him, then backed away.

As he had hoped, the little boy scrambled up and followed, as the cat slowly withdrew. But which way would they go? Back to the village—or on toward that still far place to which his need called him?

Best the village, he decided. Their journey was a slow one and Noble Warrior had to submit to a great deal of patting, and even once to the shame of a hand closing on his glossy tail. But they did come out at last on the track where he had left the caravan. There was no sign of that. Perhaps the gypsy instinct to get away from danger had taken them well ahead. But the village lay in the other direction.

Toddie sat down much more often now and had to be coaxed to follow. But before they reached the first cottages there was the thud of horse hooves on the road. The man in the lead was mounted on a tall black horse which overran the spot where Toddie had taken his last rest, but he reined back, jumped from the saddle, and caught up the child almost firmly.

Toddie wrapped arms around the man's neck.

"Toddie!" The man hugged him so tightly that the child squirmed.

"Dada!" yelled the little boy.

"Jus' like Miss Elizabeth said. Squire, them there gypsies had him— dropped him off when they got to know as they were being followed!"

"Lissy?" Toddie pushed a little away from his father to look up into the man's face. "Lissy said Toddie—come to woods—show him big 'prise. Then Lissy ranned away—Toddie no find her—only K–k–kitty! K–k–kitty good— brang Toddie to Dada. Lissy, she losted Toddie!"

He had flung out an arm to indicate Noble Warrior who was preparing to edge back into the bushes.

"Why—that there's the gypsy cat—" said one of the men.

But another approached Noble Warrior more closely, going down on one knee to survey him with care.

"Squire—this here's that strange cat Captain Ashley brought 'ome from foreign parts for 'is little girl. Stolen it was when they went to London to take th' train to th' seashore. The Captain, e's near been crazy trying to find it—e's offered a reward an' all."

Now the speaker turned his attention to the cat. "Noble Warrior, you knows me—Tom Jenkins as is second groom. Time you get back home— Miss Emmy now, she's near cried herself sick and th' whole place is not th' same without you walkin' out in th' mornin' to take th' air."

Noble Warrior all at once felt very tired, tired but at peace. He might not have won home all by himself, but he was certainly not far away. Willingly, he allowed Tom to pick him up carefully. For a fleeting moment he thought of Jankos and the caravan—but that was not meant to be the life of a guardian cat—no, not at all.

NOBLE WARRIOR
AND THE "GENTLEMAN"
Catfantastic V (1999) DAW

It was dark, though a number of candles had been lit in the dining room. The paneled walls, the long table, the rows of chairs and all the other heavy furniture seemed to thicken the gloom. Noble Warrior had his own chair next to Emmy's, with two pillows added to make him tall enough to see fully both the table and those gathered about it.

There were no cheerful looks tonight, nor any light or happy talk. He felt shadows as well as saw them and was alert to any clue of the dark thing that threatened Princess Emmy and her family.

It was Emmy who broke the silence first. "Why is it making us so unhappy, Father? I always thought it was a good thing to be a Lord—"

The frown on her father's face did not clear. Lady Ashley, his great-aunt, was watching him intently, as if she wished to echo that same question.

"Emmy," her father answered very slowly. He might want to make sure that his every word counted, "I was never meant to be Lord Garnley, you see. I had an uncle and two cousins, so the inheritance was never considered to possibly be mine. As a Lord, I will have many duties which I do not yet understand. I have been a sailor for many years, have lived in a far-away country. I am not the proper one to wear Garnley's coronet. Why, I am not even acquainted with his lands, the people in his employ and—" suddenly he brought his fist down hard on the table. "And—"

"You must, you know," Great-Aunt Amelia said simply. It was quiet again as if she had made plain that this was so and could not be questioned.

Emmy looked down at her plate. She had eaten very little of her serving because it seemed that one just could *not* swallow easily tonight.

Noble Warrior was alert to the feelings he sensed. His brown-gloved paw went out and touched her arm gently. Emmy swung around and gathered him into her lap, which he allowed (although such a liberty was not suited, of course, to one of his rank) because he knew she needed comfort now.

"Is the place in order? You have had some weeks to survey it all," Great-Aunt Amelia continued. "Did Garnley have a bailiff who could be trusted?"

Father shrugged, his frown still heavy. "Oh, they have reassured me, up, down, and sidewise, that all is well, both Findley and that law fellow Markson. Only—" He lifted his hand a little as if he were going to slam the table again. "What are we going to do, Aunt Amelia? I suppose I shall be tied there most of the year doing whatever is expected of me. But I can't leave Emmy and you here—"

Emmy nodded to that. She remembered only too well what had happened before when Father was doing his duty at sea for the East India Company and she and Great-Aunt Amelia had the terrible time with Miss Wyker. She hugged Noble Warrior tightly, and he nipped her arm, very lightly, to remind her that there were limits to this kind of comforting.

"It is very simple, Giles." Great-Aunt seemed to think that there was only one proper answer and she was now stating it. "I may be old; I may have to use a cane and welcome a supporting arm upon occasion. But I still run a good-sized household satisfactorily, and I shall have Asher and any other I need from Hob's Green. We'll simply visit Garlynstone for the summer and see how well it works out for all of us."

Father looked for a moment as if he were going to protest, but before he could say anything she added, "Do you forget, Giles, that I spent most of my girlhood there?

Thus it came about several weeks later that they moved—nearly as a complete household—across country to an area Emmy had never seen. This time, remembering the bad time of being catnapped and then lost, Noble Warrior was in the carriage with Emmy where she could keep an eye on him.

The road into which they turned at last was rough, so that she and Great-Aunt Amelia, as well as Aunt's maid Asher, and Lucy, the one chosen to look after Emmy's needs, had to hang onto the nearest stable part of the carriage and hope this jolting would soon end. Noble Warrior expressed his disgust with a growl and held on with *all* his claws.

Emmy cried out as a huge shadow loomed up at the window of the carriage beside her seat.

"Noooooo!" She denied that there was a big black thing reaching toward her.

"Now, now," Great-Aunt Amelia really laughed as she reached over to pat Emmy's hand.

"Those are just the Gars—strange beasts some distant ancestor of ours dreamed up to decorate his entrance posts. You'll see them pictured other places about in Garlynstone."

The carriage swept forward under an arch of trees until it came to a wide stretch of gravel. And there was Father standing on the steps waiting for them, the steps of what seemed to Emmy to be truly a castle. It was so high one could get a crick in the neck pushing one's head far enough back to eye its roof from under the edge of a bonnet.

Big it certainly was. It took Emmy several days to learn her way around so she could find the morning room they used for dining, Great-Aunt's sitting room, and the library where Father could sometimes be found. Noble Warrior, of course, was not in the least surprised that this palace had appeared in his life. He had been the protector of Princess Suphorn far across the sea and then came to Emmy—his second princess. It was only fitting that she should have such an important setting also.

He explored. Night was good for that. And he found his way into some strange places both above and below. One thing he searched for he did *not* find. Hob, the house goblin he had known at Emmy's former house, had no counterpart here.

Though there was a strangely unsettling sensation in one of the lower rooms, and he detected a Presence there—an unhappy Presence. But it was no threat to those under this room here and now.

The rain had fallen steadily during the first four days they had spent here in this—this place. Emmy found it very hard to think of it as "home." She and Noble Warrior both kept under cover, though through windows they had surveyed the world beyond. Emmy knew that the distant pounding which had kept her awake at first was really the sound of the waves, as it had been very stormy and the sea was not too far away. Father had sternly warned her to stay away from the sea shore unless someone was with her, but he had not forbidden her to go into the garden.

There were people working there. One was a boy who pushed a wheelbarrow and was grunted at by a gruff-looking man who could only be one of the gardeners. Noble Warrior raised a lip as he spied a black-and-white inferior of his race, but not his breed, who dared to slink along a terrace.

But now the day dawned fair and Emmy planned further exploits. The house was full of interesting things right enough, but she longed for the outside where there was sun and flowers. Admonishing Noble Warrior against going off where he could not be easily found, she went out.

They enjoyed a glorious week exploring the garden before there came another dark and stormy period. When it struck, this one was even worse than the first. Lamps and candles seemed unable to provide any real light, even in the house. Father mentioned that there was a shore watch out for fear of wrecks. Though he also added that those would certainly be of strange vessels as the coastal seamen here knew every twist and turn of wave and reef.

Noble Warrior stood by the door of the room they had entered shortly before for breakfast. As he pawed at it, he gave the small demanding call that always aroused Emmy to some need of his, and she did notice him. However, when she had opened the heavy door with no small effort, he did not dart away along the passage and leave her. Rather he stood looking around and she knew he wanted her company—which was usual.

Into the chamber of that Presence they went, a little swifter with every step. Then they were in the dark—or not quite dark—for there was a window against which the force of the storm beat furiously. Emmy wanted to edge back, but the feeling that there was need here held her.

Noble Warrior slipped through the shadows to face the wall just to one side of the wide fireplace. Emmy could only see his lighter patches of fur now as he stood facing the wall and looking up. She looked for a candle; surely there was a candle! The servants always kept any room lit in which the family might wish to go.

And there was one! It stood on a small round table beside a big chair near the fireplace. She felt almost as if something had pushed her in that direction.

There were some of the new matches, too. Father had shown her just how to make use of them. A moment later there was light, and she turned back to Noble Warrior.

He had raised up on his hind legs and was scraping with extended claws down the paneled wall, but whatever he was trying to reach was too far above.

His cat sight was much better, of course, than Emmy's kind and it was very plain—a round stain in the wood panel.

Then more light made it all the clearer as Emmy, with her candle, was beside him. She raised the flame closer, above the scratches, centering it on the dark spot. Holding the candle, which was beginning to flicker in the draft from the window, as close as she dared, she planted the fingers of her right hand on the dark spot. It was rough and splintery under touch as if it were broken. But that did not matter as much as the fact that, though she had only intended to touch it, she was now pushing it with all her might.

Noble Warrior again reared up on his hind legs, and it seemed he was using his front paws to aid in her efforts.

There was a sound, even above the roar of the wind. Emmy was never afterward certain whether she had actually heard that word or not:

"Open!" A cry of strength and purpose.

The panel moved, not backward, but to the side. She and the cat were looking into a dark passage into which the candlelight scarcely penetrated.

But that which had drawn them there was not satisfied. They were to go–*IN!*

Noble Warrior went first and she must follow or lose him. There were steps going down and spiderwebs which she tried to avoid. Down and down they went.

Once more they walked along a level, but very narrow passage. Only that did not last long, and that which had brought them here was still not satisfied. There were more steps and Emmy kept glancing fearfully at the candle. If it went out—!

Noble Warrior looked up at her and his lithe tail flipped up against her. She stooped and caught hold of it, taking care not to pull, and he seemed satisfied. So they kept on, linked by firm flesh and soft fur.

Even though there was only the single candle, and that was burning down so that the wax dribbled near to Emmy's fingers, she could see now that they were in a much larger space. It was not empty. Some humpy shadows along one wall proved to be small barrels. Several chests such as the one Father used to keep his things in at sea took shape also.

She could smell the sea—she was sure that that smell was from the sea. Noble Warrior suddenly took charge of his own tail again and eluded her fingers.

He marched straight for the far side of this rock-walled place. Emmy, determined not to be left alone, followed him quickly. She dared not look behind her for that thing which had sent her into this strange place followed and seemed to become more real! She could almost believe she heard footsteps.

Noble Warrior rounded the end of the row of small barrels and halted. When Emmy joined him again, he was stretched up against the wall clawing at a door impatiently. It was barred, and his eager paws were much below the barrier he strained to reach.

He gave his impatient summons for assistance. Why must a warrior of his rank be so dependant upon humans at times? It was shaming.

Emmy started at the sound of something striking the rock of the floor. In another moment her ankle was given a sharp blow and she edged back from what lay there—a big stick—thick, and one end of it rolled up in a mass of what looked to be rotting cloth and straw. It was not by any will or knowledge of hers that her hand shook, and she dropped the candle. The stick clattered against stone, but the candle appeared to pop out of the holder almost of its own will, to fall on the untidy bundle. The candle flickered and dimmed.

Then there was more fire starting up strongly, coming from the wadded end of the stick. Emmy, wanting light more than anything else, caught up the stick, and raising the burning end above her head seemed to make it burn all the brighter.

"WhaGaugh!" Noble Warrior raised his voice in the most demanding cry of his protest range. He looked back at her, his impatience plain to be read in every line of his sleek body where he stood, still upright against the barred door.

Emmy handled the torch gingerly, holding it as far away from her as she could. But they were not finished with the task that had brought them here. They must also go beyond this door. To juggle the bar from its holds and yet steady the torch in one hand was difficult. But at last the length of rusting metal also moved, striking on one of the barrels and rebounding to clang on the floor.

"Whhhhhoooo!" Emmy quavered in the moment, for surely something she had not seen, only felt, something must be helping to move the door. She shrank back against the barrels and had a hard time not dropping the torch from her shaking hands.

Noble Warrior was gone—into the dark—with the thing following him! She did not want to go, but what if—?

There was water ahead someplace; she could hear it. And smell the sea. What if Noble Warrior were to be caught in one of those pools her father had warned her against?

Grasping the torch in both hands, Emmy forced herself to go ahead. There were rock walls all around, but this passage was much wider than those they had followed within the house.

She came out on a big rock jutting above and into a pool of water, troubled water which surged in and out from some dark place beyond. Noble Warrior had gone no farther but stood staring down into the direction from which it came.

There was splashing, coming closer. Emmy swung the torch out a little farther. She did not want to see what was making that commotion in the water and yet she must.

Then—at the end of the rocky pierlike formation there was movement and something raised to claw about. Emmy could only think of a spider—a huge, sea-born, spider—but Noble Warrior made no attempt to move.

Not a spider but a hand! Someone was climbing, moaning a little at the effort of pulling a length of clammy and bruised flesh up onto the rock.

The torch showed him clearly when, gasping, he was at last out and lying on the rocky point. He was an old man, his white hair and beard plastered to his head, and now, when he tried to raise himself higher, he began to cough. But all at once his head came up and he looked straight at a point to Emmy's right.

There *was* someone else there. Though even when she tried to hold the torch so she could see that misty figure better, she was no wiser as to who—or what—it might be. He (for it appeared to be a man) was as tall as Father, but the clothes he wore were queer, not like any she had seen, except in some of the portraits along the walls of the house.

However, his face seemed to grow clearer and clearer until she was sure she would never forget him. He was not ugly, nor old, like this one from the sea. But he was sad. Something in Emmy made her throat begin to feel as it did when she was going to cry.

Noble Warrior had come away from his post on the sea edge of the rock shelf to stand before this stranger for a long moment. They seemed to meet eye to eye, the stranger even stooping a little. Then that misty shape made a slight gesture with one hardly-to-be-seen hand as if in thanks.

"Made it!" that was the voice of the man from the sea. "Never thought I would, did you?" He spoke angrily, harshly. "Thought as how old Rufe would never turn up—Cousin! I was the last as could point you out to the King's men—so—" He hesitated a moment, and then his words came as if he were spitting at the misty one. "So I found me on a slaver for the Moorish ports. Only I didn't die.

"You would have done better, Cousin, to have had the captain tap me on the head and slide me overboard. I lived—if you could call it living. And I held sure in my mind I would take what was due me out of that smooth gentleman's hide of yours. Which," he was on his hands and knees now, "is just what I'm going to do."

"Rufus"—That whisper of a voice seemed to come from very far away and the words were slow as if the speaker found it difficult to mouth them. "It was Patrick, you see. He told me after it was too late. So I waited, I was set to wait to bring you home and safe. The light brought you in—" Another misty hand movement was made in Emmy's direction.

"The child, the cat, they were all I could use when the time came. You are home safe—Rufus—at long last. Perhaps the only one of the 'Gentlemen' left now."

The man from the sea had not been able to pull himself up any farther than his knees. His head shook slowly from side to side and drops of water showered about.

"You—you're dead!" His head went back, and he uttered a cry which made Emmy whimper. "Dead—" Then he crumpled and lay still.

Emmy could no longer see the misty man either. She turned and, with Noble Warrior beside her, ran from the dark sea cave. She wanted Father. She wanted him now!

It was not until she burst into the upper hall from the room where the panel still remained open, Noble Warrior a cream-and-brown steak before her, that she found Father—just in to gather things for some wrecked sailors who had managed to make it ashore. What she tried to tell him was all mixed up, but he understood enough to take two of the footmen and return to the passage after he had seen Emmy into Great-Aunt's comforting arms.

It was not until later that Father explained things to Emmy—about the cousins who had been part of a smuggling band, even though they were gentlemen in truth and not by the nickname the townspeople called them. They had been betrayed to the riding officers in the end. And one, Manners Gerlyn, had shot himself, so it was thought. Though there was always suspicion thereafter, since another young man, a more distant relative had also disappeared.

Then it was thought that Rufus Tengarde, Garlyn's cousin, had been drowned when their ship had gone down in a storm shortly before they were denounced.

Noble Warrior listened after a fashion. It was a story he already had learned—from the Presence on his nightly trips. He bit delicately at one claw on a forefoot. The Presence was gone. Who knew what new adventure might turn up next for a very alert guardian to a princess?

ABOUT THE AUTHOR

For well over a half century, Andre Norton was one of the most popular science fiction and fantasy authors in the world. With series such as Time Traders, Solar Queen, Forerunner, Beast Master, Crosstime, and Janus, as well as many standalone novels, her tales of adventure have drawn countless readers to science fiction. Her fantasy novels, including the bestselling Witch World series, her Magic series, and many other unrelated novels, have been popular with readers for decades. Lauded as a Grand Master by the Science Fiction Writers of America, she is the recipient of a Life Achievement Award from the World Fantasy Convention. An Ohio native, Norton lived for many years in Winter Park, Florida, and died in March 2005 at her home in Murfreesboro, Tennessee.